MAYA OF THE IN-BETWEEN

MAYA RISING BOOK #1

SITA BENNETT

MYSTIC ADVENTURE PRESS

Copyright © 2020 by Sita Bennett.

All rights reserved.

No portion of this book may be reproduced in any form without written permission from the publisher or author, except as permitted by U.S. copyright law.

CONTENTS

Dedication	V
Introduction	1
Part One	3
1. Chapter 1	5
2. Chapter 2	21
3. Chapter 3	29
4. Chapter 4	43
5. Chapter 5	71
6. Chapter 6	81
7. Chapter 7	89
8. Chapter 8	99
9. Chapter 9	107
10. Chapter 10	113
Part Two	117
11. Chapter 11	119
12. Chapter 12	139
13. Chapter 13	151
14. Chapter 14	169
15. Chapter 15	179

16.	Chapter 16	187
17.	Chapter 17	195
18.	Chapter 18	205
19.	Chapter 19	211
20.	Chapter 20	217
21.	Chapter 21	225
22.	Chapter 22	237
23.	Chapter 23	241
24.	Chapter 24	251
Part Three		257
25.	Chapter 25	259
26.	Chapter 26	263
27.	Chapter 27	275
28.	Chapter 28	285
29.	Chapter 29	297
30.	Chapter 30	303
31.	Chapter 31	311
32.	Chapter 32	317
Afterword		324
More Books By		325
Acknowledgments		327
About Author		330

*Dedicated to all who sense a richer existence beneath the fabric
of what we see and accept as reality,
& those who, like Maya, seek to understand the deeper
mysteries of our world and human nature.*

*To the sensitives, the introverts,
the empaths, the feelers,
I wrote this novel for you.*

INTRODUCTION

Written here is my experience.

It's a documented account of everything I can remember learning in the valley of Santōṣha.

Everything I felt.

It's personal, but I welcome you in.

This past year the course of humanity changed dramatically, changed forever. An important moment in time.

We'd been invaded; our minds manipulated. Our true nature forgotten.

Because you are reading this, you are one of Earth's new children.

We are your ancestors.

And this is our history.

PART ONE

THE OLD WORLD

CHAPTER ONE

E VERYTHING WAS GREEN.
Every shade of green imaginable.
Wild and vivid.
Complimented by the browns of the tree's rough bark.
Dirt and earth.

A thick forest of trees covered the slopes of a trenching valley where a swollen river snaked through. Dangling vines twisted and twirled; a plague over all in their path. Stars of sunlight shimmered across the water's glassy surface while an ever-moving undercurrent surged toward a giant cliff off which the water plummeted.

I stood on the edge of the rocky cliff face where mist landed lightly around me, gazing down upon the rich expanse of nature in all her untamed sublimity. This kind of simple beauty was transcendental when you came from a place where iron, buildings, and miles of dry desert land had replaced all natural life.

A small cluster of shelters blended into the lush wilderness. Some were built of rustic wood and stone, others were dug into mounds of grassy earth. One was even built between hefty tree branches with a wooden ladder twisting up its trunk.

A tall, dark-skinned woman caught my attention. She stood boldly in the center of an ancient stone bridge that connected the village across the steep valley. Robed in golden silk she appeared luminous like the sun, radiating eternal wisdom and power. Her shiny black hair was pulled back by a golden band that complimented the rings that stacked up her arms, and her crystal green eyes, as vivid as the surrounding wilderness, sparkled.

Calling.

I had seen her there before and she was always calling. But not my name. She sung out in a language I didn't understand. A whisper, a breath, a feeling.

In a flash she stood before me, her eyes even more piercing up close. Sunlight glittered off a stud piercing her nose.

"Trust him."

She touched my arm. It was electrifying.

Her expression was severe, serious, but her presence so loving it overwhelmed me. I'd never felt pure love before. It didn't exist where I was from.

Trust who?

"Maya!" Lorraine's call startled me.

I had entered a kind of trance, so entirely absorbed in the world I was painting that it came to life inside my imagination.

I dropped my paintbrush in a jar of rainbow-colored water on the ledge of the easel where my canvas sat. I was no longer spying over the entrancing jungle but sat cross-legged on the paint-stained carpet of my small bedroom.

It was a room like every other with a bed, desk, and closet. Some people spent their rations on trinkets to decorate their bedrooms, but I spent mine on paint, brushes, canvasses and sketchbooks. As a result, my otherwise basic room was painted from wall to wall with bright landscapes from the world that only existed inside my head.

I liked it better there.

Sometimes that world was so alive, so rich, it felt real. So real that when I was there, I lost all sense of what others understood as the "real world." When I returned, it almost felt as if *this* place was the illusion. For this world was nothing like the one that covered the walls of my bedroom, where nature was bountiful, mountains grand, and oceans clean and pure.

Lands like that existed here once, but today there was barely a trace of nature left on earth.

And a deep but un-ignorable sorrow in my heart longed to experience in body, what it would feel like to stand on dense soil and breath clean air the way humankind had at the beginning of our time on the planet.

"Maya!" she called again.

I sprung to my feet, swung my backpack over my shoulder, and ran down the stairs.

The rest of the house, like my bedroom, was small, square and basic. Some of my paintings hung on the walls upstairs, but not downstairs. Lorraine and Jeff liked to have visitors, and most of the Society was repulsed by brightly-coloured art that depicted our prehistoric times. This was the electronic age. All art was black, white, and silver, and abstract. There were only ever two people legally registered as artists at a time, and I wasn't one of them.

When I began painting, I was young. In hiding. I didn't know what was right and normal. And creative expression helped me survive long days alone, stuck inside the otherwise bland house. Lorraine and Jeff never had the heart to crush my blissful ignorance. But as I grew older, they encouraged me to let go of my obsession with painting and do what other 'normal' teenagers did.

The only problem was that I didn't know how to be a normal teenager, and I was afraid I never would.

In the kitchen, Lorraine poured coffee into her mug. I was already late but stopped to scavenge for something to take for lunch. She raised an eyebrow and pushed a container across the bench.

"Oh, thank you."

"There were leftovers. I'm not going to make a habit of it, okay?"

"Of course. Thank you."

While her tone was stern, her face was soft. When Lorraine had the time, she didn't seem to mind doing the odd thing for me, but I tended to get lost in other worlds when I was meant to be in this one. Clearly, that was the "habit" she was most concerned about.

Suddenly, the TV in the living room turned itself on. A news program began.

That was all that aired on TV. Well, news, educational videos, and announcements from Control leaders. It turned itself on and off automatically, but with the mute button we at least had the choice to listen in or not.

It was always the same reporter. A middle-aged man with sparkly charcoal eyes, a charming smile, chiseled features, and a deep, expressive voice. The news station showed still images and videos of dry, barren stretches of land and the remains of cities, now dusty rubble. They were all desolate ruins left by extreme weather events that had, over time, devastated each continent.

Before I could peel my eyes away from the screen, images of Australia began to appear. Miles of bare land still blackened from the embers of all that once resided there, even the widest trees now but skeletons, crisp from death-eating flames.

The burnings were years ago, but the land remained dormant as if the damage was fresh. A giant tattoo of the fire's kiss permanently painted across its face.

Lorraine looked at the images displayed on the TV then turned to me with that *look*.

"Thanks again for packing my lunch," I said before walking quickly to the door.

Among all the continents, seeing Australia in this condition still affected me, even if just slightly, every time.

The pain in my chest.

The shortness of breath, as if choking on the smoke that choked *them*. All of them. Choked them to death.

The grief. Heartache. Horror.

Haunted by memories of everything aglow. Fire. Death. Desolation. Memories that weren't even my own yet felt so close it was as if they ran through my veins, woven into the very blood of my being.

"Enjoy the excursion." Her voice drifted with me out the door as I stepped into the day.

The sun was unusually bright, so bright it stung my eyes. A dense layer of smog usually protected us against its violent rays, but even in its absence, the air was thick with humidity. My breath became heavier the moment I stepped outside, and no amount of air I sucked in felt completely satisfying.

Identical houses lined the street, each an equal distance apart from one another. Each had iron exteriors, iron doors, and iron window shutters to protect them from wild and erratic winds. Iron fences enclosed each yard and bright synthetic grass, the color and length perfectly even, lay like a carpet.

Squinting my eyes, I ran across the empty road toward the sky train. Most transport was by train. Cars used too much fuel of which the City was already in scarce supply.

Just as I reached the station, a long train, like a silver bullet, swooped past, blinding me as the sun's reflection glared off its metal exterior.

"Damn it!" I squeeze my eyes shut for a moment's relief.

I was supposed to be on that train.

There was just one line that looped every twenty minutes. Any other day I would've been quietly pleased to miss the morning class, but I'd been looking forward to this day. It was the first time our class was permitted to leave the inner city.

I sat on the curb; a more pleasant and calm place to wait than the busy station. I leaned back and stared up at the unusually clear sky, breathing, and absorbing the sun's rays that rarely saw my skin.

"Trust him..." Her voice rang.

Trust who?

Within moments, I was somewhere else again, this time a yellow room, with walls that glowed like the sun.

No, not yellow, gold. Three walls of pure, glistening gold that met at the tip to form a triangle.

I was alone inside the soundless pyramid.

Alone until I fell.

And when I stood, the sense of danger raced through my body.

I began to run, my feet thumping on the dry dirt with each spring forward. Dust lifted, leaving a light trail behind me. While my subconscious understood this was a vision, the impact of the hard earth jolting my body felt real. It was a fully sensory vision.

The night air was cold and rough as I sucked it down my dry throat and into my tired lungs. It demanded every bit of energy to thrust my body forward. I had never felt so physically weak and fatigued. A striking pain in my wrist throbbed.

I couldn't see, the sky was black, illuminated only by the soft glow of a blood-red moon. A light flashed from behind, white suits speeding toward me, but my legs were moving at maximum speed.

The threat of capture seemed more daunting than the fear of death itself. If they caught me, I hoped they'd kill me.

I turned to check my distance from those chasing me and caught a glimpse of a face, his face. Right beside me, running for his life with me.

His rugged features, his bright blue eyes.

Hypnotized, I tripped and fell.

A white hand snatched my heel, a grip so tight that shards of pain shot up my leg from where iron-gloved fingers squeezed.

"You'll die if you travel in open land." The voice returned. *Her* voice, echoing in my ear.

My eyes flashed open to catch sight of her vivid green eyes, only to be blinded by the burning sun.

Time had passed. I leaped to my feet and hurried to the train.

Travel where in open land? I searched the infinite abyss from where her voice arose for more information.

But no, this isn't real. I shook off the images. *They're getting more vivid. I'm getting more delusional.*

Meredith said this would happen if I didn't take the medication.

Electrical devices entertained most people who rode the train. For most, it appeared more of a habit than necessity, but I'd never owned one, so I didn't understand the addiction.

In appearance, people expressed themselves with wild slick hair and artistic makeup. Women wore heavy dark eye shadow and bronzer that shaped their cheekbones sharp as edges, and both genders painted a glimmer of silver on their lids to emphasize the "sparkle" in their eyes. All clothes were basic in shades of black and white, with emphasis on how one styled themselves with loud jewelry, stiff-collared coats, or high metallic heels.

Freedom within boundaries.

The only empty seats were next to a girl from my class, Ray. I relaxed knowing I wasn't the only one who'd be late.

I sat on the aisle seat and took out my sketchbook, turning to finish a face I'd drawn many times. *His face.*

It was the eyes that drew me in. I could get lost for hours refining every detail. They were blue, clear and glassy like the most vivid ocean I could remember.

Blue was rare there. Eyes were generally as cloudy as the polluted air, and shades of murky brown or musky grey. But these eyes, they were so blue I could swim in them, swim like I used to. Swim like I longed to swim once again. I had been born by the ocean, drenched in salt, and still felt deeply connected to the sense of being held, protected, safe in the arms of the Australian waters. Safe until the heat of the scorched land erupted in countless fires, and the fires resulted in an unfathomable number of deaths.

The young man I drew wasn't from the valley, but he visited me often in visions the way the valley did, in flashes, and I was sure they were somehow interconnected. He felt so real like he, too, was calling.

"Hey girl hey." Shalom dumped her bag down beside me, her attention on Ray. They were inseparable.

Shalom's long, slender body slunk back into the seat between us, her eyes and skin smooth and dark as coffee. I caught myself staring out of the corner of my eye but knew she didn't mind; she owned her beauty. She knew just as well as anyone that she was stunning.

"What are you always drawing?" It took a moment to realize that Shalom was speaking to me. Sometimes they acknowledged my presence, but they rarely talked to me.

She was leaning over, peeking at my notebook but I shut it quickly before she could see anything. In the past, when I had been naive enough to show people my illustrations, it always backfired. It was controversial to draw things that were not real—at least not real anymore. So, I learned to keep it private.

"Just sketches of... architecture," I mumbled.

She shrugged then scanned the plain silver dress I wore, which hung loosely over my body. I was as plain as my dress. I didn't wear makeup and I wore my hair loose, flowing down my back in natural waves. At that moment it was clear we would never be friends. Shalom turned her attention to her phone and began scrolling.

Technology was the beating heart of our city. It connected everyone and was used for everything. It was what made us feel like we still lived in a functioning, alive world, but beyond this sector was only an endless desert.

"Check it out." Ray leaned over, turning her phone toward us—well, towards Shalom.

"There was another earthquake. *Huge.* Right on the border, near where they started developing our Sister City."

The images on her screen matched those shown by the news reporter earlier that morning. But again, this kind of news wasn't *new*.

At first, these events were dismissed as coincidences, but natural disasters escalated until tsunamis, hurricanes, earthquakes, floods, and like Australia, freak bush fires, started wiping out entire cities, then states.

Oceans rose as the Arctic melted and countries sank below sea level. The majority of our planet's history now lined the ocean floors, decayed beyond repair. Land that was elevated enough to survive the rising waters suffered the rising temperatures and over time, the entire earth's surface was seared dry by the scorching sun.

After scientists declared this the safest, most resourceful land left on the planet, our city was built. Now, it was the only place left on earth that supported human existence. Long ago, it was known as the Amazon—the world's largest tropical rainforest—but now all that was left was a barren wasteland with just enough farmland to keep us alive. Our City was powered by all the resources of its deforestation. When it was founded, the leadership sent out broadcasts to every state, every household across the globe, inviting all survivors to join them in creating one country. One people. Inside the confines of one City.

We were taught in school that natural disasters and extreme weather events caused the earth's state of desolation, as if nature had declared war on humanity, and we were victims, fighting to survive. And that may have been true in recent history. But we started this war, and none of the adults would acknowledge or admit it.

It was obvious to me, based on texts—many forbidden for general reading, however—on the planet's fundamental biology. Humans were the ones who cleared the vast majority of the land for agriculture, farming, housing and industry, and did not seem to take into consideration that Carbon was the chemical backbone of life on Earth. Carbon compounds in the land and sea regulated the Earth's temperature. Clearing plant-life stripped the soil of Carbon, turning it to dust. This alone pointed to the inevitability of global warming, yet it was just one of the many ways we destroyed the balance of nature that was critical to the planet's survival. It was all a ripple affect that started with *us*.

I understood why they hid this truth from general knowledge. We could not undo the past, and understanding it would only be a source for anger, like it was for me. It was easier to play the victim, and use our victimhood as a uniting force that motivated us to work together to keep our great, robust City functioning at optimal capacity.

"Looks like we're destined to be alone," Shalom said, still half engaged in a different story on her screen.

"God wouldn't create us to kill us off," Ray said.

"Thank the Lord we're safe until then." Shalom pressed her palms together, making Ray giggle.

And they truly believed it. They believed we were safe here. Everyone did. We'd all been fed the same story since arriving; that no matter many disasters erupted over the planet, they couldn't and wouldn't touch this city.

Our train stopped and we got off. We made our way to the harbor where our class was huddled by a little tour boat at the end of the dock. Our teacher, Mrs. Fletcher, stood in front of the group counting heads. The wind had gained momentum, and clouds now covered the sky.

We were in the final months of school in which we'd sit for exams that would determine our future. This field-trip was a tradition. The tour boat didn't run often due to the fuel shortage, but every year graduating students took a ride through the canal for an education into the City's history. To remind us what a stellar System we were about to be initiated into.

I tried to walk apart from the girls, but we shared the same destination and our paths merged.

"Hey, it looks like proctors are coming with us." Ray pointed toward two men in expensive uniforms; serious as always. "They were in my chemistry class yesterday too. I noticed that they were paying close attention to me. I think I might have a good chance of being chosen as a doctor."

"That's great girl," Shalom said tiredly.

"What do you want to be chosen for Maya?" Ray asked.

"Um." I paused; cheeks hot. "I don't really know . . . "

"Don't be shy, you clearly want to be an architect," she prompted.

"Oh, yeh, I guess I just don't want to get my hopes up."

I caught Mrs. Fletcher glaring at us and, on cue, Shalom dropped her bedazzled black leather bag, its contents spreading across the dock.

I bent down to help her pick up what had fallen out, two packets of "Skinny Me" food replacement drinks.

In the City, most young women were skinny. It was a great achievement to show bones. Advertising and billboards showered us with images of bony bodies, encouraging such ideals. It was clear Shalom spent most of her time and energy shaping her body so she could star on one of those billboards one day. I had a suspicion the propaganda was so we wouldn't eat so much food, therefore, sparing resources. But being underweight also made people tired and depleted, lacking the energy to spark up any trouble.

Ray whispered something that made Shalom snicker.

"Let's pack it super slow, just to aggravate her." The girls continued scheming as we huddled over Shalom's belongings. Mrs Fletcher had very little control over her anger and most of the class found it funny when she boiled over.

But the proctors were watching us too. They made me nervous.

Shalom finally zipped up her freshly packed bag, and we scurried to join the class.

Mrs. Fletcher took one glance at the cup of coffee in Shalom's hand and said, "Garbage. Now!"

"Aw! Come on! Do you really want to keep everyone waiting even longer by making me walk *all* the way over to the garbage cans, then *all* the way back?"

Mrs. Fletcher just held out her hand, eyebrow raised high. After Shalom surrendered, handing over her breakfast, Mrs. Fletcher opened the lid and poured it's contents slowly, dramatically, onto the ground, and threw the cup into the water. Clapping her hands, she turned to the class and said, "Now we're *all here*; we can finally move onto the tour boat."

The boat had a glass bottom, and beneath our feet lumps of furry algae drifted through the murky water revealing signs of life through the green-tinted haze.

But not sea life, past human life.

". . . one of Brazil's last inland cities drowned," the tour guide continued.

He stood before us on the lower deck as we passed over the ruins of the city he spoke of. We'd sped past miles of barren land through the canal, seeing for the first time a fragment of the desolation beyond the city border, to reach the sea that what was once Brazil.

"Quite spectacular. You can see the roofs of buildings slowly being covered by algae and seaweed. And up ahead, a special appearance. We'll see the statue of Christ The Redeemer. His ruins were salvaged and bought inland after Rio was wiped out. No one expected the rising waters would reach this city too.

"As you're about to see, he's been knocked over but still leans against a standing building, and he's grown quite the layer of moss."

Students leaned over each other, eager to capture a decent view as we approached. Torn plastic and objects of all kinds floated through the still water.

"The good news is," the guide said on a more serious tone, "with both the polar regions completely melted, the water can't rise any higher. We're safe here, thanks to those who took charge and created this haven for humanity's survival."

Safe.

There it was again.

"Isn't it a bad thing that the Arctic's don't exist anymore though? I mean, the polar regions were a huge part of regulating the temperature that clearly keeps getting hotter and hotter each season," I don't know what made me speak my thoughts out loud. I was usually very quiet.

"And it's not like the natural disasters have just stopped. We all heard about another one nearby just this morning."

Everyone turned and looked at me. Well, maybe not *everyone*, but it felt like it.

I only wanted answers from someone who appeared knowledgeable.

But he was only a guide. His ability to regurgitate certain paragraphs didn't mean he had a vast amount of knowledge. Still, he answered my questions with confidence. "Our metals are robust enough to ensure we survive anything that might come our way."

What about when we run out of resources? I thought. They always seemed to skip over this part. But I suppressed the urge to speak again. It was pointless. No one on the boat could fix the inevitable, nor did they appear interested in acknowledging the truth.

The Society as a whole had given up on solutions, and chose instead to fixate on our present safety.

"Ah, and here we are. Christ The Redeemer..."

My attention drifted again as I caught both proctors watching me closely. I immediately regretted opening my mouth. I should have known better than to question the way things were.

CHAPTER TWO

I BOARDED THE TRAIN in no hurry to reach my destination. I watched the robotic nature of people moving on and off, all programmed to follow their own cyclic routines like the one the train followed, the only difference being we thought we had control over our movements. And not blinded by ignorance, I was but another cog in the machine. I was still in school. I had not entered the System, yet my days were already structured to a tight schedule controlled by people I'd never met.

Is there an exit on this train? Are other ways of existing possible? But unlike the one I rode, I couldn't see any doors through which I could slip out.

Two stops into the trip the glistening glass doors slid seamlessly open and a businessman breezed aboard.

He was a middle-aged man, evident through the creases in his wintry skin and the first threads of grey striping his hair, but his body was gaunt and slinky like an undeveloped teenager. He wore a dark charcoal suit almost identical in color to his grave eyes. A chilling frost swept outward from his body as he slumped down beside me, his bony back hunching over. He mumbled aggressively to himself, and for a moment, his skin glimmered the same metallic silver as the rings on his fingers.

I tore my eyes away.

Who is he? Or more accurately, what?

But when I glanced back in his direction through the corner of my eyes, the silver glimmer vanished. I let out a breath knowing he was human but somehow felt no relief.

A dark, toxic feeling surged in the air. It was too dense to ignore and I felt it like a storm cloud enveloping me. It seeped through my skin and throbbed inside my chest. Pain. Then, amid my confusion, my eyes burned with a heat that caused them to leak.

No, no, no, no! Maya not in public, you can't cry in public! But the tears fell beyond my control, breath flailing to help me remain centred.

I yanked an emergency pair of sunglasses from my backpack in an attempt to cover the evidence.

If anyone catches me crying in public . . . I was permanently haunted by the memory of the first time Aunt Lorraine found me crying. She threatened to take me to the hospital, or worse. She was confused. She thought my emotional overwhelm meant I was severely ill. *"Mentally unstable,"* were the words she had used when she first took me to see the phycologist, Meredith.

The train slid to a stop. I sprung to my feet preparing to exit, even though it wasn't my station. I sprinted through the sliding door, dodging my way through the cluster of people that crowded the platform, and didn't slow until I reached the harbor.

I wandered along the harbor-side pavement, catching my breath. I removed my sunglasses once my eyes had dried. The harbor was man-made, dug to open a channel from the city to the sea, but our location was far from any ocean.

I wished it was. I felt calm by the water. The swell of my emotions eased. I didn't mind crying; in fact, there was a certain beauty in sadness I almost enjoyed. It felt like an opening, an allowing. It was cleansing. But no one could know that.

The strange, etherial cloud that had consumed me on the train had cleared, while the previously sunny skies were now overcast with a heavy cloud-cover. Raindrops falling on the grey water, followed by a sweeping mist. The gloomy boardwalk was empty except for scattered patrol officers. Danger signs littered the wire fencing reading:

"WARNING; STALE WATER. DO NOT ENTER."

"MAY CAUSE ILLNESS OR DEATH."

"YOU ARE VALUABLE TO OUR GREAT CITY. WE DO NOT WANT TO RISK LOSING YOU."

For a long time I'd believed the warnings and was afraid of contact, but the water intrigued me, drew me in, and I ached to be held by it again, even if it made me sick.

But it didn't. It became a ritual to wash away a difficult day at school in the water.

I reached a hidden cove that was usually unpatrolled and dumped my bag against the concrete wall. Quickly stripping down to my underwear, I slid between the wires and sat on the edge of the boardwalk, toes dipping beneath the surface before I dropped in with a splash.

The water was always warm and murky, but it still felt fresher than the hot air. Like in the air, the deoxygenation in the water created an unstable habitat for the majority of its dependent species.

Some marine life still survived, but most species went extinct as the underwater ecosystem perished. Sea flora was the first to start dying, then the animals naturally followed. I had an old book that I read so many times it was almost imprinted in my memory, fascinated by the entire co-existing world that used to thrive in oceans and rivers. I'd read a LOT in my short existence. Especially during my years spent in hiding when I arrived in the City. Days were long, and books became another sweet escape.

At first, the plan was only to live in secret with Lorraine and Jeff until my parents came over from Australia, but when another wave of raging bushfires hit the county's last surviving colony, no one else escaped in time. The single child policy meant my existence had to remain a secret until Adam, their son, left to join the System. Adam was the one who sourced books for me. When he began training as an Officer, he had access to sections of the library that the general public did not.

In the water, I let myself sink, then effortlessly floated to the surface. This time, I dived down deeper, gliding for as long as my lungs would stretch. The moment I retreated below, everything was quiet.

Still.

Clear. Simple. Peaceful.

If there was any magic left on this earth, I felt its presence in the water. It may have been dormant, but it was still water, and water felt sacred to me. It felt like home. A truer home than this one. But even still, I wasn't sure I'd ever felt *truly* at home anywhere.

Distant memories flickered across my mind. Learning to swim as a small child in Australia with my birth parents; my dad's big, cold hands holding me as I kicked my feet. It was so long ago, but the feeling was so close, engraved into my heart. An immense, ever-present love that still rested within me even though I left so young.

When I lifted my head, a little creature was at my nose, floating, her bloated stomach contracting with slow, scattered breaths.

I cupped my hands around her delicate body and closed my eyes, bringing my lips so close to hers we almost kissed.

"May you thrive in these waters . . . or pass peacefully."

I opened my eyes for one last look and then released my grasp to set her free. She kicked her tail vigorously and soared across the water, but stopped and turned her little head to look me in the eye before disappearing into the murky depths.

Maybe she was just resting.

I spun onto my back and floated upward to face the ominous sky. Rain still fell, sprinkling over my forehead and dissolving into the water. It was a positive sign to see creatures like that. It made me wonder whether the sea could have been coming back to life. It gave me a moment hope, which was a nice break from the impeding doom I usually felt.

I inhaled deeply, and felt my whole body expand with the breath. My mind stopped, and I was just floating.

Breathing.

Inhale. Exhale.

For a moment, the sensation of the water disappeared and we merged into one.

A flash of lightning sparked in the sky, startling me out of my trance. I'd lost all awareness of time and paddled in quickly. The wind was harsh against my bare skin. I stripped off my underwear and slipped on my dress.

Thunder clapped as I walked briskly along the desolate harbor. In the distance, a muffled call pierced the silence. Footsteps echoed on the pavement. At the rising symphony of gruff male voices, I deviated off the path and ducked behind the cover of a low wall, crawling close to the ground until finding a gap to peep through.

Three officers came into view, their facial expressions as serious and urgent as their strides.

"Stop!" one ordered. The other two lowered an unconscious body to the ground.

I froze.

"Check his pulse."

One officer placed his fingers on the limp body's neck and looked up.

"One beat."

They waited. Too long.

"Another."

They waited again, but the officer checking the pulse shook his head.

"It's weak."

"I'm impressed he got this far," the officer beside him said.

"He shouldn't have," their leader said. "The voltage should have been instant death."

He crossed the border. He tried to escape the System.

"Should we kill him before the governor sees?"

Silence.

"He knew the consequences." They all stared downward at the body.

Suddenly, the man on the ground jolted. A bright blue bolt flashed beneath the skin of his wrist and electricity rippled through his body.

"Pick him up."

Again, the two officers followed their leader's command. I ducked lower as they jogged past me, boots thumping in rhythm. My breathing was fast. I hesitated a moment before emerging. I'd never seen a dead body before. I'd also never heard someone speak of death so candidly, as if it wasn't an unusual occurrence.

My steps were uneven as I continued toward the train station, body shivering, but I couldn't tell if it was out of shock or the fierce winds.

CHAPTER THREE

I WAITED ON A stiff couch in an office overlooking the city. I let myself in. I didn't think she'd mind and relaxed into the warmth of an electric fireplace. My shivering gradually calmed, and I tried to stop the excessive stream of thoughts about the dying man.

The room was OCD neat. Everything positioned just so, and as long as I'd been visiting, never an item had shifted out of place. A musky scent drifted through the room that was supposed to be relaxing, but it was a little too sweet.

A lean middle-aged woman with greyish hair and a thin pointy nose entered looking worried and exhausted.

"Oh, Maya." Meredith's hand went to her chest as she quickly composed herself. An uneasiness fell across the room.

"I didn't expect you to be here already." Her French accent was distinct, and she pressed her thin lips together in a forced smile of welcome.

"I can leave and come back when you're ready."

"Don't be silly." She took a seat on the couch across from me.

"Are you okay?" I'd overheard her arguing countless times with the man she was married to, whether cursing at him over the phone or muffled yells through the walls of the waiting room that weren't as soundproof as she believed.

"I know what you're up to young lady, you'd do anything to avoid discussing yourself."

"Isn't that what you're doing?"

"It's my job." She held my gaze, then, "Now, how has your week been?"

"Fine."

"Are you feeling more or less paranoid in comparison to last week?"

"Less. For sure," I nodded.

She raised an eyebrow, then jotted something in her notebook.

"Any unusual . . . visions?" She was almost afraid to say the word.

"Nope, just the usual," I lied.

Besides the enchanting visions of a thriving, natural world, violent images also haunted me. Ones of the entire Earth completely erased of life; black, bare, and rotting in space. I shut them out as much as possible.

Meredith jotted something else in her notebook.

"We could all be afraid if we entertained unsettling thoughts and prospects, but for now we're alive and our City is well. Find comfort in what's good. We've been safe here for decades, and there's no evidence of that changing any time soon."

I just nodded. But as much as I was able to ignore the visions in waking life, I'd often be forced to endure them as I slept. The night terrors that, even when aware I was dreaming, I couldn't wake myself from until I, too, was dead. And when I woke, the panic that stimulated my entire system would take hours to calm.

"We're very privileged to be here. Do you understand that?" Adoration for the City bled through her words.

"Of course."

"And how are you feeling about people? Have you made any friends?"

I let out a surrendered breath. I'd learned from experience that refusing to speak only caused more drama than solace.

"I just don't have much to say most of the time. But then I get nervous because I feel like I have to add something interesting."

"It makes sense to feel more comfortable with quiet after spending so much time in solitude. Adjusting takes time." She was the only person outside my family that partially knew my real history, but her job meant she was bound by a confidentiality clause. Well, Adam's best friend Cole knew too, but that was different, that was an accident, and he kind of felt like family. He kept our secret.

I nodded, somewhat comforted. We stared at each other for a few moments in silence.

"I cried on the train today, and I don't know why."

Although Meredith hid her concern, I immediately regretted sharing this information.

"Some people feel more than others," she began, "but the way you cry is abnormal and another sign of your mental instability. You especially shouldn't be crying for no apparent reason."

Her frown made me nervous.

"Perhaps it's time to try doing more things that other people do. It will be healthy to stop painting and instead go out with people your age. Have fun. Party. It will make you feel less alone."

Maybe that was the issue. I never really felt alone, even though I often was. I felt more alone surrounded by people I didn't know. People I could never know. Their shells were too thick. Their hearts too dead.

"You know when you are initiated into the System, unless you are chosen as an artist, you will legally have to stop painting anyway."

I nodded along with Meredith.

"The school socials are a great, safe environment to connect with your peers. It'd be a good idea to make the most of them before you all leave and enter the System."

"The socials. Yeah," I mumbled.

Meredith continued offering opinions, her main point: make friends, don't feel so much, stop painting, be more like the rest of the community.

My mind wandered back to the little slimy water creature I met earlier. I wondered where she might be now, whether she survived, whether she had family or friends with her. Maybe there was a little society of its own under the sea functioning under its own version of the Control. Or perhaps they were just . . . free.

The rattle of a prescription bottle full of pills drew my attention back to the present.

"These will be stronger than the ones you've been taking. They should stop the crying."

I shoved the brown plastic bottle into my bag, where I knew it would most likely stay until I found a sufficient place to dispose of its contents. It was a waste to keep supplying me with pills I never took, but when I'd refused medication in the past, it caused issues. And when I'd been submissive in taking the drugs, they made me feel numb and depressed. This was clearly the intention, but it felt wrong to suppress the life within me. I decided I'd rather feel an excessive amount than nothing at all.

The truth was, I felt an indescribable and exquisite sense of beauty in even in the most desperate moments of pain and sorrow. Each emotion felt like a portal to me, that after passing, always opened my heart wider to all the love in the world. But there was not a sole I had met to whom I could express such seemingly twisted self-observations.

A flock of bats flew over the building tops as I made my way home in the dusk of early evening. Bats adapted to the atmosphere as we did and fed on insects. They were one of the few species of animals that I'd physically seen, and emerged in the evenings when the light began to dim, squeaking acutely in their high-pitched language.

Darkness was upon the night now, and I began to walk in quicker, swifter steps through the city streets toward home as nightguards in their crisp white uniforms started to emerge.

"You best hurry home now miss," a stern voice warned. "Curfew's approaching."

I just nodded, eyes on the path as I turned down the next street.

I entered through the front door to an unusual aliveness about the house. Music played low in the background, an album we'd heard too many times in our lack of options. Lorraine and Jeff's voices echoed from the kitchen, and then another voice. My heart beating a bit faster, I dropped my bag, dashing toward them.

"Adam!"

My cousin sat at the kitchen counter while Jeff and Loraine puttered about cooking dinner together, which was always a nice sight. It was not common for couples to do more than tolerate one another's company.

Marriages were formed purely based on gene testing. When an adult was masterful enough in their field of work, they'd undergo DNA scans and other procedures to determine their genetic strengths and weaknesses. Findings would then be tested against other's results, and partners matched based on mutual strengths.

This was to ensure humankind's highest chance of survival; for each couple would then procreate their premium potential of self through a child, and every partnership was strictly limited to one child, so it was important they made it a good one. It was easier to monitor us when there was a sure three in every family, and the same rations could be distributed to every household.

I slammed into Adam, squeezing him in a tight embrace. His body was hard and tense, sculpted like a rock as a result of all his officer training.

"Happy late birthday," he said, awkwardly resting his hands around my back to return the hug.

His job as an officer for the City council required him to travel and work strange hours and strict schedules. We didn't see each other much anymore. Sadly, the work changed him. He hardened. Each time he returned home he was a little more distant.

"Are you staying for dinner?" The rich aromas filling the kitchen ignited my hunger.

"Sure am."

"We made your favorite," Jeff said. Adam and I shared the same favorite meal, brussels sprout and broccoli stew.

We didn't often get brussels sprout, and broccoli was even rarer, so when we did, it was special. Potatoes, squash, and corn dominated most of our meals—they were the only vegetables the City could depend on growing. When other vegetables *did* grow, they were offered to the upper class first, only moving down the rankings if there was enough left over.

Adam's stern expression softened as I raised my hand in the air to slap his in celebration.

After setting the table we took seats beside each other. Adam drew a small box wrapped in a silver ribbon from his pocket.

"I found this for you while I was away."

I felt a pang of guilt; it didn't feel right receiving anything more from him—he'd given and sacrificed enough for me to last a lifetime. Still, I accepted it. I could see by the look in his deep brown eyes that giving was as rewarding to him as receiving.

Inside the box was a simple, single seashell. The most beautiful gift I'd ever received.

"This is very special. Thank you." Tears threatened my eyes for the second time that day. I rested my head on his shoulder as I forced them down, his body still stiff with reserve before relaxing into my affection.

"I hope I get to see a beach again one day." Vague but sweet memories of the beaches in Australia swept across my mind as well as the seas I sailed across for months before arriving in the City. The backdrop of cream-colored sands and vast blue undulating waters were ingrained in my memory along with the smiles of my parents swimming beside me as the scorching heat made the dry land unbearable.

Lorraine started placing food on the table, followed by Jeff, who took a seat across from us.

"Maybe you'll get chosen to be a researcher," Lorraine said. "Then you'll get to go beyond the borders and travel with the officers. You're smart."

I didn't say anything, shifting uncomfortably.

"You could even train to become an officer yourself," she added as she sat down.

They both had high hopes for me, as they had with Adam.

Everyone started dishing food onto their plates, and before I could respond, Adam intervened.

"I wouldn't recommend that." His parents turned to him with a look of surprise.

I exhaled and started eating.

"You have a highly respected job. Your reputation is renowned. Even just getting through training is a great achievement," Lorraine said.

Neither Lorraine nor Jeff was overtly affectionate; they were overworked and hardened by the pressure of surviving with low ranking and paying jobs, which forced them to work redundantly for both money and social status. But they cared and were proud knowing that Adam's future would naturally be brighter than theirs.

Adam believed that being an officer was something he *had* to do; he did it for me and never complained. He enjoyed the physicality: the training, the testing of strength, but I saw the light leave his eyes when he spoke of his job. It didn't make him happy.

Then again, no one spoke with much enthusiasm about their jobs. Happiness was not a priority. Thus, my resistance toward graduating into the System.

"I am proud, Mom! Don't worry. I'm happy. I just know Maya wouldn't like it." He spooned a big mouthful of the stew into his mouth.

"Mmm, this is so good," he said.

"You bloody well should be," Jeff said bitterly. "Do you know how many people get the opportunity to raise their family status? Ungrateful is what you are, boy."

I winced, and Adam sunk a little in his chair, reverting to the timid boy I had watch Jeff strike with violent words and punches countless times in our youth.

"Dad. I'm happy."

Jeff grumbled and shoveled food into his mouth.

"Well, I'm sure you'll get some great offers. You'll be able to choose something you like," Lorraine said softly to me, ignoring her temperamental husband. I couldn't tell whether she believed it.

Based on the results of their exams, most people were only given one choice, convinced it was their one special gift to share. It was really just another instrument for people to feel proud to comply with the System.

"How was it anyway? The beach?" I asked Adam, a far more interesting topic.

"Pretty bad."

"Come on."

"No," he laughed. "I was boiling alive in my uniform and had the biggest urge to jump in the water, but we weren't allowed."

"Was it stale?"

"Yeah. To be honest, I don't think it was much cooler than the air temperature. There was steam rising from it."

"Wow, that's hot," Lorrain commented.

"No sign of life?" Jeff asked between mouthfuls.

Adam shook his head.

"Nothing has grown back since the typhoon, and sea animals were washing up all along the shore."

"How can nature just stop growing?" Lorraine shook her head, not expecting an answer.

"It's deeper than the surface damage of typhoons and whatnot. It's all in the soil. The minerals are depleted," I said before catching myself.

Lorraine and Adam both stared at me. Jeff ignored me.

At that, we were all quiet. We'd finished eating and sat staring at our plates.

Jeff was the first to stand to clear the table, followed by Lorraine.

A familiar song started playing in the background.

I took Adam's stiff hand. He was hesitant but let go with a laugh and began the first step of a routine we'd choreographed years ago in the boredom of being home alone. We continued to practice it with new moves and jumps and partner tricks. We skipped some of the tricks on their cues, considerate of our full bellies.

Lorraine emerged from the kitchen and turned up the volume. It wasn't a good song, but it had a good beat. I'd taught her the steps after Adam had left. She wasn't as practiced though and stumbled along with a light-hearted laugh.

Jeff stayed in the kitchen, occasionally glancing over our foolery, and Lorraine lost track of the steps but continued moving to the music until it finished.

Adam turned to me with the first spark of life in his eyes I'd seen all night.

"Any new paintings to show me?"

He was the only person who saw my visionary world with eyes of curiosity rather than pity.

My smile was already wide in return. "Always."

"I haven't seen what you've been working on for a while, can I come to have a quick look too?" Lorraine asked, more open than I'd seen her in a long time. She and Jeff had gone through many waves of worry over my painting habits.

"Ok." With her, I was more nervous.

We scurried upstairs to my bedroom, aware we left Jeff alone with the dishes. I watched a wide smile spread across Adam's face as we entered, shoulders relaxing as he took in the art covering the walls. Lorraine was tense, disturbed, but warmed when her eyes landed on the easel upon which rested a half-painted canvas.

It was an underwater scene, the silhouette of a whale gracefully drifting by in the background. I'd never actually seen a whale, but was fascinated by the pictures of them in books I'd read.

Silently, Lorraine and Adam admired the washes of blue and rays of sunlight that shone through its endless depths.

"It *is* beautiful," Lorraine said. "A shame you could never make a living out of it."

I nodded slowly, unsure of whether to interpret her comment as an appraisal or another gentle stab of encouragement to, instead, spend my time doing something that I *could* make a living out of.

"That's what I felt like doing," Adam gazed at the whale. "But I doubt the sea would have looked like that where we were."

He sat next to me on the floor, leaning back against the bed as he started flipping through one of my sketchbooks.

"I should help Jeff with the dishes." Lorraine slipped back down the stairs.

"Imagine if places like this still exist." He shook his head. "It would change everything."

"You'd know more than anyone. You've been out there."

"We haven't visited each country yet," he said. "We can't afford to waste the fuel on long trips. Not until we find another source to mine first." But we both knew it was a pipe dream.

The way he spoke so casually about mining whatever live resources they discovered sent alarms through my body. Clearly, the System had not learned from our past mistakes.

"Adam, I want to do something. So there's a chance for the future. But I . . ." The image of the dead man I'd seen earlier that day flashed in my mind.

"He knew the consequences," the officer had said—the consequences of rebellion.

"Maya you can't—" Adam started, his tone harsh and protective, but stopped himself. "I just mean . . . don't interfere with the System."

He was on the inside. He saw things, *knew* things about the leadership that no one else had access to. More than ever, I wanted to know what those things were.

"I don't think I can be part of the System," I blurted. Words I'd never spoken out loud before.

"What do you mean? You have no other choice."

"I don't know yet. All I do know is that when I think about graduating into a career, an allocated partner, and living out the repetitive cycle they set for my life, I feel like I can't breathe. It's suffocating."

A sadness came about him. Deep inside he understood, but he couldn't see a way out.

"The world has been in so much chaos. The Control is all we have left. It's the only way we can live in peace. And it works. We'd probably all be dead without the safety of the City." He sounded freakishly like his father.

"It doesn't feel peaceful to me." He was the only one to whom I could be totally honest with. "It feels like ignorance."

But this kind of talk was too opinionated, even for him.

"Be careful." His serious expression was unsuccessful at hiding his undercurrent worry. "It's not your duty to change what seems wrong in the world Maya. It's beyond us. It's not your weight to carry. Maybe you'd feel better if you just accepted the way things are."

His words stung. I'd already been told once that day that I should be blending in with society, but coming from Adam, the person who'd always supported me, made me feel that it's okay to be different, made me wonder if it was true.

I lay awake that night staring at my star painted ceiling, wondering if skies this clear and starry ever could exist, or if the voices that encouraged me to abandon my imagination were the wise ones. Wiser than the endless curiosity that only seemed to create distance between me and the environment that did exist around me.

I held tightly onto the seashell that Adam gave me. Just before drifting off into the divergent dreamlands of sleep, I heard a glass smash across the cold tiles of our neighbor's house and braced myself.

"I'm sick of watching you just sit there! Get out of my face. Go to bed!" a haggard female voice travelled through the metal barricades.

"Hold on a minute! Don't walk away from this mess. Who do you expect is gonna clean it up? The tooth fairy?" Though not directed at me, her words stung my chest as they did the boy she yelled at, and I wished once again for soundproof walls. It was nights when her words were the most brutal, not every night, but more that I could count.

"You're a lazy boy. You'll be a loser if you carry on the way you do!"

Sometimes he was submissive, but that night he fired back and unsurprisingly, he, too, had a bitter tongue when provoked.

"It's your mess. You clean it up fatty."

Some nights it was easier to tune out their bickering, but even still, I could always feel the pain driving it.

CHAPTER FOUR

SOME WEEKENDS I SET up a stall on the sidewalk of a busy street in the City and spread out paintings to sell. I had no permit, and it would be illegal for any adult, but I was still a minor, and I made the most of the freedoms I still had access to that I knew would dissipate in a few months time. I hadn't been told off yet, and I'd accumulated so many I needed to do *omething* with them. Lorraine and Jeff appreciated the money I earned.

"Is that an *organ*?" A man with grey eyes asked, squinting at one of my smaller canvasses.

Using a square board, I'd finely sketched a human heart in brown liner, then splashed over it with bright crimson, purple, and dark pink watercolors in an explosion of feeling.

"I think you got your biology diagrams mixed up in here." The man, wearing casual attire, was bored. He roamed the streets without company, fishing for stimulation.

"No, it's part of the collection," I said.

But he didn't get it. He didn't have a heart. Not really. His was cold, like the iron that surrounded us. I didn't know how I knew, but I could always sense the temperature of one's heart. The *aliveness*.

The man's attention drifted when I didn't bother reacting, and he continued along the sidewalk, long coat trailing behind before ducking into an electrical goods store.

The morning sun was hot and the air humid. It was a fitting day to retreat indoors.

An elderly woman sat nearby that morning with a spread of pamphlets and posters. She claimed she heard voices that told her things about the future. The urgency in her eyes when she prophesized sent chills up my spine.

Of course, most people just disregarded her. They called her "Loony Susan." Everyone mocked the things she preached. I thought that was why the officers weren't concerned about her. No one *listened* to her, so she wasn't a threat to the Control.

She caught me watching her and nodded. Her unsettling smile carried the same undercurrent as a comment she'd made to me earlier that morning.

"You see it too, don't you."

"See what?" I asked, disturbed. She just looked at me with a knowing expression. That I *knew*. She handed me a pamphlet titled *The End,* before continuing past.

I was hesitant to open it. Meredith had encouraged me not to entertain pessimistic ideas, and I was adamant not to associate myself with insanity, so I put it aside, shrugging off the frightening image of becoming an outcast like her, of being driven mad by the conflicting worlds of reality and imagination.

But as I glanced down at the cover, the bleak title was followed by *"But it doesn't have to be . . ."*

"Oh my. Look at these. They're so different," a woman said in monotone to her partner, who now stood above me, studying the paintings. Silver sparkles glittered from her eyelids, matching her shiny silver high heels. She wore a tight black dress that covered her from neck to ankle and a stiff, fitted black coat.

Their arms were linked, upholding a very civilized manner.

I shoved the pamphlet into my backpack. Although it captured my interest, to be seen associating with Loony Susan would be social suicide.

"It looks like prehistoric times." The man leaned forward, squinting his eyes. His hands were hidden in the pockets of stiff black trousers. An unbuttoned silver jacket revealed his bare white chest.

"Mmm," the woman agreed.

"Ha!" Susan let out a cackle from where she sat. "Yeah, and if we're not careful, *this* will be a prehistoric time too!" She spread her arms wide indicating the City. Her wild eyes pierced into the couple.

They scowled, sharing a look of disdain, then ignored her. She hummed out of tune and returned to her placard, spouting incomprehensible words.

I smiled apologetically at the potential buyers.

"Oh, this one's nice. What do you think?" The lady asked her partner. It was a painting of a white horse running free across a field.

"Mmmm." He lowered his voice. "If we had this in our home, our guests would think we're very charitable."

My attention drifted as they continued their quiet exchange, which I chose to ignore. I recognized a few people from school, Shalom and Ray with bedazzled totes and bulging shopping bags, and then someone else, someone unfamiliar, watching me from across the street.

He wore a white officer's uniform and helmet, but it was his eyes that caught my attention. Even from a distance their glow was surreal. I'd never seen eyes so clear, so blue, so bright. Only in my daydreams.

His gaze was intense, unsettling. I felt an impulse to break contact but at the same time infatuated by the rare moment of human connection.

"Can we buy this one?" The woman asked, forcing my attention away from the unusual man. She was already handing me the money, painting in hand.

"Thank you so much. It will be just *gorgeous* in our new home."

Ah, newlyweds. That explained their efforts to establish a 'charitable' reputation.

I smiled my gratitude in return.

Just as they left, two officers approached me with determined strides.

"Maya Turner?"

"Yes."

"I believe you turned eighteen recently?"

I was confused but repeated blankly, "Yes?"

"Good, then you won't mind coming with us."

Hands gripped my upper arms, pinching the skin and began directing me roughly away from my stand. I glanced across the street, catching a few curious eyes watching covertly from a safe distance. Shalom and Ray peered my direction, but as soon as my eyes met theirs, they darted away.

A forceful thump to one of the officer's back made him stumble forward.

"Hey! She hasn't done anything wrong! I'm the one with the signs!" Susan whacked her placard over the other officer's shoulder then hauled herself over his arm to release his grip on me.

I would've laughed if not so confused.

One officer swung his hand, striking her cheek hard. She stumbled but snarled like an animal.

"Susan stop. It's okay." I turned to the guards. "Can I at least put my paintings away?"

"I'm sure your friend here can do that for you." Spit sprayed from his lips. He picked up my backpack and tossed it at me.

"Here."

I caught it as it smacked my chest.

"All set now?" His firm grip latched back onto my arm, but I flicked it off impulsively, my forearm pressing against his to block any backlash.

"I'll come with you. Force won't be necessary." I stared into his dark, foggy eyes. His jaw tightened. He didn't want to make a scene. Neither did I.

"You don't have a choice," he whispered in my ear.

When he reached for me again, I blocked him quicker than he could grip. He swung his opposite arm, and I ducked. The second officer approached from behind and took both my arms firmly behind my back, shoulder blades jamming together.

"That's enough." His words were ice, and I surrendered, careful not to give them a legit reason to punish me.

He spun me back around to face the stand where my paintings were displayed. The other officer was now standing with one arm stretched out over them. He flicked the lighter in his hand and lowered the flame to the corner of one of the canvasses. He stared me dead in the eye. I clenched my teeth but didn't fight back against his display of authority. After a few moments, smoke began to rise from the canvas as it caught alight. Flames spread and devoured it.

The officer walked back over to me, leaving the flames to spread to the rest of the canvases on the stand. He gripped my arm again.

"Let's go," he said to his fellow officer.

"Oh, and don't worry too much sweetheart," he turned to Susan with an intimidating smile. "We'll be back for you."

"Oh, I'll be here, *darling*." She held his stare until he shifted under her eyes. I realized she had no respect for these people, and somehow, no fear.

Her whole character shifted.

"I've been looking forward to another grand trip to the castle," she continued. A pleasant smile crossed her face underlaid with all the revolt she withheld, which gave her power.

There was a history between them. The Control had taken more serious notice of her than I'd assumed.

"I do hope there have been adjustments to my usual quarters. They weren't very comfortable last time," Susan said politely. "Do be sure to make Koen aware of my dissatisfaction, won't you? Don't you agree it's unacceptable to treat visitors so poorly?"

The officer coughed attempting to muffle her words, eyes darting around to check how bystanders were responding.

She turned to me and said, "So young and sweet. What could the Control possibly want with her?"

"That's enough, Susan," he hissed.

"Poor woman," said the other officer shaking his head. "She's lost her mind."

Susan let out a spontaneous cackle that made me jump.

"Ha ha ha ha," she bellowed. "He's right everyone! I'm sorry, I've lost my mind! Don't worry, the castle is as wonderful as it looks, she'll have a pleasant time."

The officer's face was red, imploding. Het clenched his fist to keep himself from hitting her and his other hand tightened around my arm.

She spun in a dance as crazy as she declared herself. It made me wonder what they did to her, and as my imagination contemplated different scenarios, a shadow of fear crept over me.

"Don't worry dear." She touched my face, but beneath her words, her eyes spoke something like "beware."

The officer tugged firmly at my arm before she could continue.

"Like I said," his voice raised, "Poor woman."

"Back to your day everyone. Nothing to see here!" The other followed.

On synchronized cue, they drew back their shoulders, puffed up their chests, and dragged me away with the momentum of their veiled humiliation.

I looked toward the other side of the street again as we crossed.

The blue-eyed man was gone.

They brought me to the tallest building in the City.

The room, on the highest floor, was white—everything inside pristine.

A long rectangular glass table in the center featured a single vase holding a single long-stemmed yellow flower. The walls and ceiling were sheets of glass that provided a 360 view of the city and beyond.

I looked out absorbing a view that stretched further than my eyes had ever seen. Shiny iron buildings with sharp corners dominated the skyline. To anyone else, the architecture might have been breathtaking, sculpted by the most robust materials that sparkled in the sunlight. From here, the city truly appeared as invincible as it was built to be.

My body twitched, caught unaware as a man in a white suit approached. His swift strides echoing off the floor was all that gave him away until I saw his reflection in the glass. He stopped abruptly in front of me, expression stern, blocking the view as his cold white fingers wrapped around my wrist.

Before I had time to object, he twisted my wrist so it was facing upward and stuck a long, sharp needle in the center.

I gasped in response to the sting, and my surprise.

He was inserting a tracking device.

A tiny chip so rich in technology it wasn't to be underestimated.

We weren't supposed to get them until we graduated. They were part of our initiation into the duties of adulthood. These chips encouraged everyone to conform, for through them the Control had constant access to both one's whereabouts and one's livelihood. If a person was caught doing something questionable, a single press of a button would activate the chip, sending an electric jolt so painful through their body it would knock them out cold. Caught doing something unforgivable, and a single press of another button would send a higher voltage jolt, causing instant death.

Children were excluded from such harsh consequences under the protection of their naivety, but after turning eighteen, we were expected to take absolute responsibility for our actions.

Frustration boiled inside me as I stared into the officer's hazy, but fixed eyes. I *was* eighteen, but I was not yet an official adult of the System.

"Why am I here?"

He didn't respond and remained a statue, expressionless, lips pressed tight as he wiped the needle tip clean and wrapped it carefully in cloth.

"I'm sorry if my paintings offended the System, no one ever seemed to mind before . . . I'll stop selling them."

The officer activated the chip with just a few taps at his tablet. It bleeped blue beneath my skin and I felt a rush of electricity through my body. He wiped the drop of blood off my wrist, and dropped my hand. Then marched out with the same composure as he entered with.

I shifted my attention back out over the mountains of steel.

Moments after the first man's departure, an eerily authoritative voice came from behind.

"Thank you for your cooperation, Maya. What a civil offer."

It was Governor Koen.

I'd never met him personally and had only seen him speak at school assemblies or special City gatherings. He was always surrounded by a circle of his most trusted guards, so it was strange to see him alone. Somehow, he looked even more powerful.

I didn't speak.

"But you see, things have become more complicated now." He was standing directly behind me now, and while I remained unmoved, I'd been watching his approach through the glass reflection. His hands were clasped casually behind his back and he spoke in a slow and calculating manner. It was intimidating.

"Spectacular view isn't it?" He nodded toward the silver city, attempting to lighten the mood.

"Very . . . shiny," I said. Our perceptions of what was "spectacular" differed significantly.

As I turned, I saw him clearly and closely for the first time.

Strings of white spread through his grey hair and the charcoal shade of his eyes mirrored the metal he so adored. His suit was silver and reflective.

"Do sit."

I obeyed.

He took the seat directly opposite me at the long table.

"We've been watching you for some time now.

"As you know, it's crucial we watch every student in graduate year to ensure we appropriately determine your place in the System. We've identified most of your classmates. Well, as much as we can until they complete their remaining tests so we can finalize our selections. But you . . ." He paused and sat up straight.

"We're having trouble finding a place for you. Proctor Paulson told me what occurred on your school trip, and at your age I'd expect you to know better—"

"Oh, I didn't mean to challenge him sir, I just wanted to know . . ." But I drifted off, realizing that interrupting him was only proving his point. He cleared his throat and continued.

"As I was saying, we're concerned you might be showing signs of being a nonconformist. You're harmless enough now, but if this inner rebellion develops, the future mightn't be so smooth for either of us.

"Nonconformists cause problems. They make people question the way things are, and we can't afford that. There's enough chaos outside these walls. It's vital we maintain control within if nowhere else. Our System brings stability to society Maya. And through stability, peace.

"But it relies on everyone playing their part. You must see that there are too many people here to risk letting rebels disrupting the System."

I was stunned.

"Is it my paintings?" It was the only thing I was doing illegally. Well, that and swimming under the fences in the harbor . . . and the years I spent in hiding.

But no one knew about them.

"You want me to stop selling them."

"It is against customary law. But you've been a minor, so we let it slide over the years. We always assumed you'd grow out of it. Your paintings themselves however, they fill people's heads with unrealistic fantasies. Make-believe. We don't value make-believe here."

I held his gaze. "I apologize. I'll stop selling them."

He paused.

"Apart from that, I can't really think of anything I've done—"

"Ah, but that's not the point." His words remained composed and painfully detached. "See, a violent or outspoken rebel is easy to deal with, and our actions are justified by the Society when the rebellion is displayed publicly. But with you, it's subtle.

"For example. last week you gave half your rations to strangers on the street, without understanding that their situation is of their own choice and their own apathetic actions. If they don't want to work hard like the rest of Society, surely they don't deserve to live like the rest of Society, is that so irrational?"

I didn't answer, and as he stared through my eyes and into my soul, I knew he was aware of the harbor swimming too.

How could I have been so naïve?

"Anyway," he continued, bringing the conversation back to the present, "as I said, no decisions have been made. But you'll be staying here for the time being."

He stood, clicking his fingers twice, at which two offers burst through the bright white doors.

"You may escort Miss Turner to her quarters."

"Wait!" I didn't move. "My family. They'll be worried if I don't come home."

The officers paused.

"Ah, yes. Your family. Funny is it not that just the fact of you living here is an act of nonconformity? They already have one child."

My heart stopped again as I considered all he might know. Not just about me, but everyone in the Society, outside of our awareness.

"Adam left so they could adopt me."

"Of course, just after you arrived on the ship that fled Europe."

That was the story we'd decided on when Lorraine and Jeff applied for my adoption; that I'd just arrived on a ship from one of Europe's very last colonies.

Foolproof.

But apparently not. Governor Koen was far from foolish.

"And he's made a strong officer as we expected he would," Koen replied.

Then brushing it off, "Not to worry. Your family will be informed. Enjoy your stay, Miss Turner."

He turned and faced the window with a far-off gaze that signaled the end of our conversation. The officers moved toward me in long, stiff strides, taking an arm each to lift me from the chair.

I clenched my jaw tightly to avoid voicing my resistance to their aggressive grip. With the number of officers in the building, and its height, security, and location as well as the presence of Koen himself, it seemed unnecessary to be escorted this way at all.

"I'm obviously not going to attempt an escape," I told them.

As I glanced back at Koen's reflection, the corners of his lips were turned ever so subtly upward.

While being forcefully directed down clean white corridors, I attempted to process all of what just unfolded, process the idea that I might be a rebel. I'd never considered myself someone with any power to influence the Society.

They're way too paranoid.

Then again, while I'd never acted in deliberate rebellion against the Control, it was true that I had never followed their rules with high regard either. I never thought anyone noticed, but it was occurring to me that the Control had invisible eyes in hidden places.

Perhaps they're ALWAYS watching...

We reached the elevator, and as its silver doors slid open, the guards shoved me inside. After we descended a few levels the doors opened and another officer entered, staring directly at me, his uniform heavily concealing his identity. He bent his head downward, but bright blue eyes held mine from under his helmet, unmissable.

The man from the street.

When we reached our destination the doors slid open yet again. The officers shoved me out as roughly as they shoved me in, but I took one last look at the man whose eyes hadn't moved from mine since boarding.

More white corridors spread out before us, each evenly lined with white doors.

"We didn't plan it," a woman's voice echoed from the opposite end of the hall.

Moments later, two more officers appeared from around the corner, dragging a pregnant woman much like the way they dragged me.

"It's a child!" she said, exhausted, begging. "A *human being.*" She hung her head defeatedly, neck loose. I couldn't see her face.

"Not yet it's not," one of the officers replied. "Our single child policy has been clear from the beginning. No exceptions."

He looked up, acknowledging our presence with a slight nod, then opened a door and pushed the woman inside.

The door slammed shut, its bolt echoing down the hall, then silence. If the woman continued her protest, I didn't hear it. The cells were soundproofed.

I once heard of a woman becoming pregnant after she'd already birthed one child. She killed her baby before it was born by forcing herself to miscarry. I never knew if it was true. And I'd never heard of the Council killing babies, or pregnant women.

We stopped in front of a door. One of the officers opened it with a silver card and then I felt a nudge on my shoulder, an indication for me to enter.

To their defence, the cell was civilized. Simple and white as any other, but windowless.

Pristine walls, bed, chair, table, and a small cubicle in the far corner that housed a toilet and sink. I felt claustrophobic before the door even shut.

Neither officer spoke. The only sound was the thud of my backpack hitting the floor, then a high-pitched beep as the door clanged shut.

I picked my backpack up, relieved to have something familiar in the strange space. It didn't hold much; just a couple of sketchbooks, a case of pencils, my credit card and scanner, a water bottle, and the seashell Adam gave me.

I fell onto the bed, staring up at the bare ceiling, and began tossing the seashell repetitively into the air in an attempt to entertain myself.

An uneasy feeling came over me as I mulled over the conversation I had with Koen and his obsessive efforts to maintain "peace." It was as if he truly believed that if he could keep everyone and everything in the city functioning under the tightest order, the outside disorder wouldn't interfere—we'd be forever safe in his precious sanctuary.

I gave the seashell another toss, but this time it slipped through my fingers, tumbling onto the marble floor. As I rolled over to retrieve it, the pamphlet from Susan caught my eye. It must have slipped out of my backpack earlier.

Now that I was alone, I opened it. Its pages weren't covered in fear-provoking jargon as I'd expected, but rather solutions to the problems—legit solutions that specified manageable actions we could all take to reduce our negative impact on the earth.

Why is no one taking her seriously? Why is no one doing these things!?

She was smart, smarter than anyone gave her credit, and I began to think she might be the only one who saw things accurately, beyond what we were conditioned to see.

Although afraid to admit it, a lot of what she said made sense, and if that made me "loony" like Susan, I didn't know if I cared anymore. I also didn't know what was more frightening: either we were both delusional or the whole Society was.

I drifted in and out of sleep and couldn't tell how long I was there. Time dragged. I began to wonder if anyone was going to at least check on me. Suddenly, the door opened with a click.

A breath of relief.

By this time. I was sure night had fallen. Koen only mentioned one night.

As the officer stepped through the door I sprang up, backpack over my shoulder, beyond ready to leave. My heart sunk when I saw the tray he carried, realizing, as he let out an amused laugh, that he hadn't come to set me free.

"Not so fast, girly." He held the tray like a waiter would. At least he had a sense of humour.

"I'm just here to make a delivery. Can't 'av you starve." He placed the tray on the table. He was Australian too, his blokey accent about as Aussie as they get, but he hardly made the place feel homely.

"It would look bad." he added with a wink. As he turned to exit I positioned myself to bolt out of the cell beside him, but was quickly saved by my senses, which reminded me such an act would only confirm my "rebellious nature."

There were too many officers around. I'd get caught for sure.

I cringed as the door shut again, emitting a beep that confirmed its locked status. I slumped back down on the edge of the bed.

I was too anxious to eat, and the items on the tray, two cartons of meal replacement shakes, hardly looked appetizing. I did drink the bottle of water, which quenched my dry throat.

Skimming over the tray, something caught my attention.

A digital tablet.

We used them in school for note-taking. With limited trees left to make paper, the tablets created the electronic equivalent.

I stood, curious. I turned it on, and a note appeared:

Dear Maya,

You haven't been forgotten. In fact, the opposite. Over the last night I have been thinking of what should be done with you and have come to the decision that you cannot leave just yet. I have a special plan for you.

To earn your freedom, there are some things you must now do for us. If we are to let you go, we need to be able to trust that you will re-enter the System completely conformed.

I will visit you soon and explain it further.

For now, be patient and be good.

Yours sincerely,

Governor Koen

I stared at the letter for a long time. Although polite enough, the tone was threatening. What happened on the street shook some people, and he wanted to restore any loss of faith in the System. It needed for me to be in compliance.

Images of different scenarios that would serve his plan swept my mind. Frightening images in which I was no longer a prisoner, but a slave, and I couldn't decide which one would be worse. I couldn't imagine to what extreme he'd take, and trying to was draining. I felt helpless.

Instead of wasting any more time trying to figure it out, I took a deep breath and closed my eyes attempting to center myself.

I corrected my posture, straightening my spine, lifting my shoulders and drawing them back, then raising my arms above my head so slowly I felt immediately calmer. Palms pressing together, I took another deep, focused breath and let my body fall into a sequence of flowing movements taught to me long ago by a Chinese woman.

She wasn't from the City; she was from somewhere else. In my dreams she taught me tai chi.

As a child, my sleeping dreams were very vivid. So vivid that, like my waking dreams, they often felt just as real. When I'd sleep, I'd visit her in an ancient golden temple. It was small and opened to a bright isolated forest that extended for miles.

She told me it was essential to practice every day, preferably in the morning when I was freshest. She told me that if I continued practicing with discipline in my waking life, the rest of the moves would naturally become available without having to keep visiting her.

"*But I like visiting you,*" I told her, saddened. Although I only saw her in my dreams, she was the most loving presence I'd ever encountered, and spending time with her became one of the highlights of each day.

"*Even the best things have an end,*" she told me, her kind, peaceful golden eyes glowing into mine.

"*But at the same time are eternal,*" she contradicted. "*I will always live on within you. And in the distant future, we will meet again.*"

She never returned after that dream, but it was true her vibrant presence remained ever-present in my heart, and I hung on the hope of our future meeting.

The movements continued revealing themselves the longer I practiced and became an effortless flowing sequence. I sunk back into that same sense of profound presence I'd felt in the dreams, in her, where the mind was absent and, in that absence, the heart radiant.

With eyes closed, I slowly bent my knees and lowered to the floor, feeling the chi flowing, clearing, cleansing, restoring. Its purity rippled through my body, shaking off the worry and fear I'd been entertaining.

I sat still, legs crossed, focusing my complete attention inward, trying not to think too much and instead feel. Feel all that moved within the stillness. The Chinese women taught me to do this too, told me it was important.

I scanned my body from within, head to toe, catching any tension, knots, or tightness where the chi wouldn't flow. I focused on each knot, concentrating until it opened wide enough to dissolve into a clear channel.

I didn't know what I was doing or why, but I trusted her. All I knew was that it made me calm, and it was more interesting than staring at the ceiling.

Each breath I took flowed in as pure white light that washed through my body and drew out any dark mass hidden within. It disappeared on the exhale.

The longer I remained still, the lighter my body felt, and my sensory expanse of feeling widened. For the first time, I understood that the feelings I experienced weren't limited to the confines of my body, for the rage that began pulsating wasn't coming from within.

I could feel it enter from the outside. It drifted through the walls of the neighboring cell, the cell where someone was hating so heavily, I wouldn't have been surprised if they were plotting a murder.

Eyes still closed, I could feel a dwelling in the cell beside it too, and through the next wall, an immense sorrow that manifested in the pit of my belly. My womb. It was almost too much to bear, and I understood the pitch of her wailing entirely now; it was the pregnant woman, and it was only a matter of time before they killed the baby she carried.

I realized that the further my awareness spread I could feel all the pain of the entire floor at once. I'm sure I would have felt the love, too, if any was present.

A particularly dark mass approached in a brooding air of hunger, hunger for the same pain I felt in every cell. It was the appetite of the one who created it to feed off.

Koen.

My eyes sprung open. I jumped and ran to the door, pressing my eye to the tiny peephole in the center. He wasn't coming for me, not yet. He breezed straight past with his army of soldiers and disappeared into a cell a few doors down.

Fear returned, and I lost sense of whose pain was whose as it all blurred into one hazy fog.

My mind spun and raced again over all the possible "plans" he could have for me. I began to wonder whether I'd ever be free, for even when let go, I'd be entering into another kind of imprisonment. The imprisonment of laws, the Society, the System, and now, of course, Koen.

I paced the small room in spirals and circles, restless, fueled by adrenaline, by fear. An increasing sense of claustrophobia loomed, and I felt an urgency to lash out at the walls by banging, screaming, yelling, but then felt even more trapped understanding how important it was not to do that. It took every inch of discipline to suppress the emotions boiling inside me.

I tried to sit but couldn't. I looked through the peephole again to see if anyone was in the hallway, but the corridor was dead. I paced some more and digressed to shaking erratically instead of punching.

Deafened by my inner turmoil, I barely noticed the sound of the locks to my cell opening.

I froze and turned slowly, both hoping it was Koen and suddenly wishing it wasn't. As my eyes met the blindingly white silhouette of another officer, I waited. I waited for the troupe I'd seen earlier to roll in behind him, for Koen to emerge in his sparkling silver suit.

But no one followed, and the door closed.

This guard carried himself differently; there was a determination in his stride. One that strode past me, fixed on a specific point on the wall.

I followed his fixed gaze upward to a nearly hidden small black circular device, recognizing it as a security camera. I'd been naive to assume I was alone.

The man in white didn't waste a moment. He reached into his pocket and withdrew a piece of thick tape, slapping it across the camera lens.

That was unexpected. To make sense of his action, I immediately concluded it was Adam come to rescue me.

But he worked on missions outside of Council matters.

And his suit was grey, representing his lower ranking. Only the highest-ranking white suits had access to the Council building.

He spun back around and bent to unzip my backpack.

"Hey!" I warned. *What could he possibly want with my stuff? Or lack of stuff.*

He said nothing as he rummaged through, not acknowledging me or my objections, then finally stood with my sketchbook of all things, open to a detailed picture of the valley from my visions.

"How do you know about this place?" he demanded, and while covered head to toe in the same white suit every officer wore, I recognized the striking blue eyes that once again held mine.

"You were on the street . . . and in the elevator." I was distracted, now even more curious about what he wanted. *What was so important? What was so secret?*

"We don't have time." His eyes flickered from me to the hidden camera.

Again he asked, "How do you know about this place?" He was close now, holding the drawing up to my face. He had a strong accent, words sharp. German.

I pulled back a little. "I don't know what you mean. It's imaginary."

He was still, his warm, fast breath brushing my face.

"It's not . . . real." *As if anyone needs convincing of that—and an officer of all people—Right?*

His blue eyes glistened, studying me as he had on the street, but the electricity heightened as the space between us condensed.

I was infatuated again.

He broke away. "Your wrong."

He bent down, opening my backpack to shove the sketchbook back inside. Then he took the two meal replacement cartons and bottle of water, slipped them in as well, and swung the bag over his shoulder.

I'd stopped breathing and took a gulp of air just in time for him to spread a warm hand tightly over my mouth and pull me toward the door. I elbowed his gut in defence, attempting to show my disapproval, but his hand muffled the sound. I wriggled to break free, but he was too strong.

"Stop moving," he told me with a tenderness that somehow made me trust him.

I realized he might be working in my favor, and that was enough to surrender my initial resistance. As we approached the door, it was clear that he was in disguise as a Control officer and actually someone trying to help me escape.

Once in the corridor, the man stood straight and broadened his shoulders, then walked directly toward the elevator as if on strict orders.

Just as we reached it, the doors slid open to reveal another officer.

"We've got ourselves a difficult one." The man holding me remarked, avoiding eye contact, his tone grave and rough.

"Deceptive girl." I played along, squirming and elbowing his gut. He let out a grunt.

"Need a hand?" the officer in the elevator asked, sparked with concern.

"No." I've got it." He tightened his grip, voice dropping another octave conveying his capacity of unimaginable unkindness.

"Good luck then," he replied, exiting.

A nudge in my back directed us into the elevator.

Once inside, I exhaled in relief, but his hot hand remained pressed against my mouth.

Reaching the ground floor, the elevator bell dinged and the doors opened in a smooth gliding motion. Before us lay a grand, wide-open lobby with pearly white floors and a shiny desk where two women sat: the Council's guardian angels. They thoroughly examined everyone who entered before granting them access.

Guards stood at every entrance, monitoring the entire space, A few people drifted here and there. The man holding me stiffened but managed to steer us to a staff exit at the back of the lobby without much notice.

He scanned a card, his was gold, and the door unlocked with a high-pitched beep. He pushed it open to reveal a garage full of identical iron-clad cars parked in rows, each elevated high above the ground by large black tires constructed with the resilience to traverse outside the City's paved roads. They also doubled as town cars. The Control had to be resourceful.

A few officers leaned against one of these vehicles, chatting, while another was a few aisles away, loading one for a trip. All were preoccupied, but still, we were careful. My "officer" may have acted his way through so far, but I didn't know how he'd explain why he was taking a prisoner outside the building.

There was an uneasiness about him now too, which made me fear he didn't know either.

Two smartly dressed Council members, a man and woman in light conversation, walked by heading toward one of the building's entrance doors. The arm around my waist tightened, pulling me behind the nearest car. He pressed his back against the side of the vehicle, drawing me in close enough to feel his heart beating against my back.

Once they disappeared around the corner, he let out a breath of relief that tickled the skin of my neck, and for the first time he loosened his grip of me completely.

"Can I trust you to follow me?"

I glanced around, wary now of his mysterious plan, but had no other option. I couldn't go back inside, not out of wanting or safety, so I nodded.

"Good," he nodded back. He took a few steps and held a hand out behind him for me to take a hold of.

His clasp around my fingers was gentle, though unusually warm, as he guided me along the row of cars. I wondered whether he had some illness, as the only skin I'd ever been in contact with was dead cold.

We ducked around cars and slid swiftly along their sides as he checked each driver's window as we crawled passed. He stopped abruptly when we reached one with a full set of green lights flashing from the dashboard.

"Aha."

He scanned in each direction making sure no one was close enough to interfere as he unplugged a large charger from the side of the front bonnet. He then used the handle of a weapon clipped to his belt to smash the dark tinted window in one punch. He slipped his arm through the sharp shards of remaining glass to unlock the door.

"Quick!" I crawled over the driver's seat to the passenger's side as he got in and quietly shut the door behind him.

"I'm Björn by the way," he said, scanning his master key to disable the car's tracking system.

He slid off his helmet, and for the first time I saw his face. He was younger than I expected, not much older than me, but that's not what made my heart stop.

There was a reason those eyes looked so familiar. Those bright blue, ocean eyes.

I had seen them before.

But not in the City.

In my dreams.

I couldn't breathe. There was no doubt. Sitting next to me, in his white-suited disguise, was the young man from my visions. The man I'd drawn and painted countless times.

Every feature, every curve and line on his face was identical. I knew because, well, I thought I'd created him.

I was speechless. Suddenly I realized I hadn't returned the introduction, but he wasn't looking at me. He hadn't seen my reaction, which was a good thing because there's no way I would have been able to hide the tears that stung my eyes, and no way I could've explained the cause of them. My heart pounded in my ears. I tried to collect myself, regulating my breath to a steady rhythm.

As Björn slipped his card into a slot in the dashboard, the sound of the ignition grumbling to life drew me back to the present.

"Hey!" an officer yelled.

As I twisted around to see how many had caught us, Björn's gaze remained fixed ahead. He pressed down hard on the pedal.

"Give me your phone."

"I don't have one," I managed.

He scanned me carefully to be sure, before rolling down the window to throw his beneath the moving wheel, crushing it as we sped off.

CHAPTER FIVE

WE DROVE.
Fast.

Questions.

A million questions spun around in my mind, but I didn't know where to start and didn't dare break Björn's concentration. We had escaped before any other cars could have started following us, but they would be on our trail by now surely. I sat in silence, leaning back into the leather as we sped through the City back streets. One question did burn the most though: *How is this blue-eyed man beside me even real?*

I was sure I created him. He was from the world in my mind, my imagination. He even mentioned something about the world in my mind, as if he knew it too, but how could he possibly?

I tried not to indulge my fascination by staring at him, for he couldn't know I'd seen him before.

Met him.

Knew him.

Drew him.

Björn looked from the road to me for the first time, but I couldn't meet his eyes. I felt sick. We continued in silence until the traffic slowed and we pulled on to a long stretching road.

"I'm sorry for holding you so tightly," he finally spoke. "I hope I didn't hurt you."

His sincerity surprised me, but he didn't wait for me to accept the apology.

"How much do you know?"

I dared to catch his eyes, but I was confused.

"Know about what?"

"The prophesy."

I looked at him again, I couldn't help it.

"I don't even know what "prophesy" means," I said, hoping he'd stop asking and better yet, explain.

"Where are we going?" I asked again now that he was speaking, and while one of the more urgent questions I wanted answers to, I was so mesmerized by him that even if he answered something horrible, I probably would've still gone without complaint.

"The place in your drawings. The valley. It exists," he said, mystified that I didn't know about it.

He reached his hand into his jacket and pulled out a rolled sheet of old tarnished paper. As he handed it to me, his hand brushed mine, sending a jolt of heat up my wrist.

"Ouch! You—" *burnt me*. But I cut myself off and turned my attention to the scroll. The way he watched me made me think it was important, but when I unrolled it, it was blank.

When I looked at him he seemed nervous, but not quite as nervous as I felt.

"What is this supposed to be?" I asked.

His fingers tapped the wheel.

"Look again," he finally said.

This time as I studied the large, tattered paper more closely, a drop of black ink appeared in the centre and began spreading, forming lines as if they were being drawn in real time.

As I waited, eyes glued to the paper so not to lose sight of the unexplainable phenomena, I realized the lines were creating a map.

"The valley of Santōṣha," Björn said. I'd never heard such a bizarre name.

Still, my eyes remained on the drawing. It showed a long, singular strip of land surrounded by a large body of water, an island, with its own orbiting sun and moon, and a valley that ran down its centre.

It was a planet in and of itself, but located within the centre of another planet.

Earth.

I shook my head. It was fascinating to think about but positively impossible.

Horror swept over. This can't be the reason he rescued me. Anyone could draw a picture of something and give it a name. *What makes him think it's real?*

Björn's gaze shifted from the road to me. He wanted answers.

So did I.

"What *is* this?"

"You really don't know?"

My blank expression was answer enough.

He reached behind his seat, shuffled around in my backpack, then dropped my sketchbook on my lap. I opened to the first page, a painting of the valley. I carefully compared it to his map. They were almost identical, but again, anyone could paint a valley.

"I thought you must have known about it and the prophesy. Been there even!" He was the one confused now.

"These are just drawings. Björn, I . . . I've never seen this place before."

Björn stared at the road for a long time, expression shifting and changing.

"But you have," he said.

"You don't understand. This can't be coincidental." He was so sure, I almost believed him.

"It's not just the valley," he continued, reaching over to flip through my sketchbook.

"I've seen a whole bunch of pictures and sketches from this place and they're all freakishly similar to yours." He let out a laugh. "I'm sorry. I know you have no idea what I'm talking about, and it must sound insane, but somehow, some part of you knows this place."

We both sat silent, deep in thought.

After pondering this, I broke the silence. "And it's inside the earth." I was dumbfounded. "Björn, that's not—I just don't see how that could be possible. The core of the earth is solid. It's a proven fact. It's made of iron and nickel and other elements. It's hot as the sun and . . ." I racked my brain for anything scientific I'd actually retained about the planet.

Amusement tickled his eyes.

"It's not inside the earth. It's inside another dimension within the dimension of earth."

I was beyond confused now.

"Björn, I just want to know what's going on."

"So do I," he laughed. "This isn't a joke. Really."

"Santōṣha is a realm," he explained. "And only those light enough, who live in high enough states of consciousness, can travel there. Most people are too weighed down by their investment in the life they lead on earth to even consider worlds outside of it. But the map has a consciousness of its own. It revealed itself to you, and it only reveals itself to people who can meet its consciousness, and have the potential to pass through the veil."

I felt sick again.

"How do you know all this?"

"Like I said the map has a consciousness. It... communicates."

I shake my head, pretending just for now that I didn't hear that.

"So wait, it's not a physical place?"

Björn drew a breath. "It is. But only within the dimension it resides in."

He exhaled. "All beings on this planet are created to survive in the realm they are born and that realm alone. We're not supposed to cross dimensions. There are veils that keep the realms separated. But the people of the valley have been reaching out. They want to be found, and we want to know why. *I* want to know why," he corrects himself.

"They?" The image of the enchanting Indian woman on the bridge and the camouflaged shelters of the valley returned.

It still didn't make sense.

Somehow, I'd seen *him*, drawn *him*, before I knew he existed... The idea that the same could be true of this interdimensional valley seemed less impossible than it sounded. Something about his conviction was genuine and grounded, it could have been a delusion, but I was sure it wasn't a straight out lie.

"Björn, where are you taking me?" He still hadn't answered my very first question, but it was clear we were heading further away from the City and closer to the border.

"We can't stay here."

But that still didn't answer my question.

"Björn. Where are we *going*?"

His eyes darted from the road to the map. My question was answered.

"Stop the car."

"I know this sounds absolutely and utterly insane and I'm truly sorry to have dragged you into it. Seeing your paintings you were selling on the street, I was so sure you already knew—"

"No, I . . ." I squeezed my eyes shut. "I think I might believe you."

His eyes lit up with hope, but I quickly shook my head.

"But whatever your plan is, you can't take me with you." I held up my wrist to reveal the tiny bleeping blue glow trapped beneath layers of skin.

Björn slammed his foot on the brakes. The car skidded and tires screeched as he spun the wheel to steady us.

"I thought you were still in school!" he exclaimed as we came to a stop in the gravel beside the road.

"I am!"

"As soon as the Control knows you've escaped, they'll start tracking us. They probably already are." He slammed his hand against the wheel. "Damn it!"

I remained calm, and a solution quickly became apparent. I knew what I had to do.

I rummaged through the glove box, searching for something sharp, but all I could find was a screwdriver with hardly the blade I had in mind. We had no time; it'd have to do. I steadied my wrist, pointing the tip of the screwdriver over my target.

"No. Maya you can't! It will kill you!" Panic rose in his voice that vibrated the space between us, but I didn't break focus.

The tracking devices were inserted precisely into the central vein of the arm, so if anyone was rebellious or dumb enough to attempt their removal there was a high chance the vein would be severed and they'd bleed to death.

"There's no other option." Getting caught and leading them to Björn seemed like a worse repercussion. I had to get it out.

I concentrated on the task at hand, removing myself from his panic. The embedded chip was a small, dark square lump, flashing under the skin of my wrist. I traced it with the tip of the screwdriver. It would've been easier to see if the skin around it wasn't stained with the purple and yellow bruise marks of its insertion.

"Ahh!" I cried out as a high-voltage shockwave of electricity raced up my arm. I stared down at my wrist, the tracker flashing like the lights on an officer's vehicle in hot pursuit.

"They know you're the fugitive!" Björn said. We both knew it'd only be a matter of time before they checked my holding cell. Their punishment had begun.

"Ahh!" I cried out again as another shock pulsed through my system. Without further hesitation I lifted my hand holding the screwdriver and drove the tip into my arm, stabbing with enough force to break the skin.

The tip wasn't sharp enough, so I had to press and carve into my wrist to create a decent opening. The device dwelled deeper than I imagined. I winced at the sharp sting, grinding my teeth together.

Blood oozed from the wound, but I drove the blade deeper, squeezing the skin around the chip with my free hand until it finally popped out along with dark clumps of blood. I flicked it onto the seat.

"Ugh." A groan slipped through my gritted teeth as the pain caught up with me. As expected, I'd punctured something in the process, something important. I just hoped it wasn't too important.

I held my hand over the gash as warm pools of blood gushed onto my palm, leaking through the gaps between my fingers. It throbbed.

Björn picked up the sticky cube and observed it for just a second. Blood painted it crimson. It was still flashing blue. He rolled down his window, ready to toss it out into the gravel.

"Wait! Don't," I said. "If we leave it here, they'll know which way we're heading."

"They're probably already tracking it. We can't risk leaving it active."

But I couldn't risk leaving any clues.

I took the chip from him and held it carefully. I glanced out the window to see a distant car approaching in the opposite direction.

Thinking quickly, I ripped a piece of fabric from the hem of my dress and wrapped it tightly around my bleeding wrist then swung open the door and sprung from the car, hardly checking for traffic as I sprinted across the road.

I waited, adrenaline pumping as my eyes darted along the bare bitumen, well aware that the chance of another car passing was highly against my favor—and one not occupied by Council workers even more so.

A small car came into view, plodding toward me. As it got closer, I ran onto the road, waving my arms above my head. The driver slowed the vehicle to a stop in front of me, winding down the window. My heart beat fast in my chest.

"Thank you so much for stopping," I said, panting a little. "I'm sorry to bother you, but I've cut my wrist," holding it up for her to see, material already heavily blood stained.

"Oh! That looks painful," she said with annoyance rather than concern.

I hadn't planned past this point but continued on before she had a chance to pull back onto the road.

"We ah . . . don't have a first aid kit, and it won't stop bleeding. I'll have my whole dress wrapped around it soon." I laughed weakly then said, "Would you have a bandage or gauze padding you could spare, just until we get to the hospital?"

For a moment, her expression remained unreadable, then she reached under the passenger seat, pulling out a first aid kit. She swung open the lid and began rummaging through.

"You know what? Just take the whole thing."

"Are you sure? That's very generous."

"Yes. Please," she said. "They're easy enough to replace, and I don't have time to fumble through it."

I pressed myself against the passenger door, reaching through the window to retrieve the kit while simultaneously dropping the device I'd been clenching tightly inside my fist, between the crack of the driver's seat and door.

Mission accomplished.

"Thank you so much. I truly appreciate your help," I said, already turning away.

"I hope it heals," she called out the window.

"Thanks again!" I waved as she peeled back onto the road, zooming off in the opposite direction we were heading.

I held the wounded arm to my stomach, almost laughing with relief. The officers will be led off our track.

I looked back at Björn who rested tensely against the car, watching. Suddenly, my vision blurred, only the shadow of his silhouette visible.

I became lightheaded and lost my balance.

Weird.

I shook it off and jogged back across the road.

"You're safe," I said. "We're safe, I mean. They won't suspect anything in this end of the sector."

"That was brilliant."

I half smiled, then winced as the pain spread up my entire arm.

"The woman gave me this." I held out the first aid kit, genuinely thankful for it. "Can you help me wrap my wrist?"

I half stumbled as I passed the kit to him. *What's happening to me?*

He quickly caught me, arms startlingly warm and electric against my skin again.

How can a human have skin so hot?

I shivered.

"Are you okay?"

For the first time, I allowed myself to take a proper look at him, his concerned eyes piercing into mine with a kind of care I'd never received before. There was so much depth to them that suddenly I was swimming, diving, gliding, reaching something so grand, so unfathomable—*Stop!*

I'm delirious. I pulled myself away.

"Yeah. Fine." I know I sounded unconvincing.

"Just a bit dizzy.

CHAPTER SIX

WE SAT ON THE red stone gravel, using the car as a shield in case anyone followed our original route.

I winced as he unwrapped the torn red rag now glued to my skin. As soon as the pressure was released, a fresh river of blood, along with dark gelatinous clumps, flowed again, leaking from a seemingly infinite pool. My face drained to white.

"Maya, you're losing a lot of blood. You must have cut into one of the main arteries."

I couldn't do anything about that now. All we could do was try to stop the bleeding.

"Just rewrap it, tightly."

His eyes widened as he peeled off the last layer, revealing the wound.

The gash had grown, tearing open on either end. Yellow puss accompanied the gushing blood.

"How did that happen so quickly?" I didn't expect an answer.

Björn pressed his lips together, jaw tightening as he avoided my gaze.

"Björn?" He knew something I didn't.

He cleared his throat, plotting a fabricated version of the truth but then surrendered under my interrogating stare.

"You've been poisoned."

"What?"

He inhaled slowly.

"The tracking devices are installed with a dose of poison that leaks if it gets ruptured. It slowly enters the bloodstream and when it does, well, I've never heard of anyone surviving."

"Why would they do that?"

"The only way the poison can escape is if someone tries to remove the device." He shrugged. "That's the measure the Control takes to make sure no rebels survive in the System."

I squeezed my eyes shut.

Björn sifted through the kit unaffected and began cleaning the wound with whatever he could find.

"What are you doing?"

He looked up.

"You just said no one survives this poison. You should go before anyone find's us. If I'm going to die anyway—"

He gently placed his fingers on my lips. His face so close I could taste his warm breath on mine. They slipped slowly down to my chin, then without a word he turned his unwavering attention back to the wound. The tender care of the way he handled me was overwhelming.

"I'm no doctor, but I do know that there's an antiserum for every chemical they use in medical, and we're going to find the one that treats this."

He squeezed ointment onto a clean wipe, and I felt a sharp sting as he dabbed it over the raw hole in my skin.

"The people in the dimension we're traveling to are . . . different. They have powers beyond the world we know. There'll be someone there that can help us," Björn assured me. And while I still barely believed of its existence, my heart lifted with hope. In my hurry to remove the chip, I almost forgot about the valley.

"I still have to go back," I said, heart sinking again, I squeezed my eyes shut, swallowing shards of pain.

His hand froze over my wrist.

"I can't leave my family without letting them know I'm okay."

Björn finished wrapping my wrist and taped the bandage.

"You're not okay. And we can't go back."

I opened my eyes. "*We* don't have to." He looked at me as if I was crazy.

"I don't even know where this place is or how to get there or what your business with it is, let alone *my* business with it. It's highly possible it's not even real. I don't know. But my aunt and uncle, my cousin, have sacrificed everything to take care of me. It would be selfish to disappear. Especially after the trouble with the Council." I shook my head, unable to imagine what the Council might do to them in retaliation.

Before a few days ago, I thought the Council was harmless. Strict, but harmless. Now I wasn't so sure.

"The trouble with the Council is *why* you can't go back. There will be officers at your house waiting for you. I bet they're there as we speak. I think your family will be more worried if you're locked away."

I stood abruptly, knowing very well what he said was true but still paced across the dirt in no particular direction, just away.

To breathe.

But frustration possessed me.

"Why did you even help me?" I said, spinning back to face him. "I would have been fine! I didn't need saving."

I stomped back toward him as I fired off. "They would have just let me go once they realized I wasn't a threat. Now I look exactly like the rebel they accused me of being."

Björn was quick to respond. But his fire was fuelled by compassion.

"Do you honestly believe that?" He stood. "Because from what I see, every part of you is a threat. You see beyond. You see the world clearly for what it can be instead of just accepting what is. And that's more threatening than anything."

He paused for a moment, letting his words sink in, then continued.

"You would have never become a true conformer of the System, and they never would've tolerated that."

"How can you say that!" I wasn't angry with him, I was mad at the situation, but still, I took a stab. "You don't know me at all. You think you're being some kind of hero by rescuing me and bandaging my hand—"

Björn cut me off.

"You're not a victim." He remained calm, centred. "I want to protect you because I have a feeling that you're more powerful than anyone I know."

We were close now, faces only inches away.

"I rescued you because your power is wasted in the System. They'll never understand you, and they'll never allow you to be who you are. You'll either be suppressed into complacency, or punished for rebellion."

He stopped again, searching my eyes. I didn't know what to say, but his voice was soothing. Even though the truth in his words was unsettling, I knew he was right, except for the powerful part, that was an assumption for sure.

Still, I attempted to refute him, but it was weak.

"You don't . . . even know me," I drifted off, hardly even believing that myself.

"Tell me you don't want to find the world you envisioned and I'll leave you. But I think it would be a mistake. I think you have a greater purpose than to spend your life hiding in a world where you don't belong. I think there's a reason for your visions. They mean something."

I had nothing to say. I couldn't honestly ask him to leave me here.

As wrong as it felt to leave my family behind without an explanation, Björn was right: there was no way I could go back without being caught. I had to stay away at least until the Control cooled off, then I'd sneak back for them.

"But it's not even a real world, it's a . . . " My voice drifted off in weakness. I felt too lightheaded to think about what the word "dimension" entailed.

"Trust him," the majestic woman on the bridge had said. *Was she talking about Björn? Had she known he was coming?* Everything was getting trippy. It was all too intertwined.

My heartbeat slowed and everything calmed and became vague. I felt like a feather that might float away on the next gust of wind, and in contrast to the fire I'd accumulated within, a rush of icy cold swept through my body.

My head spun.

My ears rung.

My wrist stung, sharp pains shooting up my arm.

My vision blurred until everything faded to black and I felt myself falling.

Miles of dry earth swept past as we drove beyond the inner City. I was unconscious for only a short time, but the vague despondency didn't leave. My arm throbbed, but the river of blood had calmed.

Björn allowed me to process everything in silence, but I was aware of his subtle glances to check that I was still awake and breathing.

We passed crops of wheat struggling to grow and vast acres of dull farmland where people were scattered about the fields attempting to bring life forth, but with the Council's car for disguise, no one took much notice of us.

I started speaking my thoughts aloud—they were making my head ache—and found Björn to be a generous listener, more attentive than any therapist.

"I was born in Australia," I began. He was the first person I felt safe enough to share the truth of my past, without filtering every second word.

"My parents were caught in the fire. They sent me here while they stayed behind to help fight it, thinking that like any fire it would have to die out eventually. Most people assumed that.

"We were one of the last colonies there and had heard about the legend of this City. My parents wanted to give me the best chance of survival just in case things got out of hand, so they sent me here on a boat with my Aunt Lorraine and cousin Adam, who'd come back to collect the last boxes that my parents kept in storage for them. Jeff, my uncle, was already here working, they'd moved before I was born.

"They planned to hide me until Australia was stable again, or if it got worse, my parents would follow and register as the standard family of three. But it was over those next few months that the fires got way out of control and no one else escaped in time.

"Months became years, and they took care of me like a daughter, careful to keep me hidden from the Council.

"Adam shared half his rations with me, gave up his bedroom, and slept on the couch. He tried to spend time with me after school most afternoons and share things about the outside world. He snuck me out as often as he could, always investigating where guards would be less likely to detect an unrecognizable face, but for the most part, I grew up at home alone. That's when I became absorbed in painting. It was my entertainment.

"When Adam turned sixteen, he left school to train to be an officer for the Defence Force so I could register for adoption and go to school and have a normal teenage life. Even that was a risk though because my aunt and uncle had already raised one child, but they took a chance and made up a convincing story that I'd just arrived from Europe."

Officers were the only people granted the option to move out of their home before graduation and finish their final years in intensive training compounds where they'd bunk with other initiates. Otherwise, families lived together until the child was ready to marry and start their own family. There wasn't enough space or resources for them to occupy a house on their own.

I'd been gazing out the window as I spoke, and when I finally turned to Björn, his features captured the most understanding expression.

He didn't say anything.

He didn't need to.

We were fast approaching the border. The Council didn't bother installing a fence to mark it. Instead, there were thin iron poles connected by electrical currents that detected the tracking device of anyone who passed, which in turn would activate and explode. For the rest of their lives, they'd walk around with the shame of a half-blown off arm and sentenced to the lowest-ranking jobs like trash collectors, janitors, sewerage cleaners, etc.

The voltage wasn't high enough to kill the defectors. Well, that's what I believed until a few days ago. Their survival served as a warning for anyone else plotting an escape.

"We'll have to ditch the car before we pass the border," Björn said.

Just like us, Council cars had an embedded chip that activated at the border. It was activated differently though. It lay dormant until the vehicle left the City grounds. The Council would then track its movement to make sure its mission stayed on course.

I closed my eyes, still weak, trying once again to shake the image of the dying man at the canal. If I hadn't cut out the chip, I'd most likely soon be suffering the same fate. Then again, my fate may already be worse than that unfortunate man's, for although it didn't get the chance to blow my arm off, the device had performed well in leaking enough poison into my bloodstream for my descent toward death.

I nodded.

"Tell me about the prophesy."

CHAPTER SEVEN

BJORN PAUSED, THOUGHTFUL, BEFORE he began.
"It was my parents who found it," he started. "They were both scientists who studied the soil's minerals for fertility. We were originally from the last colony of Germany but they got transferred to the City to work for the Council when I was young, and after being appointed work as part of a regeneration team, they began making discoveries that gave them conflicted feelings about their research." His German ethnicity came through in his accent and rugged features.

"They found that much of the soil here was still fertile. On the surface it looked lifeless, but underneath is was rich with minerals. My parents believed it was nature's way to protect the planet from humans depleting it completely. They understood that if we continued to use all of nature's resources to fuel our city, it would cause the extinction of all living things.

But because the Control couldn't see beyond their need for fuel and resources, my parents took it upon themselves to keep nature's secret by making sure any evidence of the land's fertility remained hidden. They withheld the true results of their tests and forged reports that proved the land as dormant."

"The land is still alive!" I interrupted.

Björn nodded. I felt like a fool for underestimating the earth's competence... And intelligence.

"That would've been a dangerous secret to keep."

"That wasn't their only secret. Over time, everything they came to believe conflicted with the System, but their chips trapped them. They had more freedom than most because their jobs required travel beyond the border, but if they stepped off their set path, their devices would activate, just like any other citizen. They accepted the fact that they couldn't escape or change the System, so instead worked within it in the hope their efforts to reserve fertile land might allow it to re-grow and regenerate for the future generations.

"They found the prophesy buried at the wreckage site of an abandoned town they were sent to research. It was rolled up in a golden canister that was engraved with symbols and markings we couldn't match to anything we've ever seen in our world.

I was about eleven at the time and still remember their obsessive study of it. It consumed their spare time. They knew that it had to stay hidden from the authorities.

The prophesy confirmed their assumptions about the land, its fertility, how it's still very much alive."

He turned to me.

"No matter how bleak it seems, Earth will survive because Santōṣha does. Santōṣha, Earth's alternate dimension, fuels and feeds ours. It is sustained by a higher frequency of light than Earth, a higher frequency of consciousness that has the power to ripple into our dimension, but we have been living in an era of too much ignorance and destruction to allow it in. The beings that live in Santōṣha are the caretakers of the entire ecosystem, because they reside in a high enough consciousness and intelligence to understand we are not separate from nature. They live outside of the cycle of mere survival and suffering that we experience here as humans."

I shook my head. "So what do these beings want with us... lesser beings?" His story was incomprehensible, but with each detail he revealed, I became hooked.

"Not lesser. Just less informed." He corrected, clearly excited by my interest. "And that's exactly what we're going to find out."

But I was still sceptical.

"How could you get all that information out of one prophecy? What do you even mean by prophesy?"

"Look for yourself," he said, nodding down at the map on my lap that was a blank page once more.

I held it up again, waiting for the map to reappear.

"*This* is the prophesy?" I asked in disbelief.

"I told you, it's not just a map. It's an interdimensional communicator."

I stared, willing the map to re-appear, but it didn't.

"The page paints upon itself the information you desire to know. But it cannot be a desire of the mind. The mind is too limited to comprehend any of it. It must be a curiosity of the heart," he explained.

"I only know this because we spent a long time experimenting and working out its ways. It took a long time for anything at all to show up. So, the fact that you have already seen the map is a good sign."

I ran my fingers gently over the brownish page, considering what he meant by a curious heart, but it seemed my heart must have already been curious, for a spot of ink appeared, followed by a line that continued to draw an identical sketch of the village in the valley I'd seen many times in my mind's eye. I finally understood Björn's wonderment.

Words started to write themselves in elegant handwriting. A letter from the locals. A prophesy that dated back to the early 1900's, of all that was to unfold on Earth in the years to come.

I could barely believe the unfathomable force of magic that made the words I read possible. It was surreal. And the prophesy, impeccably accurate...

The beings from the other dimension had predicted the rapid decline of all life across the lands.

The depletion of humanity, our fall into an age of ignorance and self-obsession, and nature's attempts to shock us into action with brutal warnings, was foreseen.

If we remained complacent, the final phase of the prophesy was clear.

Natural disasters would wipe the remains of humanity from the planet for good. Problem solved.

While its writer didn't state why we were being called upon, it was clear that a different ending to this story was intended.

As we drove, Björn continued his story.

"At one point, my parents started treating me differently. For years they'd been working on a way to counteract the poisonous chemicals in the chips and deactivate the tracking signals, but it started to seem that the chips were indestructible. So, they began preparing me to make the journey to Santōṣha instead, with or without them.

"Something we learned early on about the dimension is that you can only slip through the doorway if you're "clean". Clean of the "shadows," as they're called in the prophecy. There was a lot of stress on becoming "internally empty," so a lot of my preparation was in clearing and freeing as many shadows as I could sense wrapping me. It took a long time to build up the skill of being able to feel when we're taught to numb ourselves from birth." He laughed lightly.

"It's to protect their world from the negative forces of ours slipping through," he explained, "If there are shadows trapped within us, we carry their potential for darkness, even when they're not actively being expressed."

I furrowed my brow in confusion. He was speaking a foreign language, the language of energy, the unseen, but it was making sense at the same time.

"By 'shadow' do you mean the . . . " I closed my eyes. It had always been beyond explanation, even just acknowledging it made me feel crazy.

I continued. "They're like lumps of . . . I've never really understood it, but I guess it's like a sense of an unseeable force running everyone. Like no one has full control over their actions and desires. They are driven by... shadows I guess."

I opened my eyes to find him staring at me.

"Yes." He was quiet for a moment.

"That's another reason I was sure you'd seen the prophesy because there's a sense of lightness about you that feels purer than anyone I've ever met. I could feel it from a mile away on the street that day, like an empty container among a street of concrete bricks. I was sure you'd kept yourself clear for the same reason I do, and then when I saw the paintings . . . "

He shook his head again, but continued his story, knowing I had just as little an explanation for all of this as he did.

What did he mean by "feel it"? Could he sense me the way I could sense everyone in their cells yesterday? Is that part of being clear?

My head spun again.

"If it had been up to me, I would've waited longer before leaving. I still carry shadows. Working for the leadership has bought up as many complications as benefits. Shadows seep in slowly and are transferred between people and environments so subtly its often hard to tell somethings hooking into you until you feel the full weight of its negativity. And there are a *lot* of shadows running the Control.

"But we knew my best chance of escaping would be by working my way up through the ranks and securing one of the few jobs that don't require a tracking device and that gives me access to the planes.

"So that's what I did. I was lucky because my parents were already in Governor Koen's entrusted circle. My mother and father trained me, teaching me everything about the heads of the Council so I could mirror them.

"I've been working as Koen's supreme general for two years now. I attend every Council meeting, hear every phone call and conversation, have access to every key for every lock across the City, and have ultimate authority over all the guards. Usually, my uniform would be silver, like Koen's. This is a disguise. I have no doubt I'm being hunted right now too."

I stiffened, only now realising his acts of secrecy and rebellion were far more explicit and life-threatening than mine.

He continued. "The morning I saw you on the street, my parents were captured by the Control as traitors.

"They were respected scientists, but of the land, not the lab. All their visits to and from the Council for materials unrelated to their allocated work attracted attention. They were caught in the lab after-hours testing their latest serum against the tracking chips.

"I haven't seen them since. I figured the Control would immediately distrust me as well. That's why I had to abruptly leave. Before they stuck a chip in my arm or locked me up or . . ." Björn went quiet.

I didn't dare to ask where his parents were now. If I was considered dangerous enough to be locked away for showing signs of rebellious implications, I couldn't even imagine the punishment for people forthrightly working against the System.

He stared ahead, expression tense, with a tight grip on the wheel.

"I'm sorry," Was all I said.

I respected his need for quiet as he mine earlier, but my mind was far from quiet. Our conversation stirred concerns for my own family's safety, and it began to sink in that where we were going was no simple trip across the country. Nor was it a trip to another. Our destination wasn't located upon earth at all.

"Björn, how exactly do we *pass through* into the other dimension?" I quoted the words he'd used earlier.

"There's only one entry. It's in a part of the sea called the Bermuda Triangle. The map doesn't show how we pass through, but the entrance is pinpointed."

"But we'll come back, right? If we find this place and it's safe, we can come back and get Adam and Jeff and Lorraine and anyone else. Right?" But before he had a chance to respond, a sharp pain shot up my wrist.

"Ugh." I curled inward, alarmed by a sudden burning in my heart.

My head pounded and vision blurred, sirens blaring in my brain. Blackness wiped me out again as I fell back into my seat.

When my eyes fluttered open, I knew I'd been unconscious for some time. I felt disorientated and lightheaded, my entire body ached, muscles throbbed in dense, pulsating rhythms.

It took me a moment to focus, my eyes stinging as they opened. No longer in the car, I found myself laying on rough earth, dry dirt pressed into my skin. A figure hovered above me, distorted, more like a beam of light, speaking words. Words that were all but slurring sounds to my ringing ears.

I tried to force myself to focus, understand what Björn was trying to communicate, only to fall unconscious again.

The rest of our journey slipped by in a haze as I flickered in and out of consciousness. When awake, I could feel the poison spreading through my bloodstream. It was powerful. Being unconscious was the only way to reserve enough energy to fight it.

I willed the strength to move, but my body wouldn't cooperate, and every time my eyes flashed open, the environment had changed. Sometimes when I awoke, if felt as if I was in motion.

Is Björn carrying me? Is he superhuman?

I woke and vomited. The surges of sickness escalated in waves until I finally purged, my body determined to be cleansed of the poison.

The land we traversed was barren and the sky overcast in a never-ending dusk, an ever-grey blanket of smog polluting the atmosphere. Miles of nothingness dominated, garnished by odd swamplands and small hills.

My body burned, but I couldn't discern between what was internal fire and what was the sun on my skin.

When I would awaken, Björn poured water down my throat while he had the chance before I faded into the illuminating blackness again.

CHAPTER EIGHT

IT'S NIGHT. I LAY on the floor of my bedroom, staring up at the star-painted ceiling. The solitude may have been torture to anyone else, but I'd never known anything different. I was in hiding.

And somehow, I never felt alone. There was always this presence, warm and loving. I couldn't explain it or even make sense of it; it was just there. Ever-present.

"Maya." Adam's face peeped over me. I thought everyone was asleep.

I propped myself up on my elbows as he crouched quietly next to me.

"Hi." I was wide awake.

"Wanna come to a party?" he whispered, a rebellious glint in his eye.

He was dressed in his only pair of good jeans that matched his black leather jacket. He carried a mask.

Adam didn't sneak out often. The night watchmen made it a risky feat. His school organized dances, and Adam was at social events almost every weekend (everyone adored Adam), but by eleven o'clock he'd be home, often creeping into my room to share the stories of the night.

"Don't tease me," I said, punching his arm.

"I'm not." He held up the mask to reveal not one but two.

"It's a secret masquerade gathering in an old abandoned house. We spent the last few afternoons soundproofing the walls. We'll all be wearing masks. We can't risk using lights so it'll be dark inside and we've shaded the windows. If you come, everyone will think you're just another eleventh grader."

A splash of fear and excitement simultaneously rushed through me.

This is unwise. I knew on an intellectual level the risk. No one could know I existed. That was the single most important rule in our family.

But my craving to see the outside world prevailed.

"Okay!"

Without contemplation, I sprung up, heart thudding in my chest. There wasn't much to choose from in my closet, so I slipped on a plain loose silver dress to blend in with the starry sky. I didn't own anything black.

Adam was surprised when I turned back around, expecting I'd need more convincing.

"Is this okay?" It was only then it dawned on me that I had no idea what other people wore. Or how they behaved. Or what they spoke about.

He paused before answering, analysing me, his serious resting face unreadable.

"You look great." But I sensed he, too, realized I might stand out more than I should.

"Wait. What do I say if anyone asks who I am?"

"Don't say anything. Act mysterious—that's the theme of the gathering. It's more of a dance thing anyway."

He was eager to get going, so I pushed the imploding doubts in my mind down and just nodded.

I took a breath, and he took my hand. His was big and rough and always cold to the touch, but not as icy as some others. As long as I was with him, I felt safe.

After creeping out the back door, we climbed the shiny silver fence. Adam climbed straight to the top, his athleticism showing. I took a few awkward attempts, but there was nowhere to stick my feet, they kept sliding down.

I finally managed to make it to the top, pausing for a moment to look out across the rows of identical buildings and then at the full, blood-red moon.

When I look down, a blond American boy, who I quickly recognize as Cole, was waiting on the other side of the fence, smiling sweetly up at me. Cole was Adam's closest friend, the only friend who's ever been to our house. The only friend who knows about me. He came over once to pick up Adam when no one else was home. He ran upstairs to Adam's bedroom only to find me.

Adam pretty much threatened his life on keeping my existence a secret. He proved to be a very loyal friend. Sometimes, he felt like my friend too.

On the border of freedom, I squeezed my eyes shut in anticipation, then leaped into Adam's waiting arms.

―――※※※ ※※※―――

When I opened my eyes, I was startled to be met not by the deep brown of Adam's but dark blue ones that looked like they held the ocean.

It was Björn. I swam there for a moment.

A moment that felt like forever.

A shiver rippled up my spine, and Björn pulled me in closer. I pressed my face into his welcoming chest, the warmth of his body still strange but appreciated in the crisp air.

I was conflicted. It felt wrong to leave Adam behind after all he'd sacrificed for me. But there was a deeper knowing assuring me that no matter what I had left behind, everything that was happening now was *right.*

I pulled myself from Björn's comforting embrace, his arms falling to my waist. Another shiver coursed through me as his hands brushed my hips. The ever so slight movement was enough to send my head in spins, and I couldn't discern whether the shivers were in response to Björn's touch or the chemicals in my bloodstream.

"Woah." I lay my head back on his chest, frustrated for being so useless. "I'm sorry."

"Don't be."

"How did we get here?" Disorderly clusters of scrap metal, bricks, totalled cars, and the remains of crumbled buildings spread out all around us.

"I've been carrying you." Sensing my embarrassment, he continued, "It's okay, you're very light."

I'd never had access to enough food that would make me gain weight.

"And I was trained to carry heavy loads. I'm used to it," he winked.

The sun sunk below the distant horizon as we spoke, the sky splashed with mottled hues suggestive of sunset, the smog stunting their true color. The ever blood-red moon began to cast a soft glow from the opposite side of the sky.

"We'll rest here for the night. It's not wise to travel in the dark."

The town's ruins were half-buried with sand and ever-moving earth. I'd seen them in photos on the news and in class, but it was eerie to actually be in one.

"It must've been big. We've been traveling through it for hours," Björn told me.

While my awareness was more coherent than it had been in days, I still felt dazed. The air was still and humid, but shivers racked my body.

"I didn't have time to prepare blankets or anything." Björn tucked me in closer, regretful he couldn't offer more than his body heat.

His warmth helped stabilize me.

"I haven't taken this route before. We're trained to avoid this kind of terrain." His voice was soothing, distracting me from the intensity of feelings in my body. "But it's good for cover. If the Control does think to search beyond the borders for us, I doubt they'll look here."

"You'll die if you travel in open land," The saintly woman's voice returned.

"She warned you too?" I asked before thinking, lifting my head.

He looked at me oddly.

"Who?"

"Oh, nothing," I pressed my cheek back into his chest where he couldn't see my face.

"I agree. Let's avoid open land," I reaffirmed.

He nodded. "Don't worry, I'm taking every precaution to stay out of sight."

"Trust him," I was sure now that she had meant Björn.

I relaxed, appreciating the space both around and above as we gazed up at the stars that twinkled intermittently through the smog, watching us as we watched them. If I remained still, consciousness was bearable.

I looked down at my arm, expecting to see evidence of healing, but instead, the poison had spread, reaching towards my shoulder. A shard of fear struck, the blood draining from my face.

"I don't know what to do for it," Björn said quietly.

"It's spreading slow enough though, and I've been revisiting the prophecy," he said with urgency. I tilted my head toward the tough paper spread open beside him and wondered if the same images would be revealed to us both at once.

"What do you see?" I asked. All I saw was the map.

"It speaks of a Shaman who knows medicine more powerful than anything we've seen in this dimension. I know she'll be able to treat you. We just have to get there before—" He cut himself off, protecting me from something.

Before the poison reaches my heart. That's where it was headed, snaking its way through my blackening veins. I tried to calm my pulse; panic would only stimulate its speed.

"I didn't want to stop, but it's safer here," Björn said. "It'll only take another day to reach the first base camp."

"You have to rest," I said.

"I'm okay," he assured me.

Just then, I remembered something Adam did when Lorraine once cut herself cooking. Slowly, carefully, I reached down with my healthy arm and ripped my dress with the little strength I still had, handing the rag to Björn.

"Tie it tight enough around my shoulder to cut the circulation."

Björn was gentle as he lifted my limp arm, my skin pinching as he tightened the fabric.

I fell back into him, closing my eyes, suddenly fatigued. I didn't want to sleep, afraid I wouldn't wake up. I *had* to walk tomorrow's stretch of the journey.

"Don't you question the logistics of traveling somewhere that's invisible?" I had to ask.

"I *did*," he replied. "But at some point I accepted that it's beyond logic. The prophesy has already proven accurate in a lot of ways. I mean shadows that are trapped in our bodies and feed us thoughts that dictate our lives? That doesn't sound logical either," he said.

"I can't say I *understand* any of it, but I do trust it. You sensed the shadows without being told about them. It's been your experience even though it makes no sense."

A shard of pain pulsed up my arm. I couldn't help but wince. Björn continued to distract me.

"As humans, we've barely cracked the surface of understanding what's possible, and have pretty much destroyed this planet before uncovering any of its greatest discoveries."

As he spoke, the sky looked even more monumental than ever before, even more infinite, the stars more mystifying.

"I've never really been interested in material wealth or technology. I'm not interested at all in what we can see. I'm fascinated by the possibility of everything we can't see. Fascinated enough to at least look and find out." He paused.

"I'd rather die in the Bermuda Triangle than waste an entire life living out the same routine that's been lived by a multitude of people before me."

By the time he finished, it was as if the gap between us and the stars had dissolved completely.

"You should sleep now. I'll stay awake and keep watch," I finally said. "You must be exhausted."

He placed two square pieces of tin around us, blending our presence into the surrounding junkyard then relaxed, leaning backward against the rigid metal.

"You can sleep too," he told me as he closed his eyes. "No one will find us here tonight."

Regardless, I forced myself to stay awake, feeling through the pulsating pains and aches, heat, tremors, and cold flushes, but somewhere in my delirium, reality began to blend into dreamland, and I drifted back into unconsciousness.

Just before I fell, I made sure to tell Björn, "If I don't wake up tomorrow, you have to leave me here."

It was clear that my chances of survival were bleak, and I was only slowing his journey.

CHAPTER NINE

THE FOLLOWING DAY'S WALK was treacherous. I was delirious, more aware of the blood pumping loudly through my veins than my surroundings.

I wanted so desperately to curl up somewhere soft and quiet and sleep without disturbance. But it was more important to move, for if we didn't arrive in the valley soon, there was a good chance I may never awaken from that quiet, undisturbed sleep.

My body trembled, both vision and hearing blurring in and out of focus. I leaned on Björn the entire way, trying not to drag my feet as my body lost the ability to support itself, and his movement became my motivation to keep moving.

Finally, structures appeared in the distance. I couldn't be sure if it was a mirage or not, but as we got closer, it became clear that we'd reached the base camp.

"There are no missions scheduled this week," Björn said, his arm wrapped securely around my waist. "But I can't promise that no one will be here."

His uniform was now a creamier, dust and dirt-stained shade of white. He removed his helmet that was clipped to his belt and placed it on his head, fastening its straps under his chin.

Domed iron buildings dotted the camp and a small plane perched on a round platform. There was no evident movement, but we crouched close to the ground anyway, hopping from one domed structure to the next. Björn was on high alert, while I barely maintained any alertness at all.

We reached the last dome, only space between us and the plane now.

"Wait here," he instructed.

I slumped against the hot wall, sliding down to the ground. I watched Björn stealthily enter one of the domed buildings, quietly sliding the door shut behind him. A few moments later, the door slid open from another building and a grey-suited officer appeared, moving toward the structure that Björn was in.

Björn re-emerged with two steel drums. He set them on the ground and began talking to the officer. I could barely watch. Every officer would be on alert for him by now.

Björn swept an arm upward whacking the officer's face with a force that caught the officer by surprise. Blood splashed from his mouth and he fell to his knees.

Two more officers approached while Björn wrestled the first, but he was swift and cunning, trained in some form of martial art that was no match to his opponent.

Björn spun the first officer onto his back, knocked out just in time to meet his next two opponents. They danced around each other, throwing punches. Björn swung high kicks and struck blow after blow until they, too, were on the ground.

But the first officer rose from the ground, drawing a knife from his belt.

Get up. Do something! I willed myself, but before gathering the momentum to move, Björn had already knocked him to the ground and stole his knife.

The other two officers rose. Björn threatened the knife on them and they hesitated, but didn't stop. After fighting them both at once, he pulled one into a headlock and sliced his throat, then looked fiercely up at the remaining officer in warning But he only grew more determined to fight, fuelled by anger.

I froze, suddenly sick.

Björn hauled himself onto his back and they both tumbled to the ground. Björn wrapped a leg and arm around his opponent's upper body, immobilizing him. With his free hand, Björn applied force to a pressure point along the man's temple, under which his body went limp.

The surviving officer rose from the ground once more, this time slowly, drawing out a gun.

From my hiding place I couldn't help but yell out with a sudden burst of energy.

"Björn, behind!"

He spun and froze.

The man holding the gun pointed it my direction and began moving towards me, knowing he now had the upper hand. My pathetic attempt to help him had become more of a hindrance. Björn held his hands up in surrender.

I was frozen too. But after taking a few steps closer towards me, the officer stopped in his tracks.

Gun pointed in my direction, he opened his mouth as if to say something, but was too shocked. Too stunned to even lower his gun, he reached up with his opposite hand and lifted his helmet, just enough to reveal a face I knew better than any other.

My heart skipped a beat with joy.

"Adam," I whispered.

His eyes expressed a combination of worry, fear, hope, and relief.

Unaware of our connection, Björn ceased Adam's moment of distraction and swiftly locked his arms back from behind, taking the gun.

"No! Wait!" I launched myself up off the ground and ran towards them.

Now, Adam's hands were up in surrender.

"I thought you were in detainment," he said in disbelief as I fell into his arms. They tightened around me, tighter than ever before.

"What are you doing here?" He was quick to check my wrist, lifting it to exam the wound. His expression changed to one of concern as he scanned first the gash, then my depleted body.

"You're poisoned."

Björn walked up slowly behind him, gun still pointed at Adam.

"Stop," I told him. "This is Adam. My brother."

"What do you want with her?" Adam's question sounded more like a death threat. He turned to face him and I fell to the ground, too weak to hold myself upright unsupported.

Björn stopped a few feet away, lowering the gun to rest readily at his thigh.

"Nothing but her freedom."

Adam's fists tightened.

"We don't have the luxury of time to explain right now," Björn's eyes flickered to my wrist then back to Adam. "You can come with us, but I can't guarantee that you'll survive the vortex." Björn words were riddles to Adam's uninformed ears.

"Did you guarantee *she'd* survive the removal of the chip? Because her chances are looking slim to me." A heavy ache ripped through Adam's chest. I felt it as if my own.

I forced words out of my mouth, head pounding. "I did it to myself Adam. Björn didn't want me to but I . . . I had to get it out."

Adam held his ground.

"Björn," he said bitterly. "Do you know how much you are worth right now? Now I know why. You kidnapped a girl."

Björn held his ground too. "She's a woman, in power of her own choices."

An officer behind Björn groaned and stood. Björn turned, lifted his arm, aimed low, and fired.

A single bullet ripped through the air, striking the man's foot. "Ahh!" He called out in pain and dropped back down to the ground.

Björn spun back around to face us.

Anger propelled Adam forward, and while Björn did his best not to fight back, he intercepted almost every blow.

Struggling to my feet, I said, "Adam, stop! What he said is true! I chose this!"

"He poisoned you!" Adam's rage was like his father's; hard to reason with once erupted.

"Maya stay there. It's okay," Björn said, but I ignored his concern. His once soothing voice now sounded deceitful. He was a killer...

Adam struck him with full force, blood bursting from another split across his cheek. Björn finally hit back.

"We have to leave. Now. Or she'll die," Björn's said urgently.

"You're not taking her anywhere."

"Adam, listen," I begged.

He turned, crouching down next to meet me.

"There's a place. The valley in my paintings. It exists." I couldn't believe I was regurgitating Björn's words before I was even sure I believed them myself.

"He's lying to you." Adam's certainty stimulated a wave of doubt, but I couldn't go back now. It was my only chance of survival.

"It's called Santōṣha, and if I don't get her there soon, she'll have no chance," Björn said.

"Come with us," I pleaded Adam.

He paused, for the first time considering the possibility of the valley, then shook his head.

"It's not possible."

"We're leaving. Now. Either come with us or . . ." There was no "or." He had to come.

"Maya," he said gently, seeing how sick I was, beginning to acknowledge that I'll be dead by nightfall either way.

"Don't go. Stay with me until . . ." He couldn't say it.

"Come, and we might both live," I whispered, his form blurring.

"Even if I wanted to . . ." Adam looked down at his wrist, at the chip bleeping under his skin, and shook his head knowing that the moment he stepped beyond the border it would activate.

I pressed my hand against my burning chest, that small movement drawing every ounce of remaining strength from my body. My head spun.

"Maya!" Björn dropped to the ground beside me, everything around me out of focus.

Against all my will, I fell out of consciousness yet again.

CHAPTER TEN

I WOKE BUT KEPT my eyes closed, too weak to attempt parting my lids. Gale-force winds blew against my face and through my hair.

The air was fresh and cold. It felt as if we were moving. Fast.

A loud sound like that of a surging engine vibrated the seat upon which I now sat. We were in the plane!

The speed, while brilliant and exhilarating, made my stomach turn. I was going to be sick again.

I reached over and found Björn's thigh, then his hand, then remembered it was the hand of a killer. I quickly pulled my hand away from his.

He said something, but his voice was muffled.

My head was hot.

My arm was hot, burning. There was no escape from the sweeping sting of the poison. Sweat dripped from my forehead while my body shivered. The fever had become a feeling that was all too familiar by now.

I felt a sudden stabbing pain, this time in my chest.

Breathing became difficult. The airway to my lungs contracted.

I started to panic.

This is it. This is the poison reaching my heart.

I stretched my torso, lifting as high as I could in attempt to open my airwaves. No matter how much oxygen I sucked in, it wouldn't fill my lungs and left me gasping.

My eyes opened to the sight of a bright, even, blue sky. We flew high above the bed of grey clouds that held down the smog. For a moment, all was calm. Wind whistled through the cracked window beside me. The glare of the unshielded sun stung my eyes, which I shut, groaning, but forced open again. If these were my final moments of life, I wanted to absorb all of it.

The plane shuddered as we descended down through the clouds. Beneath us, through dense fog, a vast, dark blue ocean became visible. Rough waves rose and thrashed in every direction, and in the distance a swirling downward spiral sucked and churned both water and air into a spinning void—a whirlpool.

We few directly toward it.

I tried calling out in warning, but my voice failed me, and I sunk back in the seat. Björn was aware of the maelstrom ahead.

The shards of pain coursing through me were beyond unbearable. My body was shutting down, and I didn't have the energy to fear death.

The noise from the rattling fuselage was deafening. We were directly above the swirling vortex, its power sucking us in a nauseating downward draw.

I looked questioningly at Björn thinking surely this wasn't part of the plan. The spinning made me dizzy. He blurred and shook out of focus.

My eyes rolled shut.

Everything still.

Quiet.

Tranquil, like when I dove underwater and all was silent, clear. I was held in the arms of something divine. Perhaps God. But not God as a being. God as a vast space that all life rested in.

Björn's voice finally registered in my distant brain. His warm hand sent an electric volt through mine.

"Hey. Hey, keep your eyes open. Look at me," he yelled urgently over the engine's roar—the mysterious, majestic murderer with ocean blue eyes.

"Don't fall asleep. Stay here. Stay here."

But I'd lost control of my body, and I stopped fighting.

I surrendered, and felt myself falling, or flying, into darkness that became a glowing, glistening pool of light.

PART TWO

COLLAPSE OF THE WORLD AS WE KNEW IT

CHAPTER ELEVEN

WHEN I OPENED MY eyes it took a few moments to realize that I wasn't asleep and dreaming. But I wasn't sure if I was alive either.

I found myself in a lush valley surrounded by a magnitude of green, looking down upon a wide, snaking river that flowed down its centre.

It didn't take me long to register that I was not in *any* valley. I was in *the* valley.

The valley from my visions.

I pressed the palm of my hands on the ground beside me. The complexity of textures felt unreal.

The grass poking up between my fingers wasn't like the plastic kind I'd known from home; this was lush, slightly wet, and naturally bright. The sun's rays warmed its tips. Below, close to the dirt, it was cooler. And the dirt wasn't the dry, dust-like kind I had known either. It was damp and rich and dense.

Death has been dear to me. Sweet and generous and kind.

The ledge upon which I lay extended out further than the others, located high along a cliff. A monstrous flood of water tumbled down the rocks beside me.

A refreshing mist sprinkled lightly upon my skin, and the clean, crisp air was invigorating like nothing I'd ever felt before. I closed my eyes and took a deep breath, so pure I was in ecstasy, heaven.

My eyes flashed open at the sound of crunching twigs. I turned my head to see where it was coming from.

Björn emerged from the wild forest of trees behind me, carrying a firm, bowl-shaped leaf. In my euphoria, he appeared to be floating, feet only just skimming the ground while his whole body glowed like an angel.

Was he an angel? Had he been an angel all along, guiding me to heaven?

"Maya." His smile was radiant with relief, but there was hesitation in his steps, eyes examining me meticulously.

"I saw you stirring and wanted you to have water when you woke," he said. As I started to sit up, he quickly knelt beside me.

"Steady," he laughed, hand resting on my shoulder. "You've been out for days and lost a lot of blood."

I met his striking eyes as he handed over nature's cup. His eyes were even brighter here in heaven, more breathtaking, as was his smile.

Why is everyone so scared of death? Heaven's great.

I bought the leaf to my mouth slowly, curious as to why leaves and other materials encased my arm. *Our cause of death must follow us here.*

As soon as the liquid hit my lips, it slid down my throat with ease. I'd never tasted anything so pure and fresh! I could feel it wash through my organs, and it was then that reality hit me with full force.

I wasn't in heaven, or at least not the heaven my spirit might reside when my body perished.

I *hadn't* died. Not entirely.

The poison hadn't killed me.

I was alive. Possibly more alive than ever before and breathing.

Here.

In my own heaven.

Heaven on Earth.

Or more accurately, heaven within Earth.

"We didn't drown?" An image of the Bermuda whirlpool flashed across my memory. Everything before that was a blur.

I searched his eyes in disbelief, but my heart knew it true. "You did it. You got us here. And I'm still, *alive*."

He searched my eyes in return, looking for a trace of something that I couldn't place. He tilted his head, opening his mouth as if to say something but closed it before any words escaped.

"We made it through." He relaxed, his arms wrapping around me in a tender embrace. I was taken aback at first, but sunk into the warmth of his body against mine.

I looked down, patting my hands along the curves of my own body.

"It feels the same."

He lifted his shoulders shaking his head. He didn't have an explanation.

"I was sure I had it wrong. The water sucked us under. You were already passed out. It kept spinning us downward. I began to drown. I must've been dead for a few minutes before taking my first breath here."

"So we *did* drown?"

He chuckled.

"No, we jumped. I didn't know this before, but to enter, to leave our world, we had to die. Only for a moment. I think people who carry a lot of shadows die and don't wake up, but that's where the thing about being 'clear' comes in. We were light enough to fall through."

It didn't make sense, but we were here, so maybe it didn't have to.

"When we got here, you were still dying. I guess the poison jumped too. But here, the Shaman knows more advanced medicine than anything we've ever seen. She healed you. She's real, Maya. It's all real!"

He'd been preparing for this journey for most of his life, and it was all based on hope. His reverence in knowing it was real was evident in every crease of his glowing expression.

I lifted my head to gaze upon the valley. It was an unbelievable replica of my paintings. This exact angle, this very ledge was where I looked upon it from in my visions.

Without having to search for them, I saw familiar homes and structures. The ancient stone bridge spanning high across the river was there too. I knew it well, and my heart squeezed with the highest of love, for it already felt like home.

The images I'd seen in my dreams were not born of my imagination alone. A force I didn't yet understand sent them to me as a way to connect to this place. Goose bumps rippled across my skin. My perception of the world expanded, encompassing an unexplainable divinity I never knew existed.

"Maya, welcome to Santōṣha," a powerful voice came from above.

I swivelled to give the voice a body and then to Björn in confusion. It was only when following my initial instinct to look upward that I placed it.

Behind me, a man of giant proportion stood. At eye level were his knees. His body toned like a Greek god. Strapped around his waist hung a soft brown hide that wrapped into loose pants.

As my eyes continued upward, his bare, muscular chest was the product of an active lifestyle, radiant skin stained dark from regular sun exposure, and his face was familiar, eyes so clear they revealed his essence—a warm essence.

His lips broke into a smile, baring gleaming teeth. He voiced a hearty chuckle. Although gentle, it boomed through the air.

"I'm Ṭarō. Son of Chief Hân and Athêna, our tribe leaders." His thin, pointed nose crinkled and his silky hair shone in the sunlight. A ring of golden vines twisted around the crown of his head, dipping to a tip at the center of his forehead.

"I've been showing Björny around while you've been healing." He bent to ruffle Björn's hair, and while doing so with as little force as possible, it still knocked him to the ground.

"Oh. Sorry." He pulled Björn upright. "Humans." He rolled his eyes.

I didn't quite know how to respond to his humor. Humor was foreign to me.

"You're not human?" I asked.

He settled down beside us crossing his legs.

"Yes and no. In body we're *humanlike*, but many races from different dimensions are humanlike; the Sky People, the Ascendants, the Feya also all have a similar physical anatomy to humans, but we live in immensely different *consciousnesses*. Each dimension functions in a different frequency of consciousness."

His lively sky-blue eyes pierced into mine, which felt intimidating. I wasn't used to people holding eye-contact.

"So this isn't the only... dimension?"

He laughed at my apparently obvious question.

"We're the Samādhi People. We've been calling to your kind during the years of Earth's disease. Until now, contact was unnecessary. It goes against the nature of our creation to interfere, but as the earth continued to weaken, we had no choice but to lift the veil to allow for interdimensional communication."

"That's what my visions were? Your calls? They came from you?"

He grinned.

"In your realm, communication is predominantly through words. Over time, many of you have forgotten *how* to communicate without them.

"Only those with quiet minds can hear our calls. The metals of your city act as armor that shield our access to heavily preoccupied minds. Individuals will always receive differently, for example, receiving our messages as imagery reveals your creative, visual nature.

"Björn's parents were intellectuals, so they received it as evidential data in the form of a document. We were in close contact with a woman by the name of Susan for years. We believe she heard our messages as voices."

"Susan. She knew . . ." Loony Susan's warnings weren't so loony after all, but the world couldn't *hear* them. The Control *wouldn't* hear them. The truth was too inconvenient.

"Why didn't you ever come to us physically?"

"We can't survive on your land just as you can't in space. The oxygen levels are lower than here and our lung capacity is high because of all the forests and trees, and the weather is too harsh. Can you feel how the air here is so still you can hardly feel it on your skin? It rests, unchanging at neutral body temperature. The Mother created it this way intentionally. It's important for our people to remain still."

My brain processed information like a computer loading multiple documents at once.

"Who's The Mother?"

He sensed my fear. Fear that they, too, might be under the tight reigns of a force of authority like the Control.

"The essence of planet Earth is feminine, creative, and nurturing by nature, so we call her the Earth Mother. You'll sense her presence over time, the closer to nature you become. She's the force that governs every gust of wind, every movement, every breath."

Ṭarō paused and I found myself staring out, admiring the rolling peaks and dips of paradise before us, my mind blown wide open.

He broke his silence before too long.

"Have you tried standing yet? How do you feel about going wandering?"

"Yes," I said without hesitation. "I mean no. I haven't, but I feel up to it."

Ṭarō chuckled. Björn was quick to jump to his feet beside me, lending his hand.

"The Shaman said to take it slow," he reminded me, as if the word was a trigger, a memory that flashed over my mind's eye.

It only lasted a moment, but it knocked the breath from my chest.

⇢⇢⇢⇢ ⇠⇠⇠⇠

I'm lying here, on this ledge. Well, my body is, but somehow I'm not in my body at all. I watch it from above.

Dark purple veins crawl out from the black wound in my wrist and reach all the way up my neck and across my chest. It is obvious I am dying.

A white-cloaked being kneels over me—the Shaman. I can't see her face, but hear unrhythmic chanting as her hands wave over my body. Water falls and flows down beside me. The sound is soothing, meditative, and the ever-present mist and occasional splash of pure, clean water provides constant cooling.

The air is still, yet wind lifts my hair and blows my dress that is pulled down around my waist, and a small pit fire burns beside me, undisturbed by neither water nor wind. As the cloaked Shaman presses ruthlessly into my wound, an array of ointments spread around us, the earth rumbles. The force of all of nature's elements are present with us, as if working alongside the Shaman, uniting with her intention to heal me.

Like an electric shock, I was forced back to the present, back to my body. I looked to both Björn and Ṭarō, but they hadn't noticed my brief disappearance into a memory I wasn't consciously present for.

Björn wrapped an arm around my waist, stabilizing me once more, and I couldn't help but melt in the warmth of his skin, his touch electric. Even in such a profound environment, his closeness consumed me.

I tried to contain the racing feelings, avidly avoiding eye contact, knowing then I'd be truly lost. Instead, I drew attention to my bare feet, each touch of their contact with the ground varying. My tender skin was sensitive to the symphony of textures. The air was cooler beneath the shade of the twisting trees, and I was captivated by carpets of bright moss that crawled up the bark that encased their trunks.

While Björn had traveled this path before, his experience was as fresh and alive as mine, wide eyes sparkling.

"You okay?" He felt me watching him again.

I just nodded, quickly shifting my gaze.

The ground steepened as we descended the valley slope, and I had to focus on where I placed my feet, stepping carefully over sticks, rocks, and cavities, while Ṭarō swung from low branches, apelike and in his element. Everything about his movements suggested a deep awareness and appreciation of the nature around him. He breathed it in like it was medicine.

Inhale, exhale.

We came to an opening where the frequency of shuffling feet had carved a twisting dirt path and branches reached across on each side, creating a tunnel of shade. It was cool beneath.

As I stepped out, the first human structure became visible. And then another. And while they all featured high roofs to accommodate the giants, each home was just one level making our multilevel houses in the City seem like mansions. Each home was unique, built with creative flair.

Lavender flowers burst in bunches through cracks in the rough stone-tessellated walls, their potent scent drenching the air as we approached one of the homes. Its wood-planked door was embellished by textured carvings, and swung open to reveal two striking women, but not in the way one would be judged back home.

Like Ṭarō, they were enchanting, both wild and sophisticated; skin dark and bodies tall, lean but muscular with full thighs and hips that enriched their feminine frames.

One of the women wore her hair in plaits intermittently strewn through her long wavy mane. She wore a lightweight fabric that twisted at her chest and fell to her shins. At her waist was a strip of rose gold rope that matched her jewelry. Her eyes were a dark, electric shade of blue and as clear as glass.

The other woman wore a plain skirt that fell to her ankles. Her exposed breasts fell slightly under the laws of gravity. A necklace of lapis lazuli adorned her chest. She was short and stocky but had an identical pair of electric blue eyes that matched the stones in her necklace.

"That's Gingēr and Petãl. They're sisters who carry ancient plant knowledge that has been passed down through the generations. They work with the Shaman to supply medicines." Ṭarō was unfazed by Petãl's lack of clothing.

They didn't smile or move to greet us. Their expressions were pensive and wary as they leaned against the doorframe, watching us pass.

Other locals we passed were equally fascinating. They carried a sense of hyper-awareness of everything around them, eyes piercingly present. Some were welcoming while others as cautious as Gingēr and Petãl. It had been naive of me to think that everyone in the village would be the smiling, friendly creatures I'd imagined. These people were almost the opposite; fierce, and warrior-like. And we were foreigners. *Humans.*

"I hope you're not afraid of heights!" Ṭarō called back as he bounded onto a rustic wooden bridge that connected the village to both sides of the valley.

The bridge's floor was a mosaic of smooth stones. Soft tufts of moss grew between them that padded each step like a soft carpet. Mist rose from the wide river below, curling around the arched wood railings. We crossed without urgency, invigorated by the elevation and when I looked down, I saw people bathing below.

Tall, tan, wild people.

I hardly noticed Björn's arm fall from my waist, but his hand now wrapped comfortably around mine. It felt natural. There were no words; we didn't need them. Just a simple look between us revealed our mutual reverence.

We paused at the centre and turned to face the sheet of water cascading down from the cliff's edge high above. Its force gushed into a pool downstream, the sound drowning out all other noise. I blinked as spray splashed my face, my laughter echoing off the wall.

Björn, amused, gently wiped the droplets of water from my face. His grin wide, he beamed down at me, eyes crinkling at the corners while all the while searching mine for a trace of . . . *something*.

I was at a loss for what. He looked away.

We continued across the bridge to the other side of the valley where a grand marble archway welcomed us. Passing through, we entered a large round field. Tall, elegantly engraved stone pillars lined the perimeter. Each featured a gold-rimmed fire bowl.

"This is the communal arena," Ṭarō gestured.

He waved and moved toward two people who sat before a spread of tools and sat beside them. They seemed fixated on the items laying before them. Björn followed, but I stopped to take in the scene.

Most in the arena paused from their tasks and looked up with a variety of expressions before returning to their work. I felt nervous. No one moved to greet us. Eyes were cautious.

A pile of branches and dried leaves lay in the center of the arena marking the site of a bonfire. It was surrounded by artistically carved logs used as benches. The ground was compact from frequent use, but still, small flowers sprung up all around.

Two older men sat by a well, one washing rustic bowls and cups then passing them to the other to wipe dry and stack.

A middle-aged woman sat upon one of the logs braiding long strips of leather. A child sat at her feet threading small amber stones on the thin strands. They were making jewelry. The mother looked up, sensing my gaze, and smiled, welcoming, radiant. I let out a breath of relief.

A little farther off a group of women sat on the ground weaving baskets, others hand-sewing, some dying fabric green, bleaching it white, or staining it deep red. They talked expressively and passionately, while happily laughing and petting each other.

Two large fountaining trees as old as time itself stood just outside of the ring. Behind them, a giant pyramid captured my attention.

As if in a trance, I found myself at its base, observing the deeply engraved symbols that detailed each stone brick, some strung into stories, others incomprehensible.

As I stepped onto the lowest platform step, I sensed a vibration emanating from its walls. I could feel it, hear it almost, as I skirted around the triangular base searching for an entrance, while simultaneously hypnotized by the emblematic images of this foreign and apparently ancient civilization.

"Maya!" I faintly heard Ṭarō call my name.

I peeled my eyes from the structure and followed his voice to a small group of people.

As I approached, I asked of the Pyramid, "What is that?"

He glanced at the man beside him, then down at his hands before answering.

"It's ahh . . . an old talisman. A statue," Ṭarō nodded.

But it wasn't just any statue.

"This is Phŏenix and Cayenne," he said quickly, changing the subject, and I let it go, for now.

Björn was engaged in a conversation about the tool Phŏenix held, its wooden handle carved with such detail it looked like a piece of art.

"Did you make all these?" I asked Cayenne of the assortment laid out before us, admiring the time and care defining each one.

"This is Phŏenix's collection. She's one of our finest carvers."

Phŏenix looked up at the sound of her name, nodding once in greeting before returning to her discussion with Björn.

She was small. Human.

"Cayenne is our lead hunter. Phŏenix supplies the hunters with most of their tools and weapons," Ṭarō explained of the trading that was taking place.

"I'll soon pass the role of lead hunter to Wolfé," Cayenne said, his warm, peaceful eyes wrinkling in response. A savage white scar cut down the line of his cheek and continued down his neck, disappearing under his shirt.

"My body has slowed with age, and he is strong and ready." Cayenne's gaze flickered up in the direction of the trees, sensing movement.

Two muscular people appeared, carrying a large furry animal, followed by a tiny older woman. Well, tiny in comparison to the giants. Another human.

They placed the animal in front of the pyramid on a round stone bench that was stained crimson and lowered to their knees, closing their eyes, and praying or chanting something beyond my ear's reach.

Then they both looked up and began circling the stone bench, moving and sweeping their hands over the dark-furred mass. They stopped opposite each other and clasped hands, arms hanging loosely, and closed their eyes once more before two men approached to lift the beast from its resting place, carrying it off for skinning.

Emerging from their trance, both looked over at Cayenne and then moved in our direction while the little woman disappeared silently back into the trees.

"Found one near the river." The man's expression was rough and rugged beneath silk black hair, clearly afraid of little. A necklace of teeth hung around his neck, a sharp stone dagger still gripped in his palm.

"We were only tracking the dead this morning. This was the only one still fresh enough to take," he told Cayenne. "We thought it looked like enough, but we'll go hunting if you think we need more." He looked to the woman who nodded in agreement.

She wore her dark hair tied back in braids and had long curling eyelashes that demanded attention, dark and thick, fluttering with butterfly beauty.

"No. One is enough," Cayenne nodded.

The man dropped his hunting belt on the dirt floor. It held an impressive array of weapons. The woman lifted a well-worn wooden bow and woven pocket of arrows from her broad shoulders. Unlike the man, she placed them down carefully, a most precious possession.

Around her shoulders was a hooded cape that tied at her neck. She pulled the string, and the cape fell away, revealing a light-brown swath of fabric across her breasts that laced in the center. Her exposed torso was impressively muscular and fit. Tight fitting pants gripped her wide hips.

"Wolfé and Katanä, meet Maya," Ṭarō continued playing host.

The man and woman sat close, knees touching, romance dancing about them now that their duties were complete.

A warm pink haze flickered between their bodies and I blinked, shaking off the strange illusion.

"Pleased to meet you Maya," Wolfé said, his voice husky and deep. His chiseled jawline paired with transparent brown eyes and a smooth dark complexion intimidated me.

"Hello," I replied, quickly smiling when I realized I'd just been staring.

Engraved on his chest was a carefully designed white scar that caught my attention.

Catching my gaze, he said, "It's a symbol of peace and protection."

Katanä had an identical tattoo just above her left breast, her heart.

I nodded slowly, unsure of how any form of killing could be an act of peace or protection.

"It communicates to the animal spirits that we abide by natural law. We take what we need. Nothing more, nothing less." He read my scepticism.

"We hunt the dead before the living, and if we fall upon the ill, we'll take the body to Hopi, our animal whisperer. You might have seen her when we carried in the carcass," Katana continued, giving a name to the human. Her voice was unexpectedly sweet and girlish.

"But anything beyond her care we'll claim for the tribe, and the energy that moved through its body is recycled as the Great Mother intended," she explained, but my attention kept drifting back to the odd pink hue that hung in the air around them. No matter how many times I blinked, the aura remained.

"What do you see?" Ṭarō asked, noticing my fixation.

"Oh. I can't really explain," I said, but decided this was a safer place than the City to try.

"It's like a pinkish mist floating between them."

Wolfé and Katanä smiled sweetly at each other, their tough exteriors melting.

"We call it Light Matter," Ṭarō said.

"Is it around everyone?" I asked, looking from person to person.

"It would be more accurate to say Light Matter *is* everyone," he grinned.

"It's just the visual expressions of energy, and energy is the foundation of all physical form. The shades change with our moods. The color you see now is fleeting, an expression of the romance between them, but most beings walk with a dominant shade of mist too."

"Is it only of your world?" I asked.

"The foundational substance of all realms is the same; you just can't see it on earth because the expanse of light isn't strong enough there. Here, everything is held together by less density, so clearer representations of the energetic workings beneath form are exposed."

Katanä leaned in, focussing.

"You're embodied by a silver-blue color."

Ṭarō's eyes glazed as he stared at me for a moment before agreeing. "Yeah."

Ṭarō and Katanä exchanged glances.

"Is that bad?"

They both laughed.

"Nothing is good or bad. All energy is equally important to the balance of nature," Ṭarō said. "Once you get used to seeing it, it kind of just is what it is." He shrugged.

Wolfe joined the conversation, and Björn and Phŏenix's attention also turned our way.

"Blue Light Matter is of the purer of the spirits. Those clearer of negative karma. The element of air runs through you more intimately than others." Wolfé delivered his words with careful articulation, then Katanä continued where he left off.

"The silver streams are what's most endearing. They only appear when a being and pure Light have merged. It's the source of life itself and lives in and around the Nõahl's of the earth, those dedicated to the practice of sorcery. We have four in our tribe. One is the Shaman that healed you.

"It usually takes years before the silver Light Matter merges with them. It's not common to be born with it, and even more uncommon for someone from your world." She looked to the others for a moment before continuing, also giving me a moment to process everything.

"We've never seen it. Your world has been dominated by dark forces that have been repressing the presence of light for decades. The Matter surrounding most of humanity now is black."

"Does black mean full of the shadows?" I remembered that's what they called them there.

Wolfé nodded slowly.

"You have powerful protection with you, Maya." His words carried the power of which he spoke.

"What are the shadows?"

But no one answered me. Two warm hands wrapped around my head and I jumped, looking up to see Ṭarō towering above.

"I think that's enough for the moment," he said patting my head affectionately.

Katanä put her hand on my knee, speaking for both herself and Wolfé, and said, "We have much time to share our knowledge with you. Our hearts are swelled to have you here."

I didn't know what that meant, but my heart definitely swelled with *something...*

Ṭarō led us onward, slipping between two pillars into an enclosed hexagonal shelter with grand open archways, a domed roof, and a stone fireplace. A long bench ran along one side, piled high with leafy greens from the morning's harvest. Stored in woven baskets under the bench was a rainbow of assorted vegetables. Sun-dried herbs, fruits, and ground spices were organized by color on shelves.

But my attention was drawn away by the colors that weaved and danced in and around the room. Colors that weren't of earth as I'd always known it; shades my eyes had never seen in the natural world. They flickered in and out of sight in sparks that I now knew to call Light Matter.

Ṭarō dropped his hand into a bowl of raw nuts, flinging one into the air and catching it in his mouth. He crunched down, cracking the outer shell, and spat it on the ground.

"Nuts?" he offered, but before I could answer, he threw one at my mouth. It hit my lip with a hard knock before falling to the ground.

"Ṭarō," a feminine voice sounded from behind. "Were you not supposed to be *welcoming* the humans?"

She glided toward us, carrying the weight of her large frame elegantly. Amusement seeped through her thin, transparent mint eyes. Her posture was dead straight, shoulders drawn back.

"Funny you should say that, mother. I'm welcoming them into a world where nothing is as serious as they were taught it to be, including the consumption of food." Ṭarō redeemed himself.

"Well, I apologize for interrupting then," she said lightly before her attention drifted down to me.

"Maya." She took my hands tenderly in hers and I knew that standing before me was the tribe's headwoman, Athêna.

"I'm glad to see you awake and moving." She was magnificent. Her hair jet black, falling in a straight line just above her shoulders. A finely woven gold wreath sat on the crown of her head, dipping to a point like Ṭarō's in the center of her forehead.

She freed one hand to reach for Björn. They'd already met.

"You risked your lives to be here, and we are grateful you did. Welcome."

Athêna squeezed our hands, devouring them completely for hers were double the size. She raised a quick eyebrow at Ṭarō.

I hadn't looked at it that way before, that we risked our lives.

I suppose I did almost die. Well, in truth we *both* died.

"You should rest," she said intuitively, and I trusted her. I couldn't help but want to follow her lead for there was no force pushing it, only pure power.

"We're celebrating your arrival tonight, and I wouldn't want to see your energy exhausted."

"Oh." My face felt hot. For so many years, it had been dangerous for anyone to know I existed, let alone *celebrate* my existence.

"But first, we'll take you to see the Shaman."

CHAPTER TWELVE

ANOTHER TRAIL LED US to an ancient stone staircase at the foot of a green hill. Rows of elegant sky-blue flowers lined the steps, and resilient plants shot through the bricks, leaving crooked cracks.

"We'll leave you here," Athêna said. She'd hardly spoken over the walk, but her presence was so pronounced it was hard to ignore her careful observations of me and Björn.

"We shall see you tonight," she nodded before turning.

Ṭarō waved with the charismatic grin I was already getting used to and followed his mother's lead, leaving Björn and I alone.

"I'll see you later." For a moment, his caring eyes sunk into mine, causing an overwhelming sensation in my chest.

"See you later." I turned to face the uphill trek that didn't yet reveal its end.

The air dampened the higher I climbed. The mist that drifted off the surrounding waterfalls cooled my body from its cultivating heat. I could taste the spray as their quiet rumble bellowed through the valley.

The sky cleared as I broke through a cloud of fog. It drifted aimlessly between a number of tall green hills that from my new height, appeared to be floating. Pungent aromas scented the air, and soon enough, a cottage appeared at the peak, surrounded by bright gardens.

Handwoven baskets with painted labels hung from shepherd's hooks around the perimeter. Echinacea, olive leaf, rose-hip, and the same sky-blue and vivid purple flowers that lined the path snaked along the windowsills in plant boxes. A tree blossomed near the door bearing an abundance of odd-shaped yellow and green fruits. Long rectangular boxes of dense soil lay on the ground where basic vegetables and edible roots bedded.

Toward the far edge of the property, a tall woman stood cloaked in a long pale cape, and a loose white fur-lined hood hung from her shoulders. She was so still and silent that she could have been a statue. I jumped when she turned to face me as if patiently awaiting my arrival.

Her expression was blank. I had expected someone elderly, as if wrinkled skin was the only indicator of wisdom, but she was young—both in appearance and zest. Her skin was smooth and radiant, glowing a shade I'd never seen skin glow. And snow-white, unlike the rest of the tribe I'd seen.

Her hair and eyelashes were white. Hair shiny as pure silk, and tied back from her face with rope and feathers, which accentuated her eyes that were a transparent shade of violet. She had the same thin, pointed nose and high, defined cheekbones as the rest of the tribe. A small white scar ran down one of her temples.

Before I knew it, she stood over me, bending to embrace me. Just the spark of her touch sent ripples through my body.

"Maya, I'm Nirmala." Her voice was lyrical, suffused with grace, femininity, and power. It hummed through the air like a musical note.

While her expression was unchanged, her eyes twinkled. After only a short time in her presence, I realized the twinkle was permanent. It was the twinkle of divinity that resided within and around her.

Her simple appearance reflected her inner majesty. Beneath the cape, a lightweight material wrapped around her chest, and loose cream pants fell from her waist. A white symbol was tattooed below her collarbone, and equally explicit scars embellished the top of her hands and up the lengths of her arms.

As I scanned downward, her belt caught my eye. Long claws hung from it, as well as canine teeth and miniature skulls; all real.

Her face broke into a vibrant smile. "Come inside," she said before spinning with a buoyant skip towards the door.

Inside her lodging, fresh air flushed through open windows, and the entire space was pristine.

Flickers of candlelight glowed brilliantly under hand-painted glass domes and richly scented oils burned in small bowls, making me feel calm and relaxed as I breathed them in. Bottles of potions, medicines, and dried herbs tied in bunches lined the shelves, alongside feathers, skulls, bones, and sharp weapons.

"It's a Shaman's responsibility to take care of the dark forces in the world just as much as the light. They both exist within the One substance," she said, acknowledging my fixation on the skulls. I shivered, having no idea yet of what dark forces existed, and both afraid and desperate to find out.

"You can lay down."

She collected a coconut shell of premixed oils from an aged wooden workbench. In the center of the room I climbed onto a high table covered with furs and lay back into them.

"How do you feel?" Nirmala spread her silky hands around my feet.

"My body is pretty stiff, and I'm a bit dizzy again."

"That's to be expected." She pressed into my calves, massaging out the tightness.

Her touch was soothing, but at the same time, unusually electrifying as she worked her way up my legs. She dipped her hand into the shell and rubbed the lotion into her palms, then over my skin in smooth strokes. It burned, stimulating heat deep within my muscles, and expelled a scent of rosemary, sage, and citrus that invigorated my lungs as it did my body.

She continued up my body and pressed carefully into my belly. It was so sensitive I couldn't decide whether it was pleasant or uncomfortable, then a well of emotions stirred.

I was confused, embarrassed. I couldn't cry with someone as respected as a Shaman standing over me! I felt trapped. I wriggled, prompting her to continue up the line of my body, but her hands remained at my stomach.

"It's okay. Stay still. It's safe for you to feel here," Nirmala encouraged. "When emotions aren't acknowledged, they get stored in the body, but I'm setting them free now," she said, and I trusted her, surrendering, even though I'd come to see her to heal my *arm*, not my emotions.

I don't know how long I lay on the table. After letting go, I became lost in space and time, falling into a meditation of feeling. Feeling the shadows, and I soon understood the sensations I felt, were the shadows uprooting under the spell of her touch. Her very presence drew them from their hiding places.

Memories flashed involuntarily in my mind's eye.

People.

Pain.

People in pain. Pain I had, on countless occasions, experienced as my own, but with the detachment of revisiting, was it really? The feelings were somehow interwoven.

That man on the train. That woman alone. No love. No life. Jeff; his anger. Our neighbor, her resentment.

It was all the same. Pain created by the shadows.

The visions zoomed out, from individuals to groups, to an aerial view of the City, then the round earth itself. I knew what was coming. I knew it too well.

First, the flames. My birth parent's faces flickered, then vanished. The entire earth was on fire. The flames burned out and all that remained of our one blue and green planet was a charred sphere floating in space.

Rotting.

Death.

All I could feel was death.

"Stop!" I finally called out. It was too much.

Behind closed lids all went white. Clear. Pristine. But I was too alarmed to rest there.

"I have to go back. I have get the others. I have to bring Adam here." I shuffled to sit upright but Nirmala held me down as her hands moved up to press into my chest, then shoulders. She exhaled a deep chesty hum, chanting something quietly.

"Not yet," she said.

I tried to calm my heavy breathing while hands continued to press into my chest. My body twitched and convulsed, rattled by whatever it was she now uprooted. Anxiety. All my anxiety about the world's end was stored inside my chest.

The visions weren't unfamiliar, but that didn't mean I understood them.

Why so much pain? Where did it come from? And why did it follow me here? I felt haunted by the shadows that had lingered over me for as long as I could remember.

"*I'm setting them free,*" she'd said. I hoped she was talking about the shadows.

Would Adam be too weighed down by the shadows to survive the vortex? But I couldn't even consider the thought. *Of course not. Of course Adam will make it through.*

"Where did the plane land?" I asked.

"Metals can't survive in this realm. The plane didn't fall through. It's at the bottom of the Bermuda Triangle, with your Earth bodies."

"So I did die?" I felt overwhelmed by confusion. How could she drop such information so calmly?

"Your body here is only a projection of your spirit. No different to what it was on earth. But you had to shed your Earth body to arrive here in a form that matches the frequency of our dimension."

I had read many science and physics texts, but this was too complicated to grasp. It was *metaphysics*, which, until this moment, only existed in speculation and theory.

"How will I get back?" Panic rose again, but Nirmala's voice was stern, cutting through it.

"You can't go back. Not yet. I can't tell you why, but if you wait, you'll understand."

"But I *can* go back? It is possible?"

"It is much easier to accumulate density than to shed it. Your body will re-adapt to the density of Earth realm if you return. It becomes a question of whether you *want* to carry the extra pressure and weight that is required to exist there. Earth realm is... like an obstacle course." The word sounded foreign in her mouth. "Filled with many challenges and much adversity. The Mother created it this way with intention – a constant dance between both extremes of love and pain. You will learn that our realm is a much stabler place. Both our physical environment and the mechanics of our internal biological systems are less erratic. Yours will adapt in time, and the idea of going back may become less appealing."

I didn't argue the point any further. *I wouldn't go back for myself. It would be to save the rest of my people.*

She pressed the tip of her finger into my forehead and the tension building there softened.

"Rest for now in knowing that we're still calling. Anyone ready, like you were, will hear."

I was silent for only a moment, but I could not rest my mind.

"Can you call Adam?"

"Our connection to you can help us form a stronger connection to Adam, yes, but like I said, we can only send messages. He must be open and willing to hear."

"I'm going to look at your wound now." The Shaman lifted my arm with the gentlest touch and peeled away the leaves. As the blood flowed again, fire flooded through my veins, burning, but the pain was far more manageable than before.

"The leaves have been coated with a numbing paste. You'll still feel pain, but it should be milder."

She's reading my mind.

Nirmala inspected my arm and continued. "The poison hasn't resurfaced, it's been flushing out of your system well, but the damage lingers. I've kept you unconscious with heavy sleeping potions so you could heal."

When my eyes adjusted to the soft rays of light coming in through the window, I lowered my gaze to my wrist. Faint purple stains crept up my forearm that gradually faded to yellow. The wound itself was now just a small pink indentation in my wrist. I traced the sensitive skin with my finger.

"Have you ever treated someone poisoned like this?"

"Not from your world. But we have poisonous plants here that have infected our tribe members severely. Nature can be ruthless too; she awards no special mercy on any species."

"But your case is different because it's not just one poison." As she spoke, she gently applied ointments over my healing arm.

"Björn didn't want to leave your side." She looked up, pausing for a moment.

He probably felt guilty for dragging me across the border in the first place.

The Shaman smiled and let go of my hand to retrieve two more concoctions from her workbench.

"For your internal healing. They're strong," she warned, handing me the first cup. I drank it in one swallow, shivering in response to its bitterness.

When she handed me the second, I paused, wary, then downed it like the first. This one was different; sickeningly thick and sweet.

"You will drink these three times a day until you regain your strength."

I lay back down on the table and stared up at the wooden ceiling while Nirmala pulled over a stool. Her hand drowned mine in a gesture that felt like friendship, and a tender touch of tears warmed my eyes.

We were quiet for some time.

"How did you learn all this knowledge about plants and potions, and . . .?" I didn't know what to call the other stuff.

"I didn't learn it, nor did I choose it. It passes through me. I become the channel to transfer knowledge into form," she interrupted.

"Magic is a frequency of light, and some bodies are in direct tune with it.

"The Mother chooses only one Shaman for each village, and through them the ancient knowledge of every Shaman before transfers. The tribe assumed my Shamanic nature from a young age. I'd spend most of my time wandering the forest, collecting plants, and talking to the elements rather than other children." she laughed.

"When I was transitioning into womanhood, a bolt of lightning struck me. My heart stopped for a number of minutes, and the tribe believed the miracle of my return to body was an omen." The scar at her temple began to glow as she revisited the memory. I was sure it wasn't my imagination. She touched it, and the glow ceased immediately.

"It wasn't until the past Shaman died that the transfer of knowledge began. It hit me like a fever that made me bedridden. Lifetimes of visions flashed across my mind's eye for days. I couldn't move or eat or drink or sleep. I was a vessel, downloading information and memories. When I awoke it was like I'd lived all those lifetimes, learned all their wisdom through personal experience. It was like awakening and remembering and discovering all in one." She went quiet. Still. No words truly able to convey the experience, but the emotion expressed through her words did.

The sky splashed with color as evening set in, like a painting through the frame of the window. A wash of radiant reds, pinks, and yellows drifted opaquely with the sun as it fell further behind the distant mountains.

I wandered outside, gazing at the moon as it rose, a majestic mist of violet and magenta washing the horizon.

Against the vivid green of the lush forestry and the fading blue sky, the picture became a rainbow of color.

Before darkness replaced it, Nirmala walked me back down the stone steps and along the trail to the guest cottage.

Björn awaited my arrival and appeared at the front door to meet us.

"Welcome back."

"I'll see you tonight," Nirmala turned to leave.

"Thank you, Nirmala."

She nodded. "You can call me Nala." Then walked swiftly back up the trail.

After watching her disappear into the tall, majestic trees, I followed Björn inside the cottage.

Small fire sticks and a few candles lit the room. Their warm orange glow was dim but luminous enough to see. The circular living area had large windows that opened to a moonlit garden. It was a rustic and uncluttered space. Natural-edged wooden paneling lined the walls and a stone fireplace was built in at its centre. All the tables, chairs, and cupboards were cut from softwood and embellished with elaborate carvings.

I could *feel* Björn's presence beside me, grounding me back down to earth.

"I haven't had a chance to thank you yet either, but the way you've taken care of me—"

"It's okay. I know. You don't have to thank me. Of course I'd take care of you."

"Björn, you saved my life. You didn't even know if I would survive."

"Like I said, it wasn't a question. I wouldn't have left you. You had to make it here just as much as I did, possibly more so." The intensity of our eyes in contact caused my face to burn and my hands to sweat.

"And why would I go through the trouble to bail you out of the Council building just to leave you when things got a little complicated?"

I shook my head and looked away. He stepped away even though part of me wished he had stepped closer.

"Athena left clothes for you on the bed," he said, drawing my attention to the only bedroom in the cottage.

I noticed he was dressed like the Samadhi People. He wore loose-fitting pants made from thin brown hide. The neckline of his thin cloth shirt exposed his chest. He was fit, I assumed, from all his training.

I peeled my eyes away from him and examined myself. The same ripped silver dress still hung from my shoulders, unraveling in tatters at the bottom. I could no longer call it silver either; more of a sweaty, stained grey. I reached up to my tangled, oily hair and ran my fingers through it a few times before braiding a long plait.

"I'll wait outside for you." Björn moved courteously toward the door.

"Thanks."

He hovered beneath the doorframe. "I'll sleep out here," he said. A bed was already made on the couch beneath the window. "The bedroom is yours."

"Oh, no, I don't need all this space. You're bigger than me. I'll sleep on the couch."

But he wouldn't hear of it. "I've already set it up. I'll be sleeping out here," he repeated, then disappeared.

I shook my head in surrender even though it felt uncomfortable to receive the kindness of others. In the City, there was always a catch, something expected in return, but here, giving seemed free.

I lifted the dress from the bed, shaking it open. It was thin and light brown with a braided rope hanging down one side.

I slipped the rag I wore off my shoulders, stepping out of the heap it made on the floor, then wrapped the dress around my body, tying the string around my waist.

Simple.

It fell just above my ankles and flowed when I moved, softly brushing my skin.

I looked around the room and located a basin filled with water where I was grateful to wash my face. Careful not to leave Björn waiting too long, I made my way to the door feeling a little cleaner.

"Hey, there's something I've wanted to talk about," Björn began as we walked toward the arena.

"It's about . . . What's the last thing you remember before the Bermuda Triangle?"

I looked up to the sky as if it held the memories I'd lost in my delirium.

"I remember . . . passing out in the car . . . being carried . . . stumbling through the desert. You were supporting my weight, taking care of me . . ."

I shrugged, not bothered by the loss of memory for I was just glad to have survived, but he looked away, jaw clenched as if my appreciation offended him.

"You don't remember reaching base camp?"

I racked my brain for any images that resembled a base camp but saw only a blank page.

I shook my head. "Kind of. Not really."

He nodded slowly.

"Did I miss something important?"

He let out a breath and opened his mouth only to close it again.

"I just . . . want to make sure you're okay."

I broke into a grin. "I'm more than okay. I'm alive."

CHAPTER THIRTEEN

NIGHT HAD FALLEN AND a ring of golden fires already flickered beneath each of the grand stone pillars. By the time Björn and I arrived, huge, wild but graceful beings already filled the arena, and sounds of relaxed joy rode the airwaves, enlarged white teeth flashing in the darkness.

A long spread of food was set along the length of an elevated wooden slab as well as stacks of coconut shells. The rainbow of color was so vibrant that it looked fake. When the sky darkened, Wolfé lit the bonfire.

My heart raced, ached. Familiar pain pressing down on my chest, lungs choked, the air suddenly thick, hot, violent.

I'd never seen live flames so large before. The first thing I saw in their exuberant dance was my birth parents' faces, their smiles, then their smiling faces burning.

I squeezed my eyes shut for as long as it took for my ears to stop ringing, drawing in slower breaths to force the threatening tears from falling. Calling on my inner strength, I opened my eyes, forcing them to stare first at the orange flames, then coals, then ashes, until the pain slowly dissipated and the flames became compelling, mystifying, their power *beautiful*.

"Björn! Maya!" A voice called. Walking directly toward us was Phŏenix, arms extended in greeting.

"How do you like your cottage?" Her smile was charming, and her wild blonde hair fell in waves around her face.

"It's perfect," Björn replied.

"I can't believe someone spent the time to carve such detail in the wood," he said.

I nodded in agreement. A triangular strip of brown leather around her chest drew my attention to her midriff, where a large symbol was tattooed down her side.

"It was the first cottage built here. There've been upgrades and additions since, but it's mostly all our first chief and headwoman's original work." She spoke with an ever-present glimmer in her vivid green eyes.

"I'd love to be able to carve like that."

"With our small hands we make the best fine designs," she winked. "I'll introduce you to Alfrigg our head builder."

"This way," she directed us.

I would have followed, but something drew my attention away.

Standing among the crowd was a small woman having a spirited conversation with taller folk. Like Phõenix, she looked like a tribe member but less wild, and dressed in simpler native attire.

Where did all these humans come from?

I weaved through the tall bodies toward her.

"Hi," I said, catching her alone as her previous conversation had just ended.

"Hi, Maya," she said, her smile wide, then noticing my look. "This is *your* welcoming ceremony."

"Oh, yeh." My eyes darted down to the dirt for a moment, then, "But who are you? You're human."

"How *ever* could you tell?" she laughed. "I've been here for some time. It's always nice to talk to another person of the same height. I swear my neck will permanently lock upwards one day." She tilted her head back, long orange hair falling below her hips, then laughed again.

She was about to go on, but something behind me caught her attention. Dimples formed on her lightly freckled cheeks and wrinkles pulled at the corners of her eyes as a young girl with matching orange hair slid around me.

"This is my daughter, Moānā."

"Hey." The young girl smiled innocently.

A young man also emerged from behind me, followed by a small boy who peeped out from behind his leg. His big, round yellow eyes stared up at me, strawberry blond curls falling away from his forehead.

"And her younger brother Ṭasmai." The woman said, then leaned in, more quietly, "He's shy in crowds."

I smiled at the boy, understanding, and crouched down.

"Hi, Ṭasmai. I'm Maya."

He giggled, the sound pure and sweet.

"I'm so sorry. I didn't introduce myself! I'm Chaṅtara, and this is Bŏdhi," she said as I stretched my legs to stand.

Bŏdhi smiled with a sense of mysterious reserve that immediately drew me in.

"It's a pleasure to meet you, Maya." I felt his presence in a more pronounced way than others; like a calm, but deep ocean. While human, he had dark skin and exotic features. His vivid, jungle green eyes glowed with an untamed sense of wildness, almost identical to Phŏenix's eyes.

"Did you come here together?" I asked.

A loud gong rang through the arena.

"Ooh! That means the feast is ready. Let's walk and talk," Chaṅtara said before answering. "We met when I arrived. He grew up here."

I glanced back at the man who trailed behind with Moānā's hand in his. His piercing eyes were as alive as the surrounding wilderness.

"How long have our kind lived down here?"

"Only a couple of decades. When Bŏdhi's parents followed the call, they were the first after the veil lifted. Phŏenix is his sister."

She lifted Ṭasmai up on her hip, who snuggled into her chest like a monkey. She stroked his hair as she walked.

"I came on my own. My parents both died from the chip when we crossed the border. I was seventeen so I didn't have one yet. They were rebels, traitors of the Control. As you can probably imagine, they were under death threats for their lack of conformity, so were basically forced to escape the System. We were sure the fences were down, but . . . to this day I still don't know what happened."

The distant look in her eyes revealed a lingering sorrow but traveling such a journey alone also explained her sense of independence.

"They would've been killed if they stayed anyway," she justified. "At least this way, they went out with integrity."

"I roamed the desert until I was starving and close to death myself, and that's when the voices started guiding me here. I obviously just thought I was delusional," she laughed.

"But they led me to a couple of bandits who had access to a tiny stolen boat and were already searching for this place. They had a map and a lot of information. They drowned too, but they weren't light enough to fall through the vortex."

Her story ended with a heavy weight. Her eyes searched the arena, landing on an elderly couple sitting on a log across the fire. They were the most visually aged people I'd seen in the village, and significantly small.

"That's Bŏdhi's parents," Chantara pointed. "Çusack and Hopi."

I recognized Hopi as the tribe's animal whisperer I'd seen earlier.

"How did they get here?"

Our walk slowed.

"The only entrance is through the Bermuda Triangle," she said. "We all drowned before falling through." She looked back over at Çusack and Hopi.

"And what about . . . the exit?" I asked more quietly. "Do you return through the Bermuda Triangle as well?"

"Exit?" she laughed. "I don't know of anyone who's gone back. I don't know why anyone would want to, or if it's even possible."

"Çusack and Hopi were from Florida before the extreme weather events wiped it out. They saw the prison that the City was, and avoided going there for as long as possible. They were explorers and obsessed with myths, particularly tales of the Bermuda Triangle. They were sure the disappearances led to somewhere."

"When Florida became unstable, and everyone that was left started evacuating to the City, they decided they'd rather die and know the mystery of the Bermuda Triangle than be trapped in one place for the rest of their lives."

I studied the couple more closely, their rich histories written across their wrinkled faces.

"It would seem their 'obsession' was another way of hearing the call though, right? A call they heard and felt in their heart. They chose to act, but when you listen to them tell their story, it seems as if that wasn't even a choice. Not an intellectual one anyway. The call was so strong it was embedded into them; they *had* to take action."

Moānā let out a high-pitched laugh, and I turned to see Phŏenix walking beside her brother, Bŏdhi, teasing and tickling Moānā lightly from her dad's tight embrace.

My eyes lit up when we reached the long table—it was the most epic feast I'd ever seen. The tribe moved along in a relaxed manner filling their bowls, while some already sat but yet eating. Björn perched himself on a log behind the growing flames that swam in the air between us.

I didn't quite understand what it meant to listen to my body yet when it came to eating. All I knew was that I needed sustenance, so I filled my bowl with hearty spiced vegetables, avocado, and coconut yogurt. I tonged one thin slice of meat since it was collected especially for the celebration, although I was still hesitant to try it.

The only meat I'd ever eaten had been a whole, skinned, and skewered bat which was tough, chewy and tasted like dirt. It felt wrong to kill one of the last surviving mammals just for our own consumption. In the past, the City farmed cows, pigs, sheep, and chickens, but their fields dried out and the City ran too low on resources to keep the animals alive.

Just as I settled on the log beside Björn, the headwoman moved in graceful strides to stand before the pyramid.

The fire blazed before her, bestowing a light glow around Athêna's body while casting an enlarged shadow over the triangular wall behind her. Her silhouette was just visible through a long shear gown that looped around her neck where a thick bronze-plated necklace rested. An opaque, hooded veil hung from her shoulders and a vibrant green emerald embellished the wreath resting on the crown of her head.

"May tonight we eat in the warm welcome of Björn and Maya's arrival and celebration of their journey here," she started.

My face blushed. All eyes turned our way, many still wary of our presence, while others kind and welcoming. I was relieved when she declared us free to eat.

Before beginning their meal, every Samādhi took a moment of silent gratitude. I was suddenly overwhelmed by things I was grateful for, but tuned my attention to the simple meal I held.

Thank you for this energy and healing, I thought, even though it felt a little strange speaking to food.

Most people ate quietly, and as I took the time to chew and taste each bite, I began to feel the pure pleasure of the food as it moved through and nourished my weak body. The meat was surprisingly soft and tender in comparison to bat meat, but it was too fleshy, too creepy for me to totally enjoy, especially after seeing its carcass in the arena earlier.

As we finished our meals, conversation slowly filled the arena.

"I wish we were taught that kind of thing in school," I said in response to a comment made by one of the younger Samādhi's, Cherokee, who'd been sitting with us most of the evening.

The night had progressed, the moon now full and bright above, glowing against the black sky. We'd long finished eating but remained seated as each tribe member approached to introduce themselves.

A group gathered around us lounging casually, attentively interested in what life was like for us in the City.

"They taught us the most irrelevant things," I said, the madness alarmingly clear in comparison. Björn chuckled beside me.

Was there a beginning to the madness? Or were the way things were just the nature of our dimension? Erratic, like Nala had described.

"There was a time when earthlings lived in similar ways to us." An unfamiliar male voice entered the conversation as if hearing and answering my silent contemplations.

I didn't know when he approached or how long he'd been listening, but as I looked up, an elderly man stood before me.

Although only lit by the firelight, his frame was almost a replica of Ṭarō's but bigger, and while aged, his physical strength was evident and even further pronounced through his bass-like voice. Like Athêna, his dark skin still appeared youthful beneath supple wrinkles.

Small animals carved from ivory hung around his belt and dark fur fell over his broad shoulders, secured at his collarbone by a blood-red ruby. He held a twisted staff that was adorned with roughly hewn tree sap, shaped into a sharp-tipped triangle that glittered, pointing skyward.

"I'm Hân. We haven't officially met yet." The chief sat beside his son and rested his staff against the log. He moved slowly, with intent, and carried himself with air of wisdom, and life experience.

The beings here aged slower and lived far longer than humans, so even though his physical body didn't appear particularly ancient, his transparent blue eyes indicated his knowledge and exuded peace.

"For a long time, humankind also lived in tribes of different colors and races across the planet with only the raw resources of nature to survive," he continued, articulating each word with clarity and purpose.

"They lived simply and consciously, with little knowledge of the vastness of the planet and its continents, but in touch with nature, and their own true nature. Your planet was a peaceful place."

"How could everything change so much? Why?" I asked, finally in the company of someone with answers.

He let out a long breath.

"Understand, every light frequency has its opposite and equal potential in dark. So, while human's natural state is love, they are also easily tempted by greed, power, and self-inflation. There are two potential centres of consciousness a human can live from. One is the heart. The other is the ego. One is open, eternally loving, and aware of the abundance in the world. The other is limited and self-absorbed. It cannot see beyond its own wants and needs. The heart is an immense force of Light. The ego can be destructive, and attract the dominant emotions of desire, fear, anger and hatred as a result of its competitive nature," he explained.

"As you can see, the potential for light and dark has always been within you. And understand this; the ego itself is not a force of negative charge. It is only a self-obsessed ego that becomes dangerous. Otherwise, it serves it's purpose to propel your kind into action and evolution. The change that occurred on a global scale, was not as simple as a collective shift towards a more ego-centric existence. The expanse of light and positive charge across the planet gradually shifted into the negative under the influence of intruding forces. The dominant universal frequency shifted from love, to fear. And fear is one of the most destructive of all the dark forces."

He paused again, then answered my question more directly.

"It began with an all-powerful sorceress, Revãthi, who played with the darkest of black magic. She had a rare gift of inter-dimensional communication, and was contacted at a young age by the consciousness of the Sky People, who were a race of beings from a realm of highly advanced technology, electricity and material industrialization. Earth, at this time, was still primitive, and she envisioned a future where humankind adopted the intelligence of the Sky realm to run their civilizations. To her, it was grand and revolutionary in comparison to their primitive ways. But their sharing of intelligence came with a price.

The Sky People's planet deteriorated long ago, as all form eventually does, and their consciousness drifted through space for some time before becoming desperate for a home again. A body. A source of energy. And the most potent source of energy to their species is of a negative charge, as opposed to this realm, which can only exist by a positive charge. They are our polar opposite." He paused to diverge again into a more in-depth explanation.

"See, in terms of geographic location, your planet, Earth is the middle dimension between the Sky realm and Santoṣha, which is why your potential to function on either positive or negative charge is weighed somewhat equally. Negative charge weakens you and in time, because the fundamental frequency of your realm is still light, excessive negatively-charged emotions make your bodies and minds ill. But it is a source of energy that is available to you all the same."

He returned to the story of the black sorceress.

"In exchange for access to the Sky People's knowledge, Revãthi was asked to open a portal between the realms, so their consciousnesses could enter Earth and implant themselves into the human mind. There, their consciousness could share your bodies as a 'temporary' home and energy source, while sharing with you in return, ideas in the form of thoughts and visions that would advance your race.

But because their consciousness is of a lower, negative frequency, as I explained earlier, Revăthi sealed the deal by casting an additional veil that limited access to forces of light on Earth, so that nothing, including persuasion from us, could interfere with the Sky People's implantation."

As he spoke, there was a loud crack. A tall shoot of smoke erupted from the bonfire, and the fluorescent flames grew. I could see the story of human history coming to life, flickering into shapes that looked like the very spirits of Revăthi and the Sky People.

More Samādhi gathered, and children sat on the ground in front of us, backs soaking in the fire's comforting warmth. I wasn't sure what interested them more, Chief Hân's story of humans, or humans ourselves.

"It was the beginning of the dark ages, but rays of light still lived in the form of white witches and sorcerers. The union of their power was enough to rise up against Revăthi, expelling her to a realm of utter emptiness that they created for her alone.

The sorcerers didn't realize when they exiled her, that she was the only one who could lift the veil. And by the time they had successfully closed the channel that gave the Sky People ongoing access, it was too late. Their consciousness had already entered your realm. They had already been implanted into your minds." Hân paused again, allowing the information to sink in.

"You said earlier humans were a temporary home. Why temporary?" Björn asked.

"Their intentions are not clear to us. We cannot be sure of their plan. Our consciousness can't pass through metals and therefore can't reach theirs. Metals block light, and light is the essence of our being—the substance of our dimension. Because Earth dimension is denser than ours, you can function around a certain amount of metal, just as you can with a certain amount of negative charge. But it interferes with your connection to the true expanse of light available within you. And that is precisely what happened over time. You lost that connection.

"The Sky realm was built on metal, and the Sky People can only survive in physical form if they are surrounded by metal, just like human's can only survive in their full potential when surrounded by nature and clean air. So the only explanation we've developed is that the part of the Sky consciousness implanted in your minds has been using human bodies as mediators to transform Earth into a replica of their metal planet, so they can manifest fully in their original iron forms."

At that moment, I saw in the flames an image of an iron being, just a flicker.

"Sky consciousness showed you electricity and metal, fuel and technology, but subconsciously. The thoughts they send are so convincing that you believe they are yours, because they are intertwined into your own minds. But really, you've been mere puppets in a greater plan, instruments of your own demise," he finished, his expression raw.

While listening to Hân speak, my emotions ranged from impassioned anger to sorrow to compassion. I finally understood that beneath the veil of ignorance, every human held the same connection to light within them as the Samãdhi People.

We'd just forgotten.

Stillness settled over the group.

"So Sky Consciousness is implanted in our minds too?" My eyes darted between Björn and Hân. It was frightening but also made sense. Sense of the shadows . . . *Were the "shadows" another term for the Sky Consciousness?*

"Don't worry yourself with it now," Hân said. "More will be revealed to you when you're ready. All you need to know now is that Sky Consciousness can't exist here just as we can't exist up there. When surrounded by nature in its rich and pure form, they perish. You're safe here."

Ṭarō spoke, breaking the heaviness of the moment.

"All right, enough of all that." He slapped his hands on his knees and pushed himself up.

I looked to Björn who appeared content with what we'd learned, and while part of me burned to have all the gaps filled in, I let it go. Ṭarō was right, it was an extensive subject, and we were supposed to be celebrating.

"More Kakáu anyone?" he asked.

A few tribe members stood to refill their mugs, but I was still on my first. Kakáu, the ceremony drink, was bitter and vibrantly spiced, while sweet and chocolatey. It generated a warm sensation both on my tongue and throughout my body. Its warmth surged through me, relaxing, while at the same time stimulating invigorating endorphins. I was no longer worried about Hân's message. Everything felt okay.

And peaceful. Lovely.

I turned back to where Hân sat, but he had disappeared.

I swivelled to face the fire that shimmied as if it had a consciousness of its own. I felt hypnotized by the flames. Projections of the story continued to play in my mind as if they were being painted upon the night sky by golden brushstrokes.

Revāthi appeared and disappeared before my eyes, momentarily embodying the flames before dissolving back into the ether. Visuals of the Sky People returned in iron forms, tall like the tribe but plated in silver armour. Their features were sharp and distinctive.

Suddenly, the face of the Mother appeared. She stared directly into the most central essence of who and what I was, through eyes that encapsulated the purest expression of eternal love.

The sense of an intense presence behind me stole my attention. I turned my head, but nothing was there. Nothing but the pyramid a distance away, its outline glowing from behind the ancient guardian trees that stood before it. I turned back around, but the Mother's face in the flames was gone.

The feeling though . . .

It remained alive in my veins all night.

I was safe, supported by love itself.

I was free.

The story of Earth that Hân had told fell away from my focus. I left my seat to go to Björn. His eyes were lost in the fire as mine had been, but his expression was troubled. He must not have seen the Mother, must not have felt her nurturing embrace.

Reaching downward, a stream of mist extended from my hand toward Björn, swimming like a ghost in the night.

"Dance with me?" My words carried a liveliness I'd rarely expressed before.

Our hands made contact, sparking before the mist evaporated. But I was the only one who seemed to notice. I drew him from the log toward a gathering of bodies that now danced around the fire to the beating of a bongo drum.

I could feel every beat, every note, every rhythm vibrating through my body.

The light and airy notes of a flute joined in, whistling on the wind.

"*Aaooouuuuummmmm.*" A deep, earthy male voice hummed, complimenting the high stringing sounds of a guitar. Then a female voice chimed in, offering an ethereal harmony. There were no words, just sounds. Beautiful, resonant, powerful sounds.

My body swayed and rolled to the music, feeling its rhythm reaching the core of my being. I led Björn around the fire to where the musicians gathered on the ground, lost in the sounds they generated.

Almost half their size, we had to dodge the Samãdhi's free, untamed movements as huge feet stomped the ground, their long muscular legs gliding in both rhythmic and chaotic motion. Some were graceful, floating, like they might levitate and dance upon the very air we breathed, while others were rough and heavy, thrusting their weight around in the ultimate outpour of freedom.

Bŏdhi and Chaṅtara sat just beyond the dancers with Çusack and Hopi while Phŏenix danced with enough awareness not to get knocked by the giant bodies. Children ran around the arena, playing, laughing, and calling to each other over the music.

Björn's hand fell from mine, but his eyes kept flickering over to meet mine. Raw and free, we flowed through space and time.

The music increased in tempo.

Louder.

Faster.

More instruments joined in an amplifying symphony. More bodies gathered forcing Björn and I apart, lost in the expression of body to sound while others started dancing more intimately.

There was a sense of freedom in the way the Samādhi held each other and moved as one, rotating between partners. Women swayed their hips sensually, drawing the men toward them, and men were unafraid to express their attraction.

I didn't know how to move like that.

The night grew darker and the moon brighter. Time passed quickly. My body tired and my limbs became heavy, while inside, I felt so light I could have been floating.

I stumbled out from the crowd in a strange euphoria.

Phŏenix caught my attention as I quenched my thirst with water, swaying her body like a temptress. She twirled around Björn, drawing him closer with her striking eyes.

My body reacted in a way that was protective over him, but I forced my eyes away before fully acknowledging what it meant. I caught the piercing eyes of a willowy, feline-like woman with jet-black hair. She stood next to a fit young man with a friendly smile, but her face was not friendly, nor was she smiling.

I looked away again, not knowing where to rest my eyes, but I could not escape the sense of her steady stare. My heart began to beat faster as I watched her approach me from the corner of my eye, suddenly wishing I wasn't alone by the water stand.

But she didn't stop to confront me. She simply brushed by me, hissing, "Your kind is a poison here," before disappearing into the dancers.

I didn't dare follow her, and instead left the arena with a skip propelling each step.

I wandered along the dirt path toward the cottage, staring up at the black sky that was surprisingly bright considering the only light came from the radiant blue glow of the moon.

The woman's voice played over in my mind.

Was she suggesting we go back? Was it even possible to go back?

At least it gave me an indication as to why some others were also cautious of our arrival. After hearing Hân's story, I didn't blame them. But he promised, just as the Shaman had, that we would heal there, whatever healing involved...

I was tired, exhausted, by the time I reached the cottage. I crawled into bed and under the furs, and fell asleep too quickly to contemplate anything any further.

CHAPTER FOURTEEN

THE SOUND OF BIRDS chirping woke me. It was a melody I had not heard before.

Before opening my eyes, I rolled in the warm furs, appreciating their texture against my cheek. Vitality burst within for the day ahead. Waking up in the valley and simply being alive for another day all felt like pure magic.

That was the only comprehensible explanation for any of it; that magic is *real*.

I opened my eyes to the rough wooden ceiling high above, reminding me of how small I was in a home fit for giants. A large cloth art piece hung on the wall directly opposite the bed, stained with splashes of rich beetroot purple and berry reds. Wooden shelves with rugged, natural edges curved out from the wall, decorated with simple, hand-made ornaments.

I slid from the bed and stretched, muscles stiff from dancing. The leather daybed where Björn slept was already neatly made.

The Samādhi People assumed he and I were close before arriving, and I didn't want to cause inconvenience by requesting separate quarters, but it felt strange to be living with a stranger. Especially when the stranger felt more familiar than anyone I'd ever known.

Through the open window I could hear noises from outside.

"Hua! Ha!" It sounded as if Björn was fighting someone, but when I looked out into the garden, he was alone.

He punched the air with force, eyes sharp and fiercely focussed.

I wandered quietly over to the open door and leaned my shoulder against its frame. He was shirtless, skin already shiny with sweat and white/blonde hair catching the early morning sun. I watched his muscles tighten and contract with his movements. He moved two steps and swung his leg into a high kick, spun, then stepped again, each one meticulous and precise.

He caught my gaze and paused.

"Where did you learn that?" I asked. The movements looked familiar, but at the same time, foreign.

He didn't answer, kicking the air twice more to finish the sequence.

"Ha! Ha!"

I turned to go back into the house. I was distracting him.

"A Chinese woman," he finally replied, and I froze.

"Some kind of martial art?" I turned back and stepped onto the porch.

He nodded.

"I learned in secret." In the City, martial arts were a lost fighting form. It was banned.

"And the Chinese woman was she . . . How did you meet her?"

He hesitated and scratched his cheek.

"It ah . . . It's bizarre, and will probably sound crazy but . . ."

"She visited you in your dreams." I blurted out the moment he said, "I met her in a dream."

He cocked his head questioningly and moved toward me.
"How did you . . .?"

"She visited me in my dreams too."

We simply stared at one another, a new level of connection forming.

"How often did she visit?" I asked, breaking the silence.

"More times than I can count. It started when I was around ten and continued through my teenage years. She helped me stay centered in myself, while at the same time build the fighting skills she somehow knew I'd need in the future."

I understood well the incomprehensible nature of her wisdom and foresight.

"She stopped visiting around the time I was initiated as an officer." His gaze drifted to a distant memory, the muscles on his face tightening with some kind of pain. "I thought she abandoned me for choosing the wrong path."

Before I could ask what he meant, he asked;

"She taught you to fight too?" His tone was surprised.

"Hey, don't underestimate me," I warned, swinging a roundhouse kick in front of his face.

He ducked, catching my ankle with one hand and twisting my leg.

"Ouch," I laughed. He let go.

"No. She taught me tai chi," I said, laughter still in my eyes. "She was also the one who taught me how to feel the shadows within and how to clear them. She never explained why, but I trusted it was important, so I practiced her teachings. Pretty religiously actually, and it somehow helped me... manage."

"Huh, she taught me about the shadows too," he said. "Wow." He shook his head.

Our eyes met, mystified. A strange sense of familiarity swept over me after watching him practice his moves. The glimpse of a memory that quickly disappeared.

"What's wrong?" he asked with more concern than seemed necessary.

"Oh, just déjà vu or whatever." I brushed it off, but his concern lingered.

"I um, was supposed to meet someone early this morning," he said, turning abruptly.

His held his shoulders back, rigid, as he walked out of sight. I tried to pinpoint what triggered his change in behaviour, but I couldn't make sense of it.

I found myself alone with nowhere that I *needed* to be, so I wandered through the trees. I breathed deeper, fuller intakes of the morning air and felt the presence of the wisdom-bearing stillness resting in and around the trees envelop me.

Hân's story of the Sky People returned to my mind, and I caught myself slipping down a tunnel of paranoia. The world as I knew it was crumbling and for some moments I could hardly discern between reality and illusion.

If my thoughts aren't my thoughts, then what am I? Where am I? Who am I? And what about these thoughts I'm having now, they must be mine, right?

The beauty around me faded. My head began to pound as an uproar of thoughts battled against each other.

No, I'm dreaming. I've drifted so far into fantasies that I'm fully hallucinating. Great, now I'm even more loony than Susan! Maybe I never left the Council building, or maybe that too was a dream too and I'm—

My foot caught on an exposed tree root and I tripped forwards, my hands grazing the ground as I fell.

I knelt there, shocked back into presence. My attention returned to the exquisite beauty of the environment all around me. I wiped the debris from my palms and examined each speck of dirt that stuck to the skin and the indentations left by tiny pieces of bark, unable to recall any dream capturing such detail.

I decided that if it was a dream, it was far more pleasant than the realities of the City, so I might as well embrace it while it lasted.

The one thing I couldn't deny was the story of the Sky People. It was the only explanation that made sense of mad world operating above. Sense of why humans could not *see* the destruction our kind had imposed on our own planet, or that if we had just spent more time planting and rehabilitating the land instead of continuing to mine it, nature may have been alive and well, or at least on a road to recovery.

It also made sense of how negatively-skewed thinking had become an epidemic that caused more pain than the thinker ever realized. But I wanted to know more. I wanted to know if the Sky consciousness were the same entities that Björn called shadows. And more importantly, I wanted to know how to stop them from manipulating the minds of humankind.

Twigs and leaves crunching underfoot sounded from behind. I turned, expecting to see Björn or one of the tribe. Instead, I saw what looked like two leafless branches moving in unison behind a large fern. Accepting the possibility that I could still be dreaming, I thought to myself, *maybe trees here can walk too?*

I moved closer, discovering that the two branches were attached not to a trunk but an animal that had a slender brown body, four long, bony legs, and white fur along the underside of its neck. It was a deer. Wandering not far behind was her fawn. White spots sprinkled across its reddish spine, ears twitching to all the sounds and songs carried from tree to tree beneath their shady canopy. It stumbled over stones and sticks in spirited play, gangly legs still finding their balance in a gallop to feed its endless curiosity.

A reverberatory drumming chaperoned me to a bird with a garnet colored crest and a crown of tufted feathers that swung as it bashed its beak repetitively into the wood of a rough tree trunk. A bushy-tailed squirrel scurried along a branch, transporting an apparently precious nut. Bushes of bright berries and plentiful nut trees spread throughout the forest. An abundant assortment of mushrooms lined the damp floor and whole pumpkins grew in random patches. The scene was one of true prosperity.

The smell of rain filtered down from above. I could taste microdroplets in the air and pushed apart the feathery leaves of two ferns to reached an opening where pebbles led down to the same body of water that flowed from the falls.

In the mercy of its wake, the tumbling water sounded like thunder, cascading in buckets that spilled over a series of rocky ledges and left clouds of white mist. It echoed through the channel of the valley and I followed the riverbed towards the sound, knowing there was a wide open pool that the tribe used for bathing up ahead.

White butterflies flitted across the glassy surface of the stream. Sparks of gold and silver glittered off the scales of fish beneath rays of sun. Large, algae-coated stones and green weeds appeared distorted beneath the water.

Time seemed to have stopped. I dropped my dress when I reached the open lake and broke the still surface with my dive. But there was a deeper stillness resting below.

Rushes of energy swam through me as I swam back up to the surface. I laughed, elated, refreshed by the water, reborn to this new land that revealed its existence to me in dreams.

Memories of my swims in the City's harbor flashed back. It was barely water in comparison. This was closer to the invigorating water I remembered from *before*. The ocean.

I bent over to see my reflection, but looking back was what I remembered of my mother's face.

Do I look like her? Now that I'm older? Did my parents flee to the ocean when the fires chased them on the land? Were they boiled alive by the flames?

Her smile quickly faded, distorted under my sad eyes.

I never had the chance to know them well but I still felt their presence with me somehow. I felt it most profoundly when in water. While I'd always be grateful for the way Lorraine and Jeff took me in as their own, they never understood me, and I never understood them. Sometimes I wondered whether my parents would have understood me.

"Good morning."

Two Samādhi women floated in the shallows. I hadn't realized how close I'd drifted to them. They smiled at me, welcoming.

"We didn't get a chance to meet last night." The older woman's voice, like her eyes, revealed a depth of peace I assumed could only come with age and time.

"We didn't want to overwhelm you," said the younger woman. "You were being introduced to so many."

"I'm Wimberly," said the older woman, "and this is my daughter, Everly."

Being it was such a long walk back to Nirmala's, they offered to escort me. We walked in silence, a showing of their utter contentment, but I felt nervous, like I was supposed to say something. In the City, we were obliged to make conversation. I had always relied on others to fill the spaces with noise, which had not seemed difficult for anyone else but me.

As I slowly surrendered to their quiet presence, I felt a connection to them. One deeper than I could have made through conversation. In the silence I could *feel* them, their kind hearts.

Stopping at their cottage, I waited on the front porch as Everly ducked inside, returning promptly with a folded pile of fabric.

"For you." She handed it to me. I unfolded each piece carefully to find a traditional tribal outfit.

"A welcoming gift. We were going to give it to you last night." Wimberly said.

I looked up at them, overwhelmed with gratitude.

"We thought it'd be nice if you had options custom made to fit you," Everly explained. Her eyes skimmed over my dress, the only clothing item I owned.

"We measured you while you were unconscious," Wimberly shared with a cheeky laugh.

"I don't mind. Thank you. That's so thoughtful." Tears welled in my eyes, but I didn't let them fall.

Wimberly waved her hand. "It was truly our pleasure, Maya. Truly."

They'd made me a brown leather tunic that laced up at the front. The light-weight under-top had long, loose sleeves. They had also made me a pair of pants that flared down my legs, and flat leather boots, embroidered with flowing patterns like the tunic. Lastly, I unfolded a cream-colored woollen shawl with fringed tassels, but it wasn't cold enough to wear that yet.

They were all basic items but crafted from the most beautiful, comfortable materials I'd ever worn. Each one fit my body perfectly.

"Extracted from sandalwood and bamboo," Everly said as I admired the texture.

I changed in their living room. Warm smiles lit the women's faces as I stepped back onto the porch, pleased by how I looked in their creations.

But it wasn't just an outfit they'd gifted me, it was a sense of belonging.

I felt like a woman of the tribe.

I felt freedom.

Before leaving, I *had* to ask, confused by the tribe's conflicting feelings about our presence in the valley.

"Last night," I began, remembering. "One of the women approached me and said that our kind is a poison here."

The women looked at each other, pausing before Wimberly spoke.

"There are many reasons our realm is kept hidden from your kind. Those of you who have been infected by Sky consciousness are dangerous, a threat to our environment and our stability. Some of the tribe are more protective than others . . ." she trailed off.

"Don't worry. They'll warm to you when the see you're no threat," Everly said, her sweet voice comforting me.

CHAPTER FIFTEEN

THE CLOUDS PARTED AS I neared the hilltop, mist meandering between the crevasses below. The air was fresher at this elevation, and my breathing naturally slowed to a deeper, steadier rhythm.

By the time I trekked the stone steps to find Nirmala, she had already been up for hours. She sat in front of a vibrant plant with a basket by her side, picking leaves carefully. An enchanting golden glow emanated around her.

As I stepped closer, I realized she looked strikingly different from the day before, so different that I paused. *Is she even* Nirmala?

When she looked up, I realised she wasn't. This was an elderly Nepalese-looking woman, her long silk hair not white, but black, and her face covered in tribal tattoos. She was the woman I had seen on the bridge in my visions.

A flicker of glistening gold L·ight Matter rippled over her, and as it did, she transformed back into Nala. But I was sure it was an illusion. Either some Shamanic trick, or another side effect of the poison.

I sat beside her on the soft grass. She greeted me a "hello" but no words had been spoken. She threw her head back, laughter ringing through the air and I laughed along with her in my own utter confusion. We laughed until we couldn't anymore, then lay back on the grass, staring up at the vast blue sky. The late morning sun was hot, soaking into my skin.

I closed my eyes, noticing the scent of the plant beside me.

Nala sat up, gathered her basket, and walked toward the cottage. I watched her meticulously from the corner of my eye, searching for anything else out of the ordinary. She returned shortly with three clay cups, two were my medicine, the third was tea.

"For blood circulation."

The tea's aroma was the same as the plant from which Nala had been picking leaves.

"Thank you." I sipped the warm elixir.

She disappeared again, returning with a bowl. "You must be hungry."

It was only then that I realized I was. She had mashed together beetroot with honey, pungent spices, nuts, seeds, and sliced pink grapefruit. I noticed all of the shades of red interconnecting the theme of 'blood flow', beginning to understand that food was used for medicine as much as fuel there.

As I ate, Nala wandered through her colorful garden, sometimes humming. I continued to watch intently for any flickers of the mysterious Nepalese woman to return, but she didn't.

Nala watered the plants, drawing up buckets from a stone well, and picked up small stones and twigs as she moved along the hilltop. She wouldn't accept my help when I offered, so I rested, as ordered.

"You weren't at the gathering last night."

"There was preparation to be done," she said. "At midnight, when the rest of the tribe have cleared, I'm meeting with the Nöahls at the pyramid."

"What's inside the pyramid? Does it have an entrance?"

She paused, then answered me with a brief answer.

"There's nothing inside. And no, it doesn't."

But for some reason I didn't believe her, which made me more determined to figure out why she lied.

"You don't need to know anything about the pyramid," she said sternly.

"What are you meeting there for?" I asked, trying to sound more casual.

"The alignment of tonight's astrology will open a channel of communication between the Mother and the Cosmos." Her answer mysterious, hooking me in and making me forget about the compelling pyramid for a moment.

The Mother and the Cosmos.

I was beginning to understand that the Mother was planet Earth.

The Cosmos sounded like outerspace. The mysterious abyss above that carried the orbiting planets, stars, and moons in its sublime, unseen embrace. Where the Sky People lived until their planet perished. Where their consciousness still drifted...

"Does what you're doing have something to do with sending the Sky People back through Revăthi's portal? Or taking back the veil." I asked.

Her expression was one of surprise. She didn't expect me to know about their existence.

"Please. I want to understand what's really going on up there. In my dimension."

She paused before answering.

"The veil of ignorance was lifted by a group of powerful white sorcerers some time ago. It's what has allowed lighter beings like you and Björn to be born of Earth realm again, but the planet was already saturated by the shadows of Sky consciousness. Negatively-charged frequencies had already overpowered the light. And humans had already developed loops of thinking that compelled them to obsessively pursue technological and industrial advancement. It was too late," she concluded.

"And the Sky People?"

She paused, the ensuing silence piercing.

"At this point, it wouldn't be wise for you to know too much. All you need to know is that you're safe here."

"Hân said the Sky consciousness is implanted in our thoughts and I don't know what to believe, what voice is really mine."

Concerned, Nala replied, "If I can impart one thing to you right now it would be that no voice is really *yours*. Your true being resides far deeper than the fleeting thoughts that pass through your mind. But the voice of the heart is the truest representation of your pure essence. Your sensitive; if you tune into your body closely enough, you'll feel whether a thought is born of the heart as opposed to say, the vibration of fear, anger, or greed. It's a subtle distinction, but when you learn to become an unbiased witness of the subtleties of where each emotion sits in the body, it will become obvious. One is light and expansive, the other is tense and compressed."

Finally, something I can work with.

I'd always assumed that all the noises in my head, the voices, were mine. Were *me*. Her words left me pondering;

If I'm not the thoughts, who am I? What am I?

"The truth is, the human mind was hacked by the Sky People so long ago, the majority of thoughts that play on loop in this age serve only to keep humans imprisoned in ignorance, and as a result, allow their advancements on your species to progress," she continued.

"But you mustn't let this knowledge worry you. You've maintained much of your pure essence, Maya. I believe, from what I can sense, that you already live a very heart-centred existence. It shows up in the clarity and color of your L·ight Matter, and the fact that you passed through the void. *Even* if they influenced your thoughts above, they can't reach you here," she re-assured me.

"It will take time discipline to stop entertaining the thought patterns you have been hooked into, but that is all part of the process."

I attempted to become more aware of my thoughts, where they were coming from, and allow them to pass by instead of believing them as my own. But it was confusing, layered. It was more difficult than just blindly following them.

"Your true being is more loving and peaceful than you can imagine, but be not impatient. If it were easy to just 'stop thinking dysfunctional thoughts' all of humanity would be free." She smiled gently, and I was sure she read my thoughts. Or *the* thoughts . . . ?

"You have had powerful protection around you. I don't know what being or force has been guiding you, but it has allowed you to remain close to the voice of truth. Once you become more aware of which thoughts are not your own, you'll also be able to discern what is pure."

She touched my face tenderly, and for just a second, the Nepalese woman re-appeared in her place, her vivid green eyes wells of the eternal love of which she spoke. She was somewhat transparent, made of L·ight Matter, and I knew now that she was seperate to Nala, while somehow intertwined, like a lingering spirit.

"You are not alone. Your freedom is as important to me as it is to you."

The tension I felt started to dissolve under her benevolent words and touch. I took a deep breath, allowing myself to fall beneath the waves of worry into what felt like the depths of an eternally calm sea.

I wandered back along the path, noticing much I hadn't previously. The tiniest details, down to the compacted forest floor fascinated me. Diverse species of plants, insects, and stones enmeshed to create a unique masterpiece of each meter of the Earth I walked across. No combination was repeated.

My mind was alert, not so much with thoughts but *presence*. A deeply contented calmness drifted from nature's breath into my own. There was no pressure to be anywhere or do anything. I was just walking. Breathing. Awake. Alive.

Björn came to mind and I wondered where he might be. He had begun to occupy a space in my mind and heart untouched by anyone before. I wanted to know why he left so suddenly that morning. I wanted to see him and clear up whatever it was.

My wandering led me to the arena. As I passed the pyramid, I paused in its magnificence. I circled its perimeter again, following the stories engraved on its walls more closely. They depicted battle scenes between gods and demons, spirits of good and evil, shadows versus entities of light.

I touched the stone, but was zapped with a jolt of energy that made me take a few steps back.

To be sure I hadn't imagined it, I leaned forward, but before my hand even made contact with the pyramid, I felt the electricity extend outward. Not only did I *feel* it, I saw it manifest as a stream of glistening gold mist. The same gold mist that the Nepalese woman was made out of.

The entire structure vibrated. I knew then that it had a consciousness of its own. A force of energy struck me like a wave, so powerful it nearly knocked me off me feet. I stumbled backward, both mystified and a little afraid. I couldn't decide whether its response to me was positive or negative. I decided not to stick around and find out.

Just beyond the arena, through an outcropping of trees, I entered another open space. Many tribe members gathered in a grassy field lined by a ring of trees.

They were dancing again.

But this was a different kind of dancing.

They formed a ring around two gurus who guided them through a series of movements. It was like tai chi, but also very different. The tribe moved as one, breathing and pulsating to the same rhythm as they bent and stretched their limbs to extents I never considered possible.

As I admired the union, there was one tribe member who was significantly out of sync. I laughed when I realized it was Björn.

"This is yŏga." I felt Athêna's presence before she spoke, her warm hand gently falling upon my shoulder from where she towered behind me.

"It is an ancient practice used to purify the flow of prana, our lifeforce within, and merge with the divine."

"It is similar to tai chi." She said and I turned my head to catch her actively reading my thoughts but her gaze was casual over the tribe. I started to wonder whether it wasn't so much reading my thoughts but more so catching the idea, the essence of a thought that drifted on the airways.

"But it's more targeted at cleansing the body of dense or negative energy, and healing," She looked down at me.

"It'll be especially powerful for you and Björn, to help you clear the shadows that still linger within you from your world above. I'll introduce you to Ākaṣha and Ạmadeo after. They can teach you."

There was a tremendous power between the two gurus in the centre that held the practicing yõgis in balance. Ạmadeo embodied the force of the physical, dealing more with the alignment and self-control of each pose, while Ākaṣha connected each pose to spirit, expanding the practice beyond the physical body and into metaphysical realms.

As I looked more closely at the man and woman my heart beat faster, realizing they were the two beings I'd seen at the water stand the previous night, and I immediately dreaded our introduction.

But the longer I watched, the woman, Ākaṣha, appeared far less dangerous than she had the previous night, her feline-like femininity far more graceful as her slender body flowed in and out of postures.

"Don't worry, they'll warm to you when they see you're no threat," Everly had assured me. I hoped it was true for I deeply desired to learn the dance of yõga they practiced.

CHAPTER SIXTEEN

"BJÖRN," I WHISPERED AS I knelt by his bed. It was midnight. Wad all retreated to our bed hours earlier, but curiosity kept me awake. My mind was fixated on what might be taking place at the pyramid.

Unlike me, Björn had fallen into a deep sleep immediately upon hitting the furs. The silver glow that shone down through the window illuminated his serene face.

After arriving home we spoke extensively, sharing, elated to be in the valley. He didn't explain his detachment after our conversation that morning, but I let it go. I probably overanalyzed it.

"Björn."

He stirred, mumbling something unintelligible before opening his eyes, "Are you okay?" he asked, clearly concerned to find me next to his bed.

"Yes."

We were silent. I watched his eyes brighten as they woke more fully to the crisp night, then asked, "Do you want to go on an adventure?"

"Now?"

"Yes."

I'll admit, I was being nosy, but had no intention to interrupt anything. The farthest we'd go was to the edge of the bushes. It was harmless — pure innocence.

"I'm only coming so I can take you straight back once you've seen what you need to see." Björn was less enthusiastic about the idea of spying on a sacred ceremony.

The cool night air on my skin was energizing. Shadows of the forest masked the path, and the dark, empty silence was equally exhilarating as it was eerie. I skipped a step and spun to face him, walking backward.

"Come on. You want to know what it is just as much as I do."

He paused, thoughtful, then said, "No. Definitely not as much."

"So you're a little curious?"

"I am now." His eyes crinkled at the corners as he tried to suppress a smile. "I just assumed it was a monument or something — a talisman, like Ṭaro͞ said. I didn't question whether it could open or not."

"*I* just assumed the Control had good intentions . . . until they locked me up! Assumptions are dangerous Björn," I said pointedly.

"I can't argue with that," he replied, though just the mention of the Control made him uncomfortable.

"But I also can't imagine the pyramid being dangerous," he added, shaking it off.

"Hmmm, well you never know till you know, and *that's* why it's a good thing we're investigating!"

"*Shhh*," he chuckled.

We were getting close. On either side of the pyramid the glow of two fires flickered from pillars through the foliage.

We trod more lightly, slowing to a stop, and crouched behind a low plant. The arena was deathly still, the only movement that of the flame's shimmer and shadow.

We waited.

Finally, there was shuffling behind one of the trees. A shadow appeared followed by a body.

It was a woman, her hip-length black hair swaying against her back as she glided over the ground. She wore a tunic of golden fabric, its color striking against her smooth almond-coloured skin. Golden bracelets adorned one arm and long earrings dangled with her movements, glittering as they reflected the firelight. The diamond in her nose ring caught my attention as it, too, sparkled, connecting to a shimmering gold chain that looped up to a hairpin.

"The Nepalese woman . . ." I said under my breath as she disappeared behind the pyramid.

"You mean another human? Where? I only saw Nirmala." Björn said, confused.

It was then I realised that the race we called Nepalese only existed on Earth. So she must have been human. But she was so exotic, so divine, as tall as the Samādhi, but more . . . etheric.

I just shook my head, dismissing my comment, anticipating others to follow. But no one else appeared, which gave me a moment to wonder how and why I saw the Nepalese woman in place of Nirmala. It was as if she had the ability to shape-shift between the two identities. But Björn only saw Nirmala, which made me edge more towards the conclusion that what I saw was a delusion.

Björn was so close I could feel the heat radiating off his warm skin, but my eyes remained on the pyramid. After what seemed like an eternity, its perimeter began to glow with a rich golden aura.

"Do you see it?" I whispered; eyes still glued to the pyramid.

"See what?"

How could anyone miss it?

"The gold mist."

He looked closer, focusing, then looked back at me, confused even more.

Am I delusional?

But it was too clear, too real to doubt. And it was more exquisite than mist. It was Light Matter. Brilliant, luminous gold Light Matter.

"They're in there. It must be coming from whatever they're doing," I said. "I *knew* it had an entrance," I whispered.

"*Come.*" A voice echoed.

"What?" I turned to Björn, but the voice was feminine and sounded Nordic.

"Are you okay?" he asked.

I squeezed my eyes shut, but felt something touch my back. Something electric.

In my mind's eye I saw a woman dressed in white and silver silk, embellished with dark blue swirling patterns that accentuated her ocean blue eyes. Her fair skin was both aged and eternal and she held out her hand for me. She disappeared when I opened my eyes, but a belt of dark blue and silver mist floated around to encircle my waist from the electric sensation that touched my back.

I looked to Björn. His eyes were wide. But not because he too saw the woman.

"Let's go," he said sternly.

Ignoring him, I watched the silver ribbon of Light Matter extend from my waist to the middle of the arena. It began to tug me forwards. The pressure was firm, too firm to resist.

"I don't know what's happening, but I have to go," I said, barely able to speak.

"What do you mean? Nothing's happening Maya. Go where?"

I opened my mouth to say something, but a glimmer of gold in the distance caught my eye. Another stream of Light Matter extended from the pyramid and slithered through the arena. When the gold and silver Light Matter met at the centre, a bright spark ignited. The power jolted me forward.

"That! Surely you saw that." I pointed.

My body jerked forward again, yanked by the interlacing streams of Light Matter. I stumbled to my feet, pulled by its force. When I reached the center of the arena, another jolt of energy knocked the air from my lungs. The air and earth vibrated violently and my vision blurred in attempt to adjust. Maybe it was my body that vibrated; I couldn't tell. My ears rung so high in pitch I thought my eardrums may have burst. My insides felt like they were burning, but at the same time, my body felt light enough to lift from the ground, as if the gravitational pull of the ground had loosened.

What's happening?

The golden current urged me forward. The pyramid glowed brighter and the vibrations became more immense. My body convulsed.

Björn reached out, wrapping his hand around my wrist. His touch was painful. Unlike the gold and silver Light Matter, it stung. Black mist drifted outward from his palm. The air around me reverberated, clashing against his interference. My head pounded.

"Maya, come back." When I looked at him, Björn was blurry. A transparent sheath between us separated our worlds.

"Ahh!" I fell to the ground. I pressed my hands over my ringing ears.

"Enough!" a voice boomed from the direction of the pyramid, cutting through the shrieking rattle that distorted my hearing.

I looked up. A tall man stood with arms raised overhead as if holding up the sky. When he dropped them, every glimmer of gold Light Matter disappeared and the night was black. My body fell limp, gravity reclaiming dominance once more. My heart thumped.

It was one of the Nõahl's.

His face was youthful as a child's, but his figure was that of a full-grown man. His cheeks were smooth and rosy, his wide blue eyes innocent.

"Fools. You should not have come here tonight," he thundered, stepping toward us. Just as with Nirmala, the image of another being appeared in his place that was more fitting to his voice. This being was rugged, built like a warrior, with dark skin that blended into the night in stark contrast against the whites of his bright blue eyes.

"What you see before you is the oldest structure in the history of recorded time, built before our elders arrived. The frequency of light it exists in is higher than anything else we've encountered in any dimension and beyond anything you could possibly comprehend."

"You have no idea the danger involved in these communications we gather here for. There is a reason we wait for everyone to clear the arena before opening the portal; not for our own privacy, but for the tribe's *safety*.

"For decades we've trained to align ourselves with the vast forces of light we meet here. If you had continued, if you had attempted to enter, the vibration of the pyramid would have shattered you."

A shiver ran up my spine as he cut through the ignorance of my curiosity, his words bellowing like a clap of thunder.

One other Nõahl stood beside him now. Bright white upward-facing arrows glowed from the centre of both of their foreheads.

"It's not personal," she said. "You do not embody the capacity to merge. Not yet. Just as most humans do not embody the capacity to merge with the frequency of this realm. Inside, the pyramid is like its own dimension."

It was then I saw a shimmer of silver Light Matter ripple over her body. The face of the Nordic woman flickered over the Nõahl's face. The one who only moments ago had appeared in my mind's eye in metaphysical form, calling me toward the pyramid.

Why would she call me to the pyramid only to send me away? Did the Nõahl know this Nordic woman was somehow lingering with her? Appearing in her place? Did any of them Know? It was beginning to look as if none of the Nõahls were just one being. They all had an alternate face and form that appeared in their place at certain moments, which only I seemed to be able to see.

Were they spirits? Ghosts? Gods? Saints? Maybe they were like guardian arc-angels.

Until recently, I wouldn't have regarded any of these phenomena as real potentials. But I had seen each Nõahl shift and share form too many times to believe it was a delusion.

"Until then, your presence interferes and dilutes the purity of what's being channeled here, for you still carry much baggage from your world above." The woman eyed Björn particularly harshly, and he shrunk back.

"Do not prowl around like this again. Go home now and forget what you have seen," the youthful-looking Nõahl said with finality.

"It's okay. We didn't see anything." Björn bowed his head. "We apologize for interrupting you."

The Nõahl nodded, but his eyes drifted back toward me, acknowledging that what Björn spoke was true, but not for me. I *had* seen things, mystifying, unexplainable things. I pined to ask questions but bit my tongue. My experience was enough to vouch for the danger present, even if my mind couldn't begin to comprehend any of it.

Björn didn't say much on the way home, but inside, something loud was brewing.

"I'm so sorry, Björn. I don't know what came over me. It was like . . ." Again, I bit my tongue. The Nŏahl told us to forget it, but it was so strange. So mysterious. So profound.

"It's okay. I'm fine. I just wanted to protect you. And I think the Nŏahl's power shook me."

I nodded.

"If anything, I really should've just talked you out of going to begin with."

"This one's all on me, ok? It's not your responsibility to keep me in check."

He was quiet, the crease between his brow deepening. I almost let it go.

"Are you sure there's nothing else going on?"

"Just be careful around me. I'm not who you think I am."

"Who are you then?"

He looked away and a shiver raced up my neck as I remembered the black cloud of mist that had seeped from his hand when it touched mine. I knew, if nothing else, that it was a manifestation of the pain trapped within him.

When we reached the cottage Björn said, "I'm gonna stay up for a bit. I'm not tired. I'll stay outside though so I don't disturb you."

Before I could even respond he told me good night and shut the door, leaving me alone in the dark of our unlit home.

CHAPTER SEVENTEEN

AS THE DAYS PASSED, I adapted to the lifestyle of Santōṣha. It began to feel normal, natural. Nala began working with me even more closely, but Björn pulled further away.

While the Shaman shared with me much of the ancient wisdom she had access to, none of it involved the pyramid.

Sneaking around the only pyramid proved to her my recklessness. In order to gain her trust, I needed to mature. But that night also made my "mystic affinities" evident to her, so she began helping me uncover them.

I visited her hilltop each morning, and the healings extending far beyond that of my physical body. She began reworking my mindset so it would realign with the frequency of their world. It contradicted the way I'd been programmed to think and function in the City, but it wasn't difficult to retain her teachings. It felt more like a practice of letting go than actively learning.

Nala lived a life of solitude; she *had* to because of her work. Apart from healings or sacred ceremonies, I never saw her with the rest of the tribe, nor did they approach her, afraid to invade her communications with the gods. The revere the tribe had for her created distance. Her powers connected her to higher realms both sacred and divine, but separated her from the earth-beings she walked beside.

Of everyone in the tribe, she chose to teach *me* magi◻, preparing me for what was to come.

I didn't understand then why. She wouldn't explain. But it was clear she was training me for something.

I joined the yŏga dances. At the beginning, my body was tight and stiff, and I lacked balance. Ākaṣha was hard on me at first, but I realised later it was for my own benefit. She and Ạmadeo took the time to coach Björn and I through the correct movements and positions.

As I persevered through the discomfort of each practice, new plateaus of openness and flexibility became available. At first I noticed its affects on my body, then began to notice the profound changes to my mind.

"Björn!" I sprang to my feet to catch up to him as he was leaving after a group practice. Everyone was clearing the field to start their day's work.

"Dặo's showing me how to harvest lentils. Do you want to come too?" I asked.

He stared at me blankly, then shook his head; the response I should have expected.

"Sorry Maya." He turned and disappeared into the trees.

I watched him, wishing to understand what was beneath his cold reserve.

Is he grieving his parents? But that wouldn't make him shut me out. It had to be something else, something even more significant.

I thought of Adam, sure that if he were there, he would have been able to offer me some kind of male human perspective.

I then thought about Lorraine and Jeff. *Do they think I'm still in prison?* I considered what kind of story Koen could have spun. *When I go back for them, I'll set the story straight.*

Early one morning, before the sun had risen, Ākaṣha and I hiked to a mountainous peak to practice yŏga in full view of the sunrise over the valley. Sunrise was considered the most immaculate time of the day for connecting to the deeper aspects of both the self and the divine fabric of the universe.

The sky was still dark and the air crisp as we began our ascent. I still felt slightly uncomfortable in her presence, but she had suggested the hike. I accepted the invitation as a gesture of her trust and acceptance.

"The poses are tools that allow us to open and observe our energy body, permitting whatever's there to move through and clear, so as we reach the final meditation we can sink into stillness and silence with fewer distractions," she shared.

"It's only in silence that true truth can be heard," she continued, her voice hanging in the air.

We'd been walking at a swift pace that cultivated body heat, but the icy air was still sharp against any exposed skin. As the first hues of sunrise appeared, our surroundings became visible. A transparent haze drifted through crevasses and swept around fellow peaks. A pale wash of color in the sky enhanced the dreamy ambiance of the morning.

"Every season can be found along the Santōṣha valley," Ākaṣha told me as we climbed. "There are five significant changes in the landscape and weather, so if you travel from one end to the other, you'll experience every season. Our village resides in spring."

Beyond the grassy paddocks below, where wild horses grazed as slowly as the sun rose, there was an epic assemblage of mountains under pristine blankets of snow.

"That's winter."

"Beyond the mountains, is autumn, where leaves are always falling, and at the valley edge, it's the wet season where rain is constant. It pours into a river mouth that runs all the way through the centre of the island, to Summer at the opposite end. Summer is tropical, it's where we harvest most of our fruits and different seaweeds. Coconuts are particularly generous because we can use every part of the tree and fruit for an impressive number of purposes."

"The Mother occasionally rotates seasons to refresh the land, but primarily returns every area to its original climate. It is in this order that the valley functions as one unit, each season working to regulate balance."

"Do any other tribes live out there?"

"There used to be a tribe in all but the wet season, but as the earth sickened, we merged to form the Samādhi, our power stronger as one."

"You might have noticed subtle differences in our appearances. Athêna's ancestors are from the snowy mountains of winter, their skin is fair and soft, and bodies generally more plump to survive the cold. Cheif Hân is of pure spring heritage, the tallest of the races. Ạmadeo is from summer where skin is dark as a result of a long lineage of adaption to harsh sun exposure, and Katanä is from autumn, where bodies are generally shorter and more muscular. The other villages still exist, open for anyone making long trips or journeys to camp in. But no one lives there. There's a chance we'll separate again one day if the earth regains its full strength."

We came to a stop and settled on a flat ledge.

I turned my attention inward focusing on my breath. A sense of spaciousness and stillness expanded through my body. Presence.

"Move onto your hands and knees and arch your spine, opening your chest to the sky. Slowly draw your hips back into adho mukha svanasana."

I was familiar with the poses by now, and while Ākaṣha's directions were the guidelines, the true director of all movement was my breath, moving and opening the body on the inhale, and surrendering deeper into each pose on the exhale. We flowed into the sequence of dance she called our vinyasa.

The sun continued to rise, colors fading into one all-encompassing blue. The radiance of the lush, green landscape below brightened, and my inner life also brightened, awakening with the sun.

As did time, thoughts vanished. I closed my eyes, feeling a sense of wholeness, and lightness expanding from within. When I opened my eyes, it appeared as though the light manifested itself in stars all around me.

I'm dizzy. I assumed, bending over to place my head between my knees and ease the spinning.

Slowly, I sat up to see the stars still floating before me. As I looked closer, I realized that they weren't spinning as they might in response to the brain's loss of ample oxygen; they floated gracefully, swaying, not mere stars for they had wings.

Fireflies?

Ākaṣha laughed, and I turned to see a cluster of the luminous lights dancing with and around her to the song of the wind and land. One landed on her nose and another on her hand when she held it up.

I inched closer.

What I saw amazed me. These luminous creatures had humanlike legs and bodies, bare but for their skin's radiant glow. The one on her hand was male, his face chiseled like a porcelain doll with eyes that shone the same silver as his skin. Wings stroked the air furiously even when still and they, too, glowed, almost transparent if not for the brighter blue patterns that swirled in an eternal river of motion.

His mouth opened and he laughed, but the sound was more like chiming bells. His contagious exuberance sparked laughter from the other winged creatures, some tinkling in so high a pitch it was almost inaudible to the human ear, while others rang deeper.

He sprung from Ākaṣha's hand as she sat. Suddenly, I felt tiny feet tickle the back of my neck in the lightest massage. Another landed upon my palm, then another, and soon a cluster hovered around my body. I was elated by their presence.

Then, just as inconspicuously as they appeared, they drifted into a single floating flock that disappeared into the distance.

I knelt beside Ākaṣha whose soft gaze was serene.

After some moments, she spoke.

"We call them Fèya" she said of the tiny beings. "They have existed from the beginning of time as the purest beings to take form. They survive across all realms for they are undiluted projections of light itself, and all realms are assemblies of light."

Her gaze remained out in the direction they had disappeared.

"They've been the thread between humans and the Samādhi, living between our worlds as they choose and desire. There was a time when humankind communicated with them, seeing them in form as we do, but as they fell out of contact with their own light essence, they became invisible, only seen by those who maintained or re-awakened to their true innocence.

"As nature sickened, the Fèya also sickened, depleted by lack of light and poisoned by the prevailing darkness. They retreated here permanently where they can trust light to be ever-present, but the earth's illness affects them more intensely than other creatures, even in this realm.

"Slowly their lights continue to fade to black and their bodies dissolve to ash. We barely see them anymore; they don't often wander far from their kingdom. The ill have been losing their flight and those still in health stay close to care and provide for them. We offer what assistance we can, but there is little we can do for the cause is beyond us. Nirmala and the Nŏahls have spent much time calling upon the elements to help them heal and replenish their magic, but nature herself is scarce of supplies.

"Because the anatomy of the Fèya is so close to that of nature on Earth, they thrive and suffer as one. Only through nature's revival can the Fèya thrive again."

The sound of silence was piercing, as if all of nature concurred with Ākaṣha's words.

"They felt the purity here this morning and thought your realm might be regenerating, for the existence of humans like yourself inspires hope," she explained.

"Do you have hope too?" I asked.

Ākaṣha exhaled a long breath, looking over Santōṣha with a distant stare.

"From this view, I can't say."

Then it happened again.

A flash.

The planet.

Black.

Dead.

The people.

The pain.

"I have to do something," I blurted, snapping myself out of the vision.

Ãkaṣha eyed me closely. "There's nothing you can do."

"What do you mean?" Her comment bothered me. It was as if she didn't care. *What was this grudge she had over humankind?*

"We can't just sit back and let earth fail. We can't just let the rest of humanity fail with it."

"It is their choice. We have only the power to share information across the realms, not to force or persuade. They *have* to be open to hear our calls. Many are not aware they are trapped," she said calmly. "Intent and willingness is the driving force of all forms of freedom. Without it, there is no change."

"Surely if we went back and told them about this place, they'd have to see—"

"At this time in evolution, humans are *dangerous* Maya. Destroyers," she said.

"But . . . not all humans. There must be others like us," I was too stubborn to acknowledge the objective truth of her words. To *see* it the way I had witnessed it myself my entire life.

"Okay, let's say you go back. Why would anyone there believe you? Your story would only increase their motivation to kill you. They would think you're insane as well as a rebel."

I thought of Susan. Now I knew what she had said was true, which made me even more frustrated.

"Unless they are sensitive, unless their hearts are beating, they'll never be able to hear you."

"The reason we came here was to find help to save the planet."

To my surprise, she laughed.

"And when did that become your duty?" She shook her head.

"Who said nature needs saving? What if things only appear bad on the outside. What if the Mother has it all under control? What if there's a perfect reason for it all?"

Her questions silenced me, reminding me of what Björn had said of his parent's research.

"They found that much of the soil here is still fertile. On the surface it looks lifeless, but underneath it is rich with all the minerals it needs to regenerate."

But still, that didn't guarantee human survival.

"Then why are we here?"

She didn't answer. She didn't know.

CHAPTER EIGHTEEN

MY CONTRIBUTION TO THE tribe was cooking and gathering. I'd been learning how to grow and harvest produce, and forrage for edible wild plants.

Late one afternoon I ventured into denser terrain, where the forest became a jungle between spring and summer, in the pursuit of certain medicinal herbs that Gingēr and Petãl requested.

The impeding sense of hopelessness I felt for situation on Earth continued to grow inside me. While I walked, I wondered how one race could be living in pure paradise while another in deep suffering?

The people of Santōṣha understood wisdom beyond my wildest imagination, but their decision to ignore what was happening to humanity didn't seem like wisdom to me. I couldn't lay all my trust in this great, omniscient "Mother" like they did either.

There has to be more humans hidden away in the City that would survive the jump through Bermuda if we showed it to them. If we could somehow return...

But I had no way to return. In the epitome of freedom, I felt trapped again.

"Okay, let's say you go back. Why would anyone there believe you? Your story would only increase their motivation to kill you. They would think you're insane as well as a rebel."

"Ugh!" I released some of my frustration out loud. I knew she was right.

"Why am I *here*?" I looked up at the sky, and when no one answered I kicked my leg in into the emptiness before me. I knew it wasn't in any way helpful. But then again, it kind of was, just to let go of some stress.

I distracted myself by thinking of Björn and the small ways in which we seemed to be growing closer, unblind to the fact that we'd actually been growing miles apart.

In the mornings we often walked to the falls together to greet the day in the fresh, icy water, mostly in silence for it was so grand, so magnificent, it lived beyond words and therefore so did we. Sometimes I'd catch him looking at my body. I feigned naivety but was highly aware. I found myself looking at his body sometimes too.

Afterward, when we returned to the cottage, he always maintained a certain distance.

He was keenly interested in carving, especially tools, but quickly discovered other objects, taking inspiration from things we had access to in the City. Combined with materials available here, he was able to create new items and more efficient spins on existing tools. He spent hours in the solitude of the forest collecting wood, distancing himself not only from me but everyone.

My basket was empty but for a few elderflower leaves. Intent on finding more plants to fill it with, I ventured deeper into the jungle. Giant green plants and exotic flowers lined the jungle floor, and rainbows of bright butterflies splashed the sky with vibrant colour. Massive fallen logs lay on the ground, accumulating coats of pudgy moss.

I began to catch the faint sounds of distant voices echoing from trunk to trunk and weaving through the rustling leaves as if the trees themselves were in conversation. They were masculine voices. If not for their distinctive familiarity, I might have thought them paranormal, the sound so close yet just out of sight.

Assuming Björn wouldn't want to be found by me anyway, I steered in what I thought was the opposite direction, but a pair of tan muscular legs dangling from a curved branch high above, along with two smaller human legs, caught my attention. Nestled between them were the strikingly hairy legs of some kind of giant primate with burly leather-like feet.

A low growl rumbled.

"Hey Maya!" Ṭarō had spotted me.

Of all the Samādhi, Björn spent the most time with Ṭarō. Even as the chief's heir, he always had time to play.

Björn looked downward at me, the burnt-orange beast following suit.

A small nose with flaring nostrils was in the centre of its flat, tough-skinned face. Its black eyes fixed directly into mine. It looked like a distorted species of human, but significantly more wrinkled, brown beyond suntan, and tremendously hairy.

"She's an orangutan!" Ṭarō called. "She's harmless."

The orangutan let out a sleepy moan as if in confirmation and flopped a long hairy arm over Ṭarō's leg.

"She's a character," he chuckled. "Wanna climb up and met her?"

Although tentative, I moved toward the tree.

"I've never climbed a tree."

"That's okay, I'll show you." Gripping a branch above for support and balance, he carefully stepped down to a lower branch and jumped, landing before me with a thump.

"Wait," I said quietly, stepping closer. "Are you sure Björn won't mind?"

He looked up toward Björn between a gap in the branches, then back down.

"He won't mind," he assured me, then added. "However, the shadows in him might."

I was confused.

"But don't worry, we're working on it." He winked and turned toward the tree.

"Make sure both your hands always have something to grip and your feet a branch to stand on." He started climbing in demonstration. "When you get higher, use the branches as a ladder." He hung there for a moment, bouncing to showcase his stability, then hopped back to the ground.

"Plus," Ṭarō leaned in quietly again, "Why should it matter what Björn thinks? Do you really want to tiptoe around him for the rest of your life?"

"The rest of my life sounds a bit dramatic."

Raising his voice to speaking level, he reached into his belt and said, "Oh yeah, Björn made this. When there's no branch to hold on to, you can dig it into the trunk and use it to pull you up." He handed me a sharp dagger, the first weapon I'd ever held.

The first steps were tricky, but once I got the hang of it I felt like an animal, crawling over and around branches until reaching the one where the real wild animal rested. A humbling of my mere humanness overcame me.

As I examined the beast up close, I decided perhaps we were more alike than I originally thought. The grace of her unhurried movements and the lines creasing her face exhibited an intelligence not unlike that of humans, — more profound for all we knew, for it was silent, not spoken, but lived.

Carefully hugging the trunk, I stepped around with Ṭarō at my heels, who was quick to lend his hand any moment I wobbled. The orangutan watched me peacefully as I nestled beside her, eyes curious but accepting.

"We call her Rose." Björn said.

"She seems to like it. Ṭarō and I had been hanging out here once when she suddenly climbed down from a higher branch and sat down beside us. Now she pretty much sniffs us out every time we come back." He laughed lightly, more relaxed than he'd been around me for a while.

Ṭarō swung in-between Björn and Rose, resting his arms over their shoulders. "Ahhh. Three best friends there ever was. Right guys?"

Rose stared out over the jungle, chewing lazily on something green, and as if feeling the pressure of our gaze, opened her mouth to unleash another groan. Björn cracked a smile.

From our high, broad view it seemed that all was still, but nothing was still.

Within the branches of the omniscient trees, animals lurked, hidden—many animals. More animals than I'd ever seen. Ṭarō taught me their names as they passed, my personal encyclopedia.

Bright, exotic birds swooped and glided high and low and monkeys flung from branch to branch, tree to tree, flying in squeals of mischief. Giant leaves rustled below where marsupials shuffled to and from their hiding places.

The longer I watched, the more I saw, and although seemingly wild and exquisitely free, there was order across the jungle. A natural way that all animals by birthright seemed to understand and honor.

If humans are supposedly more intelligent than animals, why did we need to be so tightly monitored by Control for things to run smoothly in the City? If we were left free like these animals, would there be a natural way among our species too? Unspoken but understood?

"It's the shadows that need monitoring," Tarō said when I voiced my thoughts out loud. "Humans *are* dangerous, barbaric even—only when their hearts are cold. When the Sky consciousness cast shadows over the conscience of their heart, they can become ruthless."

"Before, when humans lived in connection with their hearts, the Control wasn't necessary. The heart's natural way is giving and receiving. Harmony was effortless." He shrugged.

Rose grew restless and reached for the branch overhead. She wrapped her long fingers around the limb and pulled herself up, legs dangling in mid-air. Her straggly, burnt orange hair swayed as she swung her weight backward, then reached for the branch ahead, then the next.

She turned her head and met my eyes with such humanity I swore she *knew* that we'd be seeing each other again, before disappearing branch to branch into the vast canopy of leaves.

A gap was left on the branch where she had been sitting, removing the separation between Björn and me.

CHAPTER NINETEEN

WHEN I CLIMBED DOWN from the tree, Björn dropped to the ground beside me.

"Can I walk with you?"

"Sure."

He picked up a twisted piece of wood and fiddled with it before tossing it in my basket.

"I'll use that for something," he said. "So what plants are we looking for?"

"I have a sample of each in my basket."

He examined the sample flowers, roots, and leaves Petãl had prepared for me. His face was close, the warmth of his breath brushing my skin.

"Ah. Oh! I've seen that one before." He pointed to one of the flowers then took my hand, leading me through the jungle.

We ducked under branches and leaped over burrows, swinging around tree trunks and hopping over stones. As we passed a flower patch of yellow blooms he bent down, holding one against the sample.

"What do you think Miss Turner?" he asked, pronouncing each word like an academician. I could only laugh.

He rubbed his forefinger and thumb over his chin. "Mmm, no, not quite right." He took my hand, leading onward.

"Oh, wait!" I stopped.

"Here's one that looks like this leaf," I said, dropping to my knees.

Björn knelt beside me as I dug up the plant.

He closely scanned the ground as we moved on. "Now, I'm sure this flower should be around here somewhere..."

"Aha!" Something in the distance had caught his eye.

He stopped at the base of a tree, but there were no flowers in sight.

"Strangely, it seems we have to dig for these ones."

"For flowers?" I asked, kneeling beside him.

A smile crept over his face as he sifted through the dirt. Brushing away sand and leaves, he exposed a bed of rough stones. He rubbed one against his pants, uncovering a scarlet gemstone. The brilliance of its rich color became more evident when he held it up beneath the sun's rays. He had led us to an entire cluster of them.

His eyes glistened, rewarded by my response to his game. I couldn't help but smile back, shaking my head.

"How did you know where to find them?"

"They call to me," he lifted his chin proudly. "You could call me a *crystal whisperer*."

He laughed, dropping the act.

"No, I'm kidding. See those mushrooms?" he pointed toward a patch of orange fungi near us.

"I've stumbled across a few patches of gemstones when out collecting materials for carvings. That type of mushroom seems to always grow in the same location that the gemstones are buried." He shrugged.

"You're smart," I said.

"It's just common sense," he deflected.

"You're..." He trailed off, searching for the right word as he met my eyes. "Beautiful."

I shifted uncomfortably. Beautiful had never been a word used to describe me before, or a word I'd never considered of myself. *Phoenix* was beautiful. I was just ... plain.

His expression was tender as he continued to watch me.

"The stones are beautiful," I diverted.

"Yeah," he shrugged, both of us silent as we examined them.

"Let's take some of the mushrooms back with us. I wonder if Nala knows anything about them." I plucked a few of the rubbery stalks for my basket.

"Let's keep moving then, hey." He hopped to his feet. "We've got a whole basket to fill before dark."

But we didn't return until past nightfall, losing ourselves in the wild terrain both figuratively, and then when the sky darkened beyond visibility, literally. We stumbled through the forest, slipping over loose rocks and wet leaves, laughing and elated.

Björn went straight to the arena to scavenge any leftover food, but I wasn't hungry. I returned to the cottage and my sketchbook. It had been the first time since being in the valley that I picked it up. I began drawing detailed depictions of the plant medicines, deciding to keep my own journal of records in case I ever needed any of them.

While flipping through in search of an empty page, I passed an old sketch of Björn and quickly tore it out. I scanned the room, my eyes landing on a beautiful wooden box engraved with birds in flight and decorated with golden stones. I walked over to it and ran my hand over the smooth red wood, folded the paper, and placed it in the box.

When I turned back around, I was surprised to find that on the floor lay the seashell Adam had given me. It must have fallen out of the backpack when I rummaged for pencils.

I held it close for the rest of the night.

Early the next morning Phõenix arrived carrying a long leather pouch.

"Morning Maya." Her golden eyes sparkled. An animal's tooth hung from a cord at her collarbone. "You've been at the waterfall?" She scanned my damp hair.

"Yes. We just got back." I was fuelled with enthusiasm from both the fresh spring and the closeness I felt with Björn. He had been less tense and erratic around me since the afternoon we spent in the jungle.

"Björn's here too then?" she asked, direct as always.

Before I could respond, he was next to me at the door.

"Phõe! You bought the arrows!"

Turning to me he said, "Wolfé asked if I'd engrave them and decorate a few with some gemstones. They are supposed to be a special gift for Katanä."

"Björn's hands are smaller than the other carvers so he's the best at the small details," Phõenix added.

"Come in. I want to run some ideas by you for new handles as well." Björn was already moving aside for "*Phõe*" to pass.

They sat outside in the grassy meadow where rays of morning sunshine reached for the earth through branches where bluebells hung, and apples were bountiful. Phõenix unrolled her leather wrap on the grass and Björn his pouch, revealing finely carved arrowheads and thoughtfully chosen gems.

Once dressed, I set the leaves, flowers, and buds we'd collected the previous afternoon on mats to dry in the sun. I then boiled tea, stealing glances of them when I could.

I poured two cups of tea and carried them out to the garden, catching them in a moment of shared laughter. I quietly placed the mugs on a plank of bark. I felt intrusive, but at the same time didn't want to leave them alone.

I tried to reason with my feelings, but the clenching in my gut remained. As I left the cottage that morning, their resounding laughter followed me down the trail.

CHAPTER TWENTY

I SPENT THE DAY with Nala in an enchanted area of the forest, far away from the tribe where evenly spaced trees were thin and tall.

We sat in a green field where dainty white flowers grew between soft blades of grass. The uneasiness I felt about the chemistry between Björn and Phőenix quickly dissolved as I became immersed in the mystic teachings of nature.

It was here Nala worked to help me uncover ability to sense and see the Light Matter of all things living, not just people. After seeing more clearly than ever before, the Light Matter that embodied every expression of nature, it became obvious that it was the same light that moved not just through everyone but everything in existence.

"We see separation all around us," Nala said. "We speak in tongues that highlight the sense of separation, but even our creator, the Mother, is but a creation of a vaster entity still.

The One.

All of life rests in the One."

The concept was too big to intellectually grasp, but that afternoon, I felt it. For some time, the separate sense of "Maya" began to lose its solidity. I dropped a layer deeper than my surface identity, into a space of being where all that was present was presence itself. A vast sense of eternal and unconditional love enveloped me and I allowed myself to fall more completely into it.

I felt liberated from all that ever bound me and as infinite as light itself.

Later that evening before mealtime, I stopped by our cottage to collect my journal. As I entered, Björn was changing his clothes by the far window. Even just stepping into the same room as him, his presence was grounding.

He looked up as he slipped on a shirt.

"Maya," he said, taking a seat on the edge of the daybed, his hands pressed firmly on his knees.

"Björn . . ." I walked toward him slowly.

He reached into his pocket, searching.

"I have something for you." He drew out a small pouch wrapped in a banana leaf. "I've been working on it the last few suns and just added the finishing piece."

I sat beside him, holding it in both hands, unsure what to expect. I unwrapped the leaf then the soft leather pouch.

"The seashell Adam gave me?"

"I saw you holding it last night and thought it must be special to you," he said.

I lifted the shell, finding it attached to a narrow cord. A clear blue diamond, light as the sky with hints of turquoise, hung just below it, placed precisely in the belly of a tiny, intricately carved wooden whale. He had polished the gem until it shone even without sunlight.

"Wow. It's so thoughtful Björn."

"I hope you do don't mind that I used the shell. I didn't realise it was from him."

"No, it's perfect." But I was unable to express how special it really was.

"When I found the diamond, I thought of you straight away."

He looped it around my neck, fastening it securely. The necklace fell just below my collarbone, the shell lower than the rustic pendant. I placed my hand on the diamond.

"It felt familiar," Björn said. "Light and clear. After polishing it, the color, same as your eyes, came through and I realized that's how I feel around you."

My heart pounded in my chest.

"It's like . . . a weight gets lifted. I also feel kinda exposed," he laughed. "Because I know you can see me more clearly than most people."

I didn't take my eyes off him even though part of me felt like shying away.

"It makes sense why it was hard for you in the City, in crowds . . ." He paused. "You see and feel so much. What's driving people beneath the surface. The love and pain."

I was surprised by his observations. I thought he'd been ignoring me all this time.

"I always felt too soft and weak to survive there."

"You are soft," Björn said. "But it's not a weakness. Just because they thought it was doesn't make it true."

I felt the heat of his attention. It made me feel vulnerable. I wanted him to stop, but he didn't.

"Your sensitivity is a power Maya, in case you haven't figured it out yet. It's the reason you're here. Because you wouldn't accept the world we knew as all there was. . ."

Somehow our faces were closer than before, and in our silence, I felt closer still. I felt seen—for the first time.

"You know, I don't really let myself *see* you," I said, a profound sense of stillness hanging between us. "It's something in your eyes when you look at me. I've been scared of knowing what it means. Maybe I'm in denial because I feel these things for you that I can't explain, and I don't know what would happen if, if I knew you . . . either didn't feel them at all or . . . possibly even more frightening, felt them too." My eyes darted around the room as I tried to gather the words.

Before I could say anything else, he held my face gently with his hands.

All the intensity of every time we made eye contact was present between us.

His face slowly inched closer until our lips met. First gently, then more intensely, our kiss came alive with more passion than I could contain in my body.

He pulled his face away just enough to see my eyes.

"I feel it Maya. I feel it." He kissed my forehead then cheeks, wrapping me tenderly in his arms.

It felt so warm.

So sweet.

Then, like a light switch flipping off, his brows furrowed and he went quiet, frozen. He stood abruptly.

"I'm sorry, Maya. I shouldn't have let that happen." He could hardly meet my eyes and turned his cheek.

"I'm sorry." He moved to the door without another word.

The euphoria of his touch, his kiss, was still resonant on my body.

It was such an extreme shift that I was left frozen, unable to comprehend any possible explanation.

"Björn stop!" I rushed out the door to catch him before the openness between us was closed off again by a new set of walls.

It was dark. The rest of the tribe would be at dinner. As he made his way toward the arena, I raced across the dirt path and spun in front of him, holding him by the shoulders.

"Why do you keep doing this?" I demanded, catching my breath. "You know I'll be at dinner too, *and* sleeping in the same house as you tonight. You can't really escape me."

His expression was blank, regretful if anything.

"I'm sorry. I don't want to escape you."

I raised an eyebrow.

"I'm trying to protect you."

"Protect me from what?"

"Me," he said.

"Björn, that doesn't make *sense*. If you don't feel the same, just say it. You keep repeating that you're 'not good for me,' but I can't see it. I can't see what you are trying so hard to protect me from."

We stared at each other in silence.

"If it's because you like Phöenix, I'd rather just know." It was the only explanation.

He looked at me as if I'd spoken a foreign language.

"What? No, that's not—" He closed his eyes, shaking his head, desperate for a way to escape the conversation.

He started walking again. I followed.

"Maya, you have no idea how special it is to me that you've stayed so pure all your life. I can't allow myself to taint that out of my selfish desire to be close to you." His expression *appeared* sincere, but I didn't trust it.

"I've been spending so much time alone, carving and creating things because it's my way of sitting with the demons of my past without dragging anyone down beside me, especially you."

"Demons? You spent your life dedicated to getting here, to finding the truth. You sacrificed yourself to be a slave to the Control. I would call that the actions of a warrior, not someone with demons."

"A warrior..." A deflective chuckle escaped his lips.

"Maya, I'm a killer." His words were as cold as death itself.

"And you already know it! Don't you remember what happened at base camp? What I did to the officers there? Think back. I've been waiting for you to remember, waiting for you to realize for yourself that I'm capable of inexcusable things."

Recollections of being at base camp slowly returned. A sequence of images of Björn fighting a handful of men in grey uniforms. Then the image of Björn slicing one of their throats, and—My heartbeat quickened and my throat tightened.

"It was them or us," I justified.

"They weren't the first. To maintain Koen's trust and respect, I had to prove myself."

"In what way?" I asked, even though I was now unsure I truly wanted to know.

"I killed people. Innocent people." He was testing me. I struggled to hold his stare.

"Koen didn't only punish rebels," he continued. "He punished the weak. There weren't enough rations to feed the populous, so he ordered us to hunt down anyone who wasn't contributing to the community. He made me kill them while he watched or forced me to restrain them down when he did it himself. Either way, I was always involved." His dark eyes held my gaze, forcing me to look away. "Poison. Swords to the throat. Arrows to the heart. He made a game of it."

As we neared the edge of the arena the sound of familiar voices drifted through the trees.

"All I know is that I'm toxic to you until I somehow reverse my karma."

"Björn—" but he wouldn't hear it.

"No Maya. You still don't get it."

As the night wore on, I watched Björn down cup after cup of wine, his senses fading with each one.

A small group danced to earthy beats by the fire. Ṭarō caught my eye. I admired the unrestrained nature of the way he moved.

Hypnotized by Phŏenix's more sensuous movements, Björn made his way toward her. On her next twirl he caught her arm. She fell into him, bodies pressed together, their faces so close they could touch.

They danced with hedonistic abandon. My heart dropped when they kissed. As their lips met, Björn's eyes caught mine for a moment. He then looked away, took her hand, and walked in the direction of her cottage.

Ṭarō froze for a moment as he too watched them walk off together, but quickly composed himself and shook off his wounded expression in dance. I didn't understand why *he'd* feel hurt though. Unless it hd something to do with Phŏenix.

Björn didn't come home that night. The ache of loneliness overcame me. Though I'd spent the majority of my life alone, I rarely felt lonely. This was a kind of loneliness that could only arise in response to an absence.

I was sure he had shared Phŏenix's bed. She'd wanted him since we arrived, and tonight he was giving her the gift she desired.

I curled into myself, into the pain of opening myself up to him only to be so quickly discarded.

The full memory of base camp flooded back in a dream. Earlier, I had not remembered the part that involved—

"Adam!" I sat up as if expecting him to be there.

Why would Björn leave him behind?

CHAPTER TWENTY-ONE

Heartache set in the following morning. I didn't leave our cottage, waiting.

When Björn didn't come home, I sought him out. Another kind of fire burnt within me now. The jealousy I had felt the previous night had been replaced by anger.

It was hot. After finishing their daily work, most of the tribe gathered at the waterhole. The atmosphere was lively. As I scanned over the assemblage of bodies, Katanä caught my eye and waved me over. She and Wolfé lounged on large, flat rocks, their dark skin soaking up the stone's heat in the last of the day's sun.

"You look lost," she said.

"I'm looking for Björn."

"I haven't seen him since this morning. He was with Phốe," she said, watching my reaction closely.

Wolfé stood quietly, walked toward the edge of the stone, and dived beneath the calm water.

"She's been lonely these past few years," Katanä said. "It's hard to feel fully initiated into womanhood when you haven't experienced a man, you know? Until Björn arrived, the only other human here was her brother."

I nodded, attempting to reign in my anger. Katanä could sense my fury, but she didn't understand the more prevalent cause. Still, I felt belittled knowing that last night Phoenix had been initiated into womanhood by the only man I ever felt any real affection for.

"I should really find him," I said. "I'll see you later."

The afternoon drifted into evening, and as the pink hues of dusk colored the sky, I returned home, defeated. I dressed quietly into my nightwear. The evening was already cool, so I slipped my white shawl over my shoulders for extra layering.

As I stepped into the living room, a silhouette on the back porch, so still it could have been a statue, startled me. I slid the doors open slowly.

"Maya." His voice was gentle, body unmoving.

We sat side by side. He turned to face me. I couldn't speak. It seemed that he couldn't either. He stared back out at the sinking sun.

"You left Adam behind," I said, breaking the silence. I should have been angry, but the anger had calmed over the course of the day. It was an exhausting emotion to hold onto.

"He wouldn't believe me. He thought I was taking advantage of you or something."

"You could've forced him to come, or tricked him, or knocked him out and threw him in the plane . . . *Something.* He would've cracked. I know he would have. He was *right there.*"

He shook his head in disagreement.

"It doesn't work like that Maya. You *know* there needs to be a certain amount of willingness in a person for them to survive the void. He wasn't open, and he wasn't showing any signs of opening any time soon. It would have been murder."

"You didn't seem to have a problem with murdering the other officers," I said before I could catch myself. He didn't say anything.

"The plane ride would have given him *time* to open," I argued more to the point.

"I could have better thought it through, I know. At the time, our survival was my only priority. Adam is strong. Stronger than anyone I've ever fought. He radioed for backup when you fell unconscious. I was almost unconscious myself."

"He would've taken you back to the Control. He had no idea what they would do to you. I pinched a pressure point on his neck to send him to sleep."

"And you *didn't* throw him on the plane?"

Björn stared at me, deciding whether he needed to repeat himself.

If there had been any chance of Adam opening his mind enough to consider joining us, I knew that it would have had to have been through me. But I was unconscious. And he was chipped.

"I'm sorry," Björn said, and I knew how sincerely sorry he was.

I shook my head and let out a breath.

"I want to hate you for it, but I don't think I can."

"You're allowed to be angry."

"I know."

We sat quietly for a few moments, processing.

"You were protecting me. Just like you're still trying to protect me now." I paused, thinking about our conversation from the previous night and his hang-up about "not tainting me."

"You know, everything you did in the City, everything that's been haunting you—including leaving Adam behind—was more honorable than anything I ever had the courage to do."

He shook his head, but he let me continue.

"Everything you did was so you could avoid letting them insert a chip in you. It was all a part of a greater plan, to get here. Neither of us would be here if you hadn't stuck with it."

"Some of the things I did Maya . . ." He shook his head again. "And part of me felt a sense of power from it. I'm no saint."

"I'm not afraid of you." I said, not losing eye contact. "After the ceremony, you told me you're not who I think you are. What if you're not who *you* think you are?"

I couldn't read his expression as he processed my comment.

"I'm sorry," he said finally.

"You don't have to be anymore."

"On top of everything we've just talked about, I'm sorry for hurting you."

"What did I just say!?"

"Just let me finish. I was wrong to push you away like that. It was immature. I shouldn't have played that game."

"What do you mean by 'game'?"

He exhaled, then replied, "I didn't stay with Phoenix last night."

"What?"

Liar.

"I mean, it's none of my business. You can do what you want." I spoke a little too quickly.

He hid his amusement. "Making someone jealous is childish."

"What do you mean? I'm not—" But this time I stopped myself from becoming defensive and let out a breath in defeat.

"It's okay. I'd be insanely jealous if I saw you with someone else," he admitted.

I was confused.

"She wanted you since the moment we got here. She's never been with a man . . ." I said, repeating what Katanä had shared earlier.

My brows pressed together. "You kissed her. I saw you leave with her. You looked pretty into her from the way you were dancing . . ." Another wave of anger came over me. I wasn't going to be a fool. "Did you get sick of her already? And now you're coming back to try your luck with me?"

"I understand why you would think that." He was so calm, so centered, it made it hard to detect whether he was lying or not.

"You should be mad. I deceived you. I purposely hurt you so you'd stay away from me. I'm not asking for forgiveness. It just feels wrong to lie to you." His words were so pure, so honest.

"I just want you to know that I got swept up in my own guilt and made twisted decisions that shouldn't have involved you at all."

I let his apology sink in.

"But I saw you kiss."

"Yes, to lead you astray. It was meaningless and empty."

"Maybe on your end. Even if what you're saying is true, it doesn't make it noble. It will hurt her too, you know. Probably more than me."

He shook his head.

"She's in love with Ṭarō. And I'm—" He cut himself off. "But she's human."

I remembered Ṭarō's response to their leaving together.

"It's true she was attracted to me and wanted intimacy, but when I couldn't go through with it, she realized she didn't want to either. Her body did, but not her heart."

I felt myself soften.

"That would be hard," I said, sure the love was requited between them. It made sense. I often saw Ṭarō flirting liberally with women, but very rarely the same one. His heart was with Phoenix too.

Björn nodded and reached out to touch my cheek.

"Just know I'm sorry," he repeated, and just as I felt myself melting into him, he changed the subject.

"I think we better get to the arena before all the food is gone."

"I think... you're always hungry," I said. He laughed.

◊

The arena was lit only by the roaring flames of the bonfire and the ring of torches that encircled its perimeter. As we reached what was left of the feast, two arms extended around us from behind to reveal two cups of a hot liquid, their steam rising in thin coils. We looked at each other inquisitively before taking them.

"The mushrooms you gave me. They are very healing. We call them lion's mane." I was surprised to see Ḵala tower over us as she slipped around me.

"I dried them and ground them into a powder. Sip it slowly." She advised with a mysterious glint in her eye, then disappeared into the crowd.

We tapped our clay cups together with a *clink* before taking our first sip. It was bitter and earthy but sweetened with honey. I grabbed a bowl and filled it with a spectrum of colors from earth's bounty in an expression of the spectrum of feelings bursting inside me.

The light tune from a flute and the soft thud of a bongo drum sounded through the arena, creating a lively atmosphere. Björn slipped away as Chaṅtara called me over to her. She was perched on a log beside Moānā, while Ṭasmai snuggled up on Bŏdhi's knee.

I had a particular fondness for the family. There were many families in the valley but theirs was the only one of human ancestry.

"Maya!" Tasmai leaped from his dad's knee and skipped toward me.

He stood at my feet and smiled, then reached for my hand, leading me toward the rest of the family. I chuckled as I followed him.

"He's been looking for you," Chantara said.

"I made something for you," Tasmai said excitedly.

"Did you Tassie? That's very thoughtful." I said bending down, showing him my necklace. "Björn gave this to me yesterday too. I'm being showered with gifts."

The jewel in the pendant grabbed Tasmai's attention, hypnotizing him. He touched it, then looked up at me.

"Your eye," he said, his wide.

"Aren't I lucky. Now I have three." He erupted in giggles as I held it playfully at my collarbone, but his eyes didn't move.

"It glows," he said.

I looked down to find it wasn't the stone that was glowing, but the seashell. A halo of gold mist danced around its scalloped edges. I touched it, entranced.

"Ouch!" I shook my hand. The shell was hot. The mist vanished.

I glanced at the family, gaging whether anyone else noticed what had happened, but they were preoccupied. Tasmai watched me innocently as if the sight were nothing extraordinary and lifted his hand to reveal a little bracelet tied with delicate shells.

"It matches," he smiled happily.

"Wow, it's beautiful. Thank you." I bent down to hug him. "You're right, it matches perfectly." I slipped it onto my wrist and held it up against the necklace.

He beamed.

I returned to his family and sat beside Bŏdhi to eat. I appreciated Bŏdhi's calm presence but always felt a sense of distance. I'd never seen him openly reveal himself to anyone, not even Chantara.

"We just returned from a trip to the ocean. We followed the valley to the summer season," Bŏdhi said. His wild jungle eyes were striking as they made contact with mine. "The water was calm and clear, and the sun was hotter than here, tropical."

"I collected lots of shells," Tasmai said, explaining the bracelet. "They're the bones of dead sea animals," he added, proud of his knowledge.

"We saw living ones too," Moānā chimed in excitably. She was outgoing and talkative like Chantara. "We swam in the waves, and the dolphins came in from way out the back to swim with us."

"Have you ever seen a dolphin?" she asked.

"Just once. But it was dead. It washed up on the shore where I lived in Australia."

My answer killed their excitement.

"I thought your accent sounded Australian," Chantara commented.

"I was born near a beach. After moving to the City, I never stopped longing for the ocean."

I was thoughtful.

"Whenever I think about Earth realm, I can't help but wonder what it looked like in its natural form. If it was anything like here. Do you believe that the natural world there can be restored?"

"Maybe not so much 'be restored,'" Bŏdhi said thoughtfully, "but if she chooses to revive herself, I think she has the power, yes." He'd never been to Earth realm, never seen it, and expressed no preference for whether it survived or not.

Chantara's eyes were distant. "I barely think about that world anymore. It was already so . . . dead when I left. So much pain. So much suffering and darkness. Maybe nature doesn't *want* to restore herself. Maybe it's easier, simpler for the realm to fade away . . ."

I saw an image of Adam simply 'fading away.' Just the thought of it made it too difficult to continue the conversation.

"I know you care about the people there," Bŏdhi said, watching me a little too closely.

"But we can't keep looking back. It will only rob us of what's here now. There's a point when we have to let go of the past and allow life to unfold as it will, regardless of the way we want it to."

A part of me appreciated his words. "I guess I've been stuck thinking we have the power to change their future if we just take action."

"Some actions do more harm than good," Bŏdhi said. "Ultimately what you want to do is beyond anyone's power or control."

Later, I sat alone by the bonfire, enjoying not having to entertain anyone, just watching the interplay. Björn sat on the other side with Ṭarō. We kept catching each others gaze through the flames.

I began to feel a strange sense of disorientation. My vision started distorting, as if I watched everything through a veil. The sounds became more distant.

A burning heat caught my attention on my chest. When I looked down, the seashell was glowing again and left a red welt where it rested on my skin.

I felt dizzy and confused and left the arena to find solace under the still trees. I stared up at the silver moon and all-encompassing blackness that held it.

But strange whispers drifted through the motionless air around me.

I couldn't make out the words, but I was sure they were voices and spun, searching. No one was nearby.

I followed the sounds, which led me to the base of the pyramid. The whispers grew more urgent and the triangular structure began to emanate a bright golden glow again. Certain symbols that were engraved into its walls began to light up.

I glanced around to check that no one was watching, then moved closer to get a better look at the highlighted symbols. They made no obvious sense to me, but began to excrete streams of glistening gold L·ight Matter that drifted towards me.

The whispers increased. I felt a sharp, hot heat on my chest and glancing down, the seashell glowed again. It appeared to be absorbing the golden L·ight Matter.

The pyramid is speaking to the seashell.

I stepped right up to the wall and rested against the side of the warm stone, pressing my ear against it, trying to capture the words. I couldn't understand the language.

"You okay?"

I leapt off the wall to find Björn watching me.

"Yes," I replied too quickly, pretending to brush non-existent dust off my pants.

I examined him closely, relieved to find that the veil I had felt between me and everyone else in the arena had dissipated, and exhaled.

He raised an eyebrow with a look as if to remind me of the last time I got too close to the pyramid.

"I just needed some space," I said clearing my throat, the ability to assemble words returning. If it was the mushroom drink that tripped me out, Björn didn't appear affected.

Still looking unconvinced, I said, "I was resting. Sometimes it still feels weird to be around so many people at once."

"I'll walk you home," he offered, letting it go.

I nodded slowly, scanning the pyramid once more. The gold mist had disappeared, and the whispers were no longer audible, but the seashell was still warm to the touch.

Björn wrapped his arm around my shoulders.

We meandered around the arena toward the main path that led to our cottage. The crisp night air helped clear my mind. The heat of his arm around me began to feel more and more pronounced, and his presence beside me stole my full attention.

CHAPTER TWENTY-TWO

WE DIDN'T SAY MUCH as we walked. I was processing the mystery of the pyramid, while at the same time reminding myself to let it go.

Was there something special about the seashell?

"I want to take a trip to the ocean," I said.

"I've been wanting to use shells in my carvings, but I don't have any. Can I come?" he asked casually.

"I'd love that," I smiled.

We continued walking in silence, but I felt so much electricity in the air between us.

Does he feel it too?

We arrived at the cottage, Björn stopping at the front door.

A moment of hesitation.

He turned to face me, and without thinking, I pressed my lips to his.

The kiss was soft. Sweet but passionate. He pressed his body against mine, and touched his hand gently to my jaw, my cheek, my hair, then ran his hand along the lines of my body. I shivered.

He gently gripped my hips, lifting me off the ground. I wrapped my legs around his waist as he carried me through the door, our lips locked in the kiss.

He placed me down in front of the bed and took a step back, "Goodnight Maya."

Emotions overtook me and tears began to well in my eyes. Björn wrapped his arms around me, holding me the way I'd always dreamt of being held in the tides of my unpredictable emotions.

"I got carried away. I shouldn't have — I get that you can't trust me," he said a bit mortified by his actions.

"You don't get it. I *can* trust you. I'm not sad." I shook my head, feeling stupid for crying. "You just—I just —I want this," I finally managed, unable to express my true feelings.

I wiped my eyes, stood, and collected the reddish wooden box engraved with birds in flight and golden stones. I sat on the floor facing Björn, who rested on the bed's edge, and placed the box mindfully between us. I needed for him to understand the force that drew us together. Understand that it was beyond either of our control.

After taking a deep, centering breath, I opened the lid and removed a single piece of paper.

"I drew this," was all I could manage to say as I handed it to him, monitoring his reaction.

"It's amazing. Really. It looks just like me, as if I'm looking in the mirror," he said with bewilderment, assuming I had recently drawn it.

I shook my head. "I drew it when I was in the City. Before we met. Before I even knew you existed."

He sat quietly for a moment then said, "Like the valley . . "

I nodded. "I used to see you all the time. Your face, your smile, your eyes. Your eyes always fascinated me. Painting you was the only way I could get you out of my head. Make you real somehow." I felt embarrassed.

Would this freak him out?

He didn't answer.

He thinks I'm some obsessive stalker girl.

I was tempted to bolt out the door before he got a chance to speak, but as I'd informed him earlier, it would be a pathetic attempt for an escape. He was unavoidable.

"Maya." He slid from the bed and sat beside me on the floor as I held my gaze downward, afraid to look him in the eye. When I still didn't lift my gaze, he placed his fingers gently under my chin tilting it upright.

"Maya. Look at me."

"I am."

"No, really, look. In the way you know how." I took a deep breath and did what he asked. I calmed my mind and focussed on the space just above his shoulders to the top of his head. Purple L·ight Matter.

"I'm mystified. By you. By this." He held up the drawing. "It kinda scares me," he chuckled. "But only because it's so profound."

He leaned in and kissed me gently on my forehead, then my lips.

He touched my jaw again, words no longer necessary.

His defences dropped away. My defences dropped away.

I crawled closer to him and he wrapped his arms around me. Our kiss grew more passionate but his touch remained tender, sensual. He brushed his lips over my neck then back up to my lips.

My mind was absent now, and my body more alive than ever, aching to be closer to him. Closer, closer. Our chests pressed together; bodies interlocked. He lifted me up onto the bed, and this time, did not suggest leaving.

He searched my eyes again to check if I still felt comfortable.

I was afraid.

I'd never done this before. Not even close. I had no idea what to do or how to act. But I trusted him. I felt safe.

I took a breath, relaxed and let go.

Every possible guard dissolved between us, abandoned the moment we finally allowed our bodies to unite without the interference of our minds.

We were free.

We lay looking at each other for a long time after making love, his hands still sweeping my bare skin, lips moving over my body in soft, sweet, unselfconscious kisses. I closed my eyes as his warm breath sunk in, but then opened them again, not wanting to leave his.

I felt expansive, uninterrupted contentment. Pure euphoria hung in the air and in my body, and like this, we gradually drifted to sleep.

CHAPTER TWENTY-THREE

I AWOKE IN AGONY.

My eyes fluttered open as an excruciated burning pain spread through my entire body.

I screamed, the sound so shrill it hardly sounded like mine. I tried to move, or at least roll over, but I was paralysed.

Darkness consumed me once more.

A brick crashed against the side of my body, knocking the air from my lungs.

Sharp metal prongs penetrated my skin, slicing deep gashes that gushed with hot pools of blood.

A force of wind smacked me against and iron wall. It should have knocked me out, but somehow, I survived each blow no matter how brutal, just in time for the next.

I couldn't see anything but *felt* everything, my lack of eyesight intensifying the pain.

A heavy object fell from above, crushing my limbs, then another, crushing my body. It should have meant instant death. And it did. For a moment.

Then the weight lifted and my body scraped along a corrugated surface that tore my clothes, then my flesh. I winced; teeth clenched so tight they could crack.

"Stop it!" I screamed. "Stop!"

If it was a dream, why could I not wake myself up?

The temperature dropped.

Arctic air stung my skin under the force of howling winds. An ice cold body of water enveloped me, sucking me under. The current was strong.

Sharp objects tumbled beside me in the torrent of swirling water. I couldn't hold my breath any longer and I gasped, but my lungs filled with water.

I heaved, my throat burning, choking, drowning.

I heard a distant voice calling my name in panic.

"Maya! Maya, what's wrong?"

My screams must have woken Björn.

Even if I *could* have answered, I wouldn't have had an answer. All I knew was that I was experiencing something metaphysical.

I wasn't physically crushed, drowned, burned, beaten.

But I couldn't open my eyes. I was only half there, half in the realm in which the tortures took place, and wholly in between; trapped in an empty dimension where only my consciousness resided. And pain.

Björn held my shoulders and shook me gently attempting to call my spirit back. I could feel my body to a degree, but couldn't return to it.

I couldn't wake myself, nor could I be woken.

"Hold on!" he called. "I'm going to get help!"

The black behind my lids turned to white, and a vision flashed across my mind's eye. Suddenly, everything was still and I could see. But what I could see still only existed metaphysically. It wasn't *real*.

I found myself sitting on a thin cushion in the center of a polished floor, admiring the laces of gold that weaved through the electric blue stone. Above me, three lustrous gold walls towered upward to meet in a tip.

Gold mist swirled inside the triangular room, creating an ethereal haze, before gathering in masses to form five beings.

The details of their features were so intricate they could have been solid, but I had watch them take shape out of the sweeping mist of pure golden Light Matter.

I admired their regal silk robes and glittering jewelry that stacked around their wrists, ankles, and necks. In the center of their foreheads, was a vivid white tattoo of an arrow pointing skyward. I could barely look at it directly without my eyes burning.

One of the beings was the mysterious Nepalese women I'd seen embody Nirmala. There was also the dark-skinned man, built like a warrior with bright blue eyes who stood beside the smaller white-haired Nordic woman with fair skin and eyes like ice. I'd seen them too, the night outside the pyramid, embodying the other Nöahl's.

A young boy also stood with them, bright white teeth and silver eyes twinkling like stars against black skin. They exuded pure innocence, while at the same time vast knowledge that spanned the universe itself.

An urgent voice erupted from one of the beings. I recognized her! It was the Chinese woman that used to visit me in my dreams. Her porcelain-like skin was as smooth and youthful as ever, glowing against silky black hair that was tied back by an elegant gold headpiece. She, too, had a bright white arrow tattoo on her forehead.

Her transparent golden eyes exuded the same love as always, but on the surface, they were severe. Serious.

"You must come."

Suddenly, the mirage dissolved.

My eyes flashed open, heart racing and breath rapid. I pressed my hands into the bed. The texture was comforting, unmistakable of the physical realm. I had returned.

The room was dark. I reached over for Björn, but he was gone.

A thread of gold mist slithered through the door. I watched as it moved through the air toward me and wrap around my upper body. The seashell on my chest lit up again like a bright candle in the night.

"You must come," her sovereign voice echoed in my memory. Without thinking, I rolled out of the bed, throwing my shawl over my shoulders and followed the river of mist out the door. I stumbled down the forest path and found myself at the base of the pyramid. I didn't wonder upon it for long; the golden thread continued drawing me closer. It slipped through the crack of a door that was now lit by a golden glow around its rim.

There is a door!

I wrapped my fingers around the antique handle and gave a single knock. A volt of energy shot up my arm.

The door swung open as if blown by the wind, but the air was dead still. Taking a breath, I stepped inside. The room had no lights or windows, yet it was bright. A radiant glow shone out from its walls. I stepped over the threshold, squinting until my eyes adjusted. The door swung shut behind me.

The room was empty. The supreme beings weren't there to meet me, but the same cushion I had sat on in my vision was in the center of the room. The immaculate polished stone floor seemed too precious to tarnish with my feet as I tiptoed across. Once I was seated on the cushion, the mist in the room began to take form as the Chinese woman.

Her silk robe was traditional of her culture, decorated with elegant floral patterns, soaring birds, and dragons. She pressed her palms together at her chest in a loving greeting, then bowed. I quickly stood and bowed lower than she had in return.

Qiaŏhui. Her name was Qiaŏhui.

She spread her arms out wide and said, "Follow my steps."

She flowed gracefully into a sequence of movements that were at first, familiar, then became more advanced than anything she had taught me before. I didn't have to *think* to repeat her movements. My body somehow instinctively knew how to follow her. The movements were repetitive, and after an amount of time, I did not have to watch. I closed my eyes and let my body take over.

As I sunk deeper and deeper into the vast stillness beneath the movements, realms began to flash before my mind's eye, as if each new step unlocked a different door into dimensions beyond my prior comprehension.

There were dimensions of total light and total darkness, a realm where only saints existed, and another inhabited by dragons. But I didn't stop to explore any one realm, for each movement bought me to the next, and the flow continued.

Finally, the flashing realms stopped, and I found my body had stopped too. I stood still. Still as my mind. I felt the electric warmth of dainty hands on my shoulders, guiding me to sit back down on the cushion. The projection of gold light that formed Qiaŏhui then evaporated. My vision was painted by a sheet of blinding gold light, then infinite blackness, and I fell into a realm that took me far from where I sat.

Stars. A flock of stars. But brighter, blinding. Soaring. For a moment, they were pretty.

Shooting stars?

They were all that was visible. Their faint tails sliding across a blank black sky in unison, migrating to their next location. Only once that location revealed itself, all the beauty disappeared.

The world below the stars lit up in a flash, just in time to recognise it.

The City spread out before me as I had seen it from Koen's office. I was standing once again in a glass cube at the very top of the tallest building in the City, gazing out over the land that was devoured by iron buildings.

For a moment, I thought I'd jumped dimensions again. I thought I'd returned to Earth. But the City didn't look quite the same as before. Everything was slightly hazy, dreamlike. I quickly understood I wasn't really there. I was an onlooker, watching, still trapped in all I could understand as an in-between dimension.

The stars continued to cross the sky, but now with the perspective of a location I understood they were far too close and moving closer every second, soaring not merely across the sky but *toward* the City.

Off in the distance, the closest star made contact. A fire erupted where the orb kissed the land and screeched across its surface, blazing a trail that began to catch and burn all in its path.

Meteors.

They weren't stars, they were meteors. As the rest of them crashed into the earth, I realized there was nothing I could do but stand there and watch as forces more powerful and preeminent than my tiny, fragile human body, exploded downward upon the last survivors of humankind.

This was it. The Mother was finally sending her mightiest soldiers to wipe us off her surface and into extinction.

Another meteor collided with a row of buildings and transformed the rigid structures into rubble. Another shot straight through the elevated sky-train tracks, each splitting and swinging unsteadily before crumbling to the ground. Another meteor fell close to our school, and then another directly on it.

Soon, the entire City glittered with fires. The flames didn't spread quickly, but glowed from the holes they'd embedded in the earth's crust. The metal structures that survived the attack, reflected the brilliant orange flames from their resilient shiny surfaces. I stood for a while just watching, wondering if the meteors were just another warning?

People emerged from their houses in a panic, scurrying across streets in their nightwear. Officers gestured for families to return to their beds, but before any measure of comfort could settle the chaos, the next wave of destruction thundered toward the City.

As morning dawned, the first rays of light exposed tornadoes that grew from dark waterlogged storm clouds in the distance. From where I stood, I must have been the first to see them spinning toward us.

A giant flock of bats appeared, flapping erratically past the glass I looked out through. Their shrieks were even more deafening than those echoing from the humans below.

I racked my brain for something I could do to stop the tornadoes from hitting the City, even though I knew I had no power to influence their course. I lifted my leg to step forward, but my feet were glued to the ground.

"No!" I tried to yank my feet free but as I lost balance and fell to the hard floor, I remembered that I wasn't actually there.

I couldn't feel the marble that I knew should have been cold and smooth. I couldn't feel the pressure of it beneath my body.

I lifted my head and looked out the window as the tornados tore through the border, beginning to rip the City apart.

"No!" I added to the symphony of shrieks that didn't fail to reach me from my height, while pressing my hands over my ears to drown out their cries.

I squeezed my eyes shut hoping the nightmare would disappear, but when I opened them all I saw was the black sky above.

"Mother please!" I begged. "Let the people live."

"Terminate the City, but please, let humans find the valley. . ." I drifted off, knowing it was already too late.

As the tornadoes continued sweeping up everything in their path, my plea turned to guilt.

"Why me?" I yelled, standing up. "Why do I get to stand here untouched while all these people suffer? If you won't spare them, take me too!"

As if granting my wish, the window in front of me cracked under the pressure of the wild winds. The storm roared into the room.

Shards of glass soared toward me. I accepted my destiny, watching calmly until they pierced my skin. I gritted my teeth as the shards penetrated my body, bearing the severity of pain.

In a blink of the eye, the last and deadliest shard, like the tip of a torpedo, penetrated deep into my forehead.

A deep rumble erupted as the Council building shook and crumbled to the ground beneath me.

As my vision faded back into a blanket of black, I knew the shard had reached my brain. Death was upon me.

Just like that.

All that it came to mean to live and breathe snatched away in a millisecond.

But as the blackness took me, I'd forgotten that I wasn't really there, only in consciousness and perhaps spirit, whatever that meant. My physical body still lay safely in a world below this one, so I couldn't truly die there.

And for that reason, it was only the first of many deaths I'd experience as the Old World came to an end.

CHAPTER TWENTY-FOUR

I SPENT THE REST of the day dying.
Over and over on repeat.

In every way imaginable and some so savage it was inconceivable.

I began to hear faint voices, which only amplified my confusion. First Nirmala's, then Björn's, Tarō and Athêna's, all desperately attempting to tear me from the alternate dimension where my consciousness drifted. They were distant, my ears only receiving warped words, muffled sounds, and occasionally, my name. At one point, I was sure my body was being carried and laid on a bed.

I couldn't think. My body was so overwhelmed by feeling that all I could do was lay there and die.

And die.

And die.

Die every death of every last human ion Earth. I could have tricked myself into thinking that it was just a dream—or a nightmare—but it was clearly a vision. I was somehow connected to it, lost in it. But separated enough not to be physically affected by it.

I didn't know if I'd been there mere seconds or days. Every micro moment of feeling consumed me.

Time, thoughts, emotions of my own were non-existent.

I surrendered.

I had no choice but to let go.

Even as the deaths gradually eased in intensity, my body was so exhausted that my thoughts remained inaccessible.

Nothing made sense.

I didn't care anymore.

The pain was more excruciating than I knew was possible. The only was to cope was to disassociate.

I gave up.

And with every last blow, I wished my consciousness would go ahead and die too.

But it wouldn't.

I continued waking in new bodies, to taste the sting of death once more.

Some deaths stung less than others, while some I was sure I had no chance of return. Yet I continued to wake, transported each time to another location across the City and planted in another body as it breathed its final breath.

While each body I inhabited carried a unique essence, the last thing I experienced as their spirit dissolved into me was a mist of black Light Matter. I was sure it was the shadows of Sky consciousness finally releasing each body from their grip now they were no longer sources of energy.

Once dissolved, light prevailed. At the center of every being who passed through me, was light. Pure and pristine. No matter how dense the shadows that wrapped them had been.

It was the light of the One, so peaceful it gifted me at least a moment's rest before diving into the next death.

It was irrelevant whether I knew each person or not. When Lorraine passed through, my heart broke. I saw and felt what she saw and felt in her final moments; a wave of water swallowing and smashing her body against a building. Her essence was soft, feminine, and warm beneath the armor she wore.

Koen's death was sickening. Just sharing his experience of existence for those few seconds was more painful than his death itself. His existence *was* death itself, and unlike every other human, the shadows that intoxicated him didn't lift from his being as he took his last breath.

I recognized others too. Meredith, the people I went to school with, Shalom and Ray whose lifetime spent learning ended up amounting to nothing, for they didn't even get to graduate and put all the knowledge crammed into their brains to use. Loony Susan left with an unusual amount of laughter, satisfied knowing she'd never been crazy.

By the time I felt Jeff's death, they had all merged into one, each being the same whirl of love and pain, just set at different notches. He carried a lot of aggression; his anger dial was significantly high.

As the deaths faded, everything became still again, and suddenly the space in my chest that carried the pain of my true parent's death felt empty. Empty with the knowing that even if they had survived the burnings of Australia, death would have stolen them just the same, only years later.

I waited to feel Adam pass through, but he didn't. Maybe he was already dead. It wouldn't be surprising if he was murdered just for being associated with me.

Every human on Earth had disappeared somehow through the vessel of my body. The Earth itself disappeared. My awareness expanded to encompass the whole universe, and now even that was gone.

Everything was dark.

I was floating in a void of nothingness, completely alone. I don't know how long I was astray; time lost all significance. Even the idea of time, space and separation had vanished from my perception. I was just floating, through nothing and everything all at once.

Until the familiar, rich golden mist appeared, drifting through space. I moved toward it but remembered I had no body to move with. I *was* the void of nothingness. And I soon understood that I was the golden mist too.

To my disbelief, full consciousness in the physical realm where I lay returned, although it seemed there was nothing left of me. Qiaŏhui had been a force of light in my life before I even knew the significance of the difference between light and dark. I trusted her. And she had seduced me so mysteriously into the pyramid for the purpose of torture and murder.

All I had become was vacuumed into the empty void, yet still, something returned. My body convulsed in an attempt to contain the vast expanse of space I had become within the comparatively minuscule outline of my frame. But internally, everything was still.

And blank.

And dark. And empty. And cold.

The void followed me here.

I was afraid to move in case the Mother was only humoring me, just to throw me into another death when she decided I'd regained enough strength.

I lay frozen out of choice until I knew it was safe to re-enter the world. I wasn't sure if I would even be able to truly return, for of every death I endured, one of them could surely have been my own. But there was something about the presence I felt both in my body and in the air around me that was familiar of being alive.

I had the awareness of a hand holding mine, warm and rough. It was Björn.

My other hand was held by a dainty and delicate hand, though larger than my own, and vibrating ever so subtly with the essence of divinity.

"It was a mistake to keep the secrets of the pyramid from her. I knew they were calling to her," Nirmala's enchanted voice echoed through the room.

"We were protecting her," the deeper, resonant voice of Athêna said. "You were sure you broke the bondage."

Nala's attention shifted.

"It's stopped."

"She's awake?" Björn asked.

"She's here."

There was a collective exhale followed by silence, all three of them waiting and wondering when I'd wake. I wondered if they knew I had only to choose to open my eyes. Nothing felt real anymore. I felt like a stranger, and they felt like characters of my imagination.

Something flashed across my mind—a thought. Or more like a picture, and it only took a moment to realize, that again, it wasn't mine. I was seeing through someone else's eyes. All it took was that tender squeeze of Björn's hand for his thoughts to transfer to me.

The image was of myself, lying on my back, eyes closed, sweaty, and chest pulsating softly with each breath. They had carried my body back to my bed. I was naked except for a small strip of fabric covering my pubic area, and the seashell necklace.

I hadn't seen a reflection of my body since being in the City. It had changed significantly. I had filled out, no longer a thin and fragile young girl. I was fit, my arms, legs, and stomach muscular, breasts small but full, and hips wider, a new layer of insulation around my waist and thighs.

I looked like a woman.

The room was dim and softly lit, my body enchanting under the kind glow. A river of overwhelming love poured from the eyes of which I looked through.

His heart was wide open, unafraid now, to explore the depths of love it contained. Its strength was overpowering. Too harsh a contrast to what I'd just come out of.

I tore myself from his mind's eye.

PART THREE

Beyond both Worlds

CHAPTER TWENTY-FIVE

"LIFE IN THE EARTH realm is gone," I said.

I'd been invited to gather in the leader's cavern; a sacred gathering place where they discussed critical tribal matters. It was located inside a wide opening in the earth where ancient, moss coated stone steps descended to a polished circular stone platform. Brightly embroidered cushions were positioned around its perimeter, and twisting vines dangled down from the rocky roof. Once inside, the air was damp and cool.

Athêna and Hân led the meeting. Nala and Björn sat on either side of me. Ṭarō and the three Nŏahl's were also present.

Nala lit the fire bowl in the center of the ring in honor of the Mother, calling forth her guidance. The flames flickered, casting shadows over the cream stone walls that enclosed us.

I was asked to explain in detail everything that I saw and felt, from the pain to the god-like beings, to witnessing the City's destruction. And I told them everything with transparency. Everything apart from the final vision. One so frightening that I had barely acknowledged it myself.

I spoke, emotionless, numb to the memories. I had to be, otherwise all that was left holding me together would shatter.

Athêna was the first to break the silence after I finished speaking.

"We have known the end was coming," she said, "but never with such immediate totality." She sat with her legs crossed, spine long, crown lifting.

"I can't say I'm sorry that the Mother used you as the channel," she continued. "But I am sorry for the pain that your people had to endure. It's unfortunate that your kind's existence had to come to such a harsh end."

Nala rested her hand on my knee. "I had a feeling you were a seer."

Seer? The fact that it had a name put me on edge because it meant that what I saw and experienced wasn't a one-time thing.

I was grateful that my earlier visions in life were pleasant. The valley. Björn. Now it was all beginning to make sense. The abnormalities that made me feel alienated were all connected—they were all part of the affinity of "seeing".

"Does that explain why I felt their deaths too? Is that part of seeing?" The eerie detachment of my voice echoed through the cool hollow.

Nala knew the most of mystic affinities. "I have no knowledge of this kind of seeing. It's unusual for a seer to feel their visions as well, but the seers I know of have been well practiced. They learned to work with their affinity so as not to be overwhelmed when these powerful occurrences arose."

"But she's always been a feeler too, perhaps it's a merging of gifts," the older female Nõahl said.

Turning to me, her large round eyes staring into mine, she said, "You've always felt the experience of your people, even when you weren't aware that's what was happening." She paused.

"It sounds to me the Mother used you, not just as a channel for seeing, but as an in-between entity for the spirits to pass through before returning to the One. It's odd that she used someone who can both feel and see. It would be too much; too many senses working at once."

I remembered feeling of being only half here, half there, and as a result, wholly in-between. I studied the faces around me, searching for someone to explain this phenomenon.

"I've heard of something similar once before. A long time ago, but the circumstance was very different..." Nŏahl Çrėę spoke slowly. He was the oldest man in the room. His dark bushy brows furrowed as he spoke and he shook his head, continuing.

"Any one of those deaths could have convinced your body that it was you dying, leaving your spirit trapped in-between."

Turning to Björn and me, Cheif Hân explained, "Of what we know about death, we pass through the Mother before returning to the One, or more accurately, we merge with her to become One again. I agree with the Nŏahls, it's curious that she used you as the in-between."

"She carries gifts beyond our knowledge," Nala said. "We can never expect to understand the Mother's reasons, but we can no longer regard lightly the power Maya..."

Power, gifts, "special."

I didn't feel special. I certainly didn't feel powerful. I felt weak. I felt the dark shadow of death lingering. Pain and suffering dwelled with me in a stale grey mist, consuming the air I breathed and walked.

A single drop of water fell from a hanging stalactite, echoing as it splashed onto the polished platform.

"I'm sorry, I need some air." I sprung to my feet and stumbled numbly up the moss-covered staircase and into the twilight air.

The sky was fading to dark, splashed with the dusty pink glow that only sunset can bring. But I couldn't see the beauty as I usually would, for the weight of the imposing darkness manipulated all my senses.

CHAPTER TWENTY-SIX

For the days following; I was haunted.

Haunted by death. Haunted by the shadows that were the incentive force behind of humanity's demise—the shadows of ignorance, of the Sky People.

It'd always been obvious that the citizens of the City weren't happy, but I could never have imagined the magnitude of pain the majority of them silently suffered. I didn't know how to shake the imprint of the shadows I'd felt, the shadows I'd *seen,* who'd used the negative charge of human suffering as energy like vampires. I knew, from my own intimate experience that pain and sorrow had their place in our world. Their power to unveil incredible depths of love beauty was immense and unparalleled. But the pain that the shadows condemned upon humankind was different. It was toxic. And it was constant.

Their silhouettes were like black cloaks thrown over bodies, containing their light. At first they appeared almighty, but as they lifted upon the moment of death, their frangibility was revealed. They were thin, weak, almost transparent. They evaporated into black mist so quickly under the threat of the incoming light that death inevitably exposed within each human spirit, it made me realise that they could have fought them while they were still alive. Each individual had had the power to cut through the shadows by instead cultivating the light that was like an infinite sun inside each chest.

If they had only known.

After the meeting I had walked the forest as dusk became night, only the thin crescent moon offering its light. But I didn't care for light. I didn't want to see or be seen. I'd seen enough over the previous three days. That's how long I had been dying.

I couldn't fathom sleeping again. I was afraid to, depleted of the strength to endure any more metaphysical experiences.

I walked the night until morning.

Slowly.

Numbly.

Wandering.

Drifting through space and time.

Seeing nothing.

Feeling nothing. Not even the cold, or the tear of my skin as it scratched past branches and brambles.

Nothing felt real anymore. It was as if I was walking in a dream.

Sunlight shone through the misty morning haze, signaling night's transition into day. My eyes stung in response to the unwelcomed brightness.

I curled into a dip in the earth between long, twisting tree roots, where I was protected from the sun by its leafy canopy above. I rested my cheek on the dirt. In my eye-line I could see mushrooms that had cracked through the earth, their might surprising of their supple, silken flesh. Dainty white flowers sprung from patches of furry green moss. I counted their tiny petals as I lay safely hidden in nature's womb, passing time while time passed.

I heard voices and footsteps at one point, but didn't bother to peek over the bark-coated arms that sheltered me. I curled up tighter, pressing myself against the tree trunk.

I didn't want to be seen or to see.

Too many faces.

Too many deaths.

I understood that they weren't deaths as commonly known, but transferences, each being returning to a larger entity.

A beautiful entity.

Home.

I knew it was for the best that that world I had once lived in ended, but it didn't detract from the feeling of being haunted.

Haunted by the sense of loss and grief, the taste of blood, the shadow of death. Haunted by an end of such epic proportions.

But something else haunted me even more.

So much that I shut it out completely.

The thing I was *really* running from.

That final vision. After the deaths. After the emptiness.

The one that replayed every time my vigilance drifted. Every time my guard was down it would rush over me like a flash fire.

A warning.

A warning desperate to be acknowledged.

But I couldn't acknowledge it.

Not this one.

Not yet.

I had hidden it from the tribe. If they didn't know, no one could make me take the action it called of me.

I was selfish. Cowardly. I couldn't bring myself to do what I knew was right, even though hiding it felt so wrong.

I rolled restlessly beneath the tree as the sun began to glitter through the gaps in the leaves above. Two raccoons wearing matching black masks scampered across a giant root beside me, apparently in play.

I watched fluffy grey and white rabbits hop from bush to bush, and a little wood mouse creep timidly along the dirt between two hiding hallows. A lone moose sauntered by, and an auburn-red fox shadowed a few feet behind, so low the fur of its stomach brushed the earth. I didn't bother to wonder what business it might have stalking a beast so tremendous in size. I just watched, blankly.

It was all so very magnificent.

But I still couldn't feel it the way I had in the months before.

The life, the beauty, the divinity. I couldn't *see* it anymore.

I spent a few days like this. Wandering the forest alone. Hiding. When I got hungry, I ate what I could forage.

I felt small among the indifferent trees and creatures that meandered about their business, barely acknowledging my presence.

It was nice to feel insignificant.

It felt comfortable. Familiar.

It reminded me of how I felt in the City.

Invisible. A quiet observer.

I finally stumbled upon a clearing. I realized it was the sacred ledge I was healed on when I arrived. Below was the village. I watched the tribe from where they couldn't see me, feeling like an outsider again, the way I always had *before*.

The falls tumbled down beside me, mist floating lightly all around, but it wasn't dreamy like the first time I was there. In the distance of a short climb; home in the arms of the spring village awaited me, where I could live out the rest of my life in comfort, safety, and a splash of magic.

But there was an alternative, a choice that hung heavily over my heart. While the first option was pure heaven, the other was hell. And like some wicked, twisted joke, my heart was sure that the second option was the right one.

If I followed it, the human race might have had a chance at a brand new future. If I stuck with the first option, heaven, I'd only be serving myself.

But I also knew that even if I did choose hell, I was in no state to serve anything right now. Whatever benevolent force sent the call, was deluded to thinking that I had anything left in me to offer.

I stood to move. Maybe bored, maybe restless, maybe resisting the possibility that watching them might inspire me to join them again. Mostly to avoid the choice that I still couldn't bring myself to make.

As I took a step back from the ledge, a strong wind blew with such force that it swept a wave of water across the side of my body. The earth began to rumble. I froze.

"Maya," a luminous feminine voice sounded.

Damn it! Someone's found me.

I looked around, but no one was in sight. She spoke my name again, distant, echoing, but right *here*, in my head. I knew it was the metaphysical returning.

I knew it was Qiǎohui.

I ran.

Ran to escape her.

Ran to shut her out of my mind.

"Maya."

No matter where I ran, her voice remained persistently close.

I ran faster, deep into the jungle where I hoped the plethora of nature's grandiosity might drown out Qiaŏhui's celestial messages.

"You can't escape who you are."

The sentence rung in my ears. I spun and stood my ground.

"Who am I then?" I yelled.

There was no answer.

"I don't even know anymore." I felt like . . . nothing.

"You can't escape the *truth*," she corrected, before drifting back into the grace from which she arose.

Just then, the vision I had been avoiding struck me. In broad daylight, full consciousness. A shadow cast over my eyes. Momentarily, I was blind. I stumbled to the ground. Then, I began to *see*.

The Earth.

Black.

Wiped of human existence.

All existence.

The one image I'd been seeing all my life.

The same version of it that I saw a few days earlier.

And then, from the galaxy above, giant bullets dropped down onto the planet, a cluster of silver ships—

"Stop!" With all the willpower left in me, I tore myself from what I knew would follow.

"Just stop."

My body went limp. I knelt there in silence, still blind, glad the voice had vanished, but somehow far from relieved.

Tiredness overcame me and I lay down where I was, allowing myself to doze off for the first time in days.

In my slumber I felt a presence close by, too close. My eyes flashed open as sharp teeth pierced my ankle.

The lionesses' eyes were cunning as she looked up at me, ankle gripped tight between her sharp teeth. She dragged me like a doll. I wriggled to break myself free as the surge of primal instincts raced through my body, but she only sunk her teeth in deeper.

"Hey!" I yelled, fighting back by kicking her cheek with my free foot.

She thrashed my leg in her jaws, sending jolts of pain up my body.

It felt alive.

I fought again, this time, for the purpose of receiving the reciprocation of her defence.

She stopped in her tracks to bite down harder. I kicked her shoulder again with my free leg. She snarled, enjoying the game of resistance.

Adrenaline raced through my body. I fell back onto the hard earth and let her drag me once more, curious as to where she planned to take me, unafraid if it was to my death.

But a deep rolling growl from above made the lioness stop again. My eyes flashed open just in time to see a giant hairy beast drop from a tree branch, blocking her in her tracks. She dropped my leg with a snarl, manoeuvring to guard my body as if the orangutan might steal her prey.

Rose.

Before I had time to process what was happening, Rose stood erect, lifting her orange chest intimidatingly. The lion growled, bracing herself, then pounced, her claws slicing Rose's stomach.

Rose howled in pain, only intensifying her momentum as she smacked a long, gangly arm into the lion's side, knocking her to the ground. The lion stumbled, but quickly regained her composure and bounced back, leaping forward to sink her teeth into Rose's side.

Rose was quick to intercept. She wrapped her humanlike hands around the cat's neck, pinching very specific pressure points. In seconds, the lion weakened, her legs buckling as she crumbled to the ground.

Rose stepped back and watched her closely. As the lioness came to, she forced herself up, ensuring a decent distance between herself and Rose, and crept toward me.

A death threatening growl emerged from deep in Rose's throat. The lioness hissed for losing a meal, for losing a battle, but surrendered and slunk backward warily before retreating into the trees.

Strangely, I was disappointed. The promise of easy death the lioness offered was gone.

Injured, Rose made her way to me.

She emitted a soft whine and nodded at my leg. Bending over, she carefully nudged it. When I didn't flinch, she began licking the wound.

I winced, but forced myself to lay still. She cleaned each hole thoroughly, and in time, the bleeding stopped. Her saliva soothed the pain and created a protective coating.

She sat up with a groan, looking me in the eye.

"Thank you." But the words couldn't possibly express the gratitude and reverence I felt for the consciousness that led to her actions.

We sat together for a time. My heartbeat slowed as the rush of adrenaline faded. I dreaded my return to the tribe, expecting that the mauling would need a healer's touch and knowledge. But as I examined it closer, the damage was less brutal than it felt.

Garlic, aloe vera, honey, neem leaves, goldenseal. I quickly scanned through my memory of the plants Nala had used on my wrist, and others I had gathered for the medicine sisters.

Surely I could apply a similar treatment. It would just mean finding them...

It was a more appealing option than going back. I knew if I returned, I'd have to tell the tribe the vision, and I still wasn't ready to do that. I couldn't.

Not yet.

Rose stirred. I lifted my head, suddenly afraid of the darkness I knew awaited me once her soothing company was removed. She limped toward the nearest tree and climbed it less nimbly than she was capable of, body also weakened and wounded. I watched as she swung stiffly from branch to branch out of sight.

The healing gel I extracted and mixed from nearby plants soaked into my wound. I finally had been able to sleep, this time out of sight from predators, and without any visions. The celestial forces that sent them understood I could not endure more.

Another sun passed, but the moon didn't follow. The night was black.

The wounds were healing quicker than I could've ever imagined with no sign of infection. I had the feeling there was some kind of magic in Rose's saliva.

I found a stream and soaked in its cleansing waters. The sounds of sticks crunching underfoot startled me. I whipped my head around to see Rose. She had returned.

I began to smile in welcome when something else caught my eye behind her. *Someone* else.

How could you? I shot Rose a look of disappointment.

It felt as if an arrow struck my heart. I'd been caught, or more accurately, *exposed*.

Björn was cautious, and moved toward me slowly.

"What are you doing?" I said forcefully as I lifted myself from the stream, but he didn't wince. His eyes only softened.

"Ask her. *She* led me here." Björn nodded at Rose, who quietly retreated out of sight.

"She shouldn't have."

"I disagree," he said and waited, watching, then continued.

"You don't know how relieved I am to know that you're okay. We didn't even know if you were . . ." He shook his head, stepping closer, but I stepped back.

"Well, now you know," I finally said. "And I'll continue to be okay, so you can go back to the village now."

He reached out to touch my hand, but I shrugged away.

"Maya, you don't have to go through whatever this is alone." The concern and care that flowed from his eyes repulsed me.

I didn't know what to say. I was blank. All I knew was that he was wrong. *Of course* I had to go through it alone.

His eyes scanned my figure from head to foot. My stained clothes, straggly wet hair, and mauled leg weren't as convincing an image of being "okay" as I would've hoped.

He pressed his lips together. "I won't go back unless you come with me."

Anger boiled within me.

"Well that's not going to happen," I said. "Please just leave. I can't be around people right now."

"What if that's not true? What if company and care can help you?" he said with compassion and understanding. Not too long ago he'd been adamant about protecting *me* from *his* darkness.

But I shook my head. This was different. Nothing could help me.

"You think you get it, but you don't. You don't want to be around me right now, trust me."

"Yes, I do." He dumped a backpack on the ground. Obviously, he'd been prepared for my stubbornness.

"If you won't come back with me, I'll stay here with you instead."

CHAPTER TWENTY-SEVEN

BJÖRN GATHERED MORE HEALING plants for my wound. I tried to escape from him, but my leg was weak. I couldn't get far, and he was a skilled tracker. It didn't take long for him to catch me. He was determined to take care of me, and I began cooperating for the pure sake of his happiness.

When my leg was strong enough to travel a distance, he took me to the ocean of summer, trying everything he could think of to spark a sense of joy and re-open my heart, but I couldn't force myself to feel things that no longer existed inside me. Not even the magnificence of the summer sea could inspire my heart to lighten. It was as if each death that passed through me had taken a shard of my spirit, and I was left an empty shell.

The most frightening part was that I didn't *care*. I had no desire to restore who I was. Everything seemed pointless, including love and joy, under the acute awareness that it was all so fleeting anyway.

We walked for days through lush forestry to reach the edge of the island, but the bleak shades that tinted my vision washed the color and brilliance out of everything I saw. Small but sudden movements made me jump. I felt on edge, anxious.

When I slept, memories of death flashed violently through my dreams. But the other vision hadn't returned. And for that, I was grateful.

In the flashbacks, people would call my name, begging for help, but I was always stuck, and life always left their eyes right before mine. I was *always* helpless but *always* forced to watch.

Once at the beach, we found a cave and made camp. We watched the waves form, roll, crash, and sweep back out to sea as the sun rose and set from our elevated view upon the cliffs edge.

I swam.

Far and deep. Testing my limits. Escaping the heavy weight of my body on land.

I swam so far out that Björn became but a speck on the beach, and the beach but a little bay. I floated on my back, arms wide, watching white clouds drift across the bright sky as the water hugged and held me.

I breathed in the salty air.

Inhale. Exhale.

I paddled and glided and soaked in the tranquillity.

All the while empty inside.

Björn caught fish and I dehydrated seaweed under the intense summer sun. He kept his eye on me, tried to connect, but also respected my space and didn't push me. Still, my melancholy saddened him.

"We should go back," I said one evening, staring blankly into the campfire, sipping herbal tea.

Björn sat so close we could have touched, but didn't. We hadn't since *that* night.

He turned his head to face me. I did all I could not to meet his gaze as he reached for my hand. I flinched and pulled away.

Could he not feel the wrath of the endless, violent winter within me? I was sure that the mist surrounding me now was as black as the rest of humanity's had been.

"If that's what you want."

I nodded.

"We've seen the ocean. It's nice."

I was still afraid to go back. But I couldn't let him stay stuck with me alone any longer.

"Okay, let's pack up in the morning."

"Okay."

We sipped our tea in silence and listened to the crashing waves. The moon was a sliver in the sky again, offering only the faintest light over the dark ocean.

I was able to stave off sleep, but after some time my eyes closed involuntarily. Björn became used to waking multiple times a night to my shrieks.

My dreams remained just as vivid, but evolved. I watched the lives of people that had passed through me play out like movies. I saw where they came from, how they spent their days, their families. I saw what they wanted and imagined for their life, and then watched it end.

We *had* to leave.

I couldn't disturb Björn's sleep with my screams anymore either.

The next morning, I took my last swim. As I floated offshore, a giant dark shadow loomed in the water a few feet away from me.

My heart skipped a beat, hyperaware of how small and vulnerable I was in comparison. Fear spiked my pulse. It was the first emotion I'd experienced since the channeling.

Adrenaline raced through my body as the black mass moved directly toward me. My impulse was to swim as fast as I could back to shore, but it was so big. If it were a predator, it would catch me in seconds.

A dolphin?

A chord of excitement strung my heart to life if only for one tune!

But no, dolphins are small.

And then it hit me.

Both figuratively and literally.

The sea beast was directly beneath me. Its huge rubberlike flipper rubbed against my leg. I squealed in fear, then laughed hysterically for just from the gentle nature of its slimy touch, I knew it had no intention to harm me. It exuded grace, which was odd for its size. I realized that I knew what it was. A whale!

Again, the armor around my heart cracked open, and this time, a pool of love poured out.

Color intensified around me.

Everything became brighter.

Crisper.

More alive.

I was in the presence of a great, majestic whale!

It nudged me again, and I squealed and laughed again as it made contact. Its back breached the surface and a soft spray shot up and sprinkled down over my face. A elongated wail echoed from below the water.

"Hello." I stroked my hand carefully along its blubbery skin, testing its sensitivity to touch.

As its body sunk below the surface, it lifted its great tail high into the air. I watched as it dove down and disappeared into the deep blue.

I stayed in that spot, treading water, wondering if that was goodbye, but just as I accepted the experience for what it was, it returned, using the depth of his dive to breach high into the air. Time stopped as its giant body reached for the sky, exhibiting the full brilliance of its power before crashing down with a huge splash. A ripple currents reached swept past me.

The whale made its way back toward where I floated and nudged me with the tip of its nose.

"You are ..." but there were no words. I rested my forehead on its cheek. "Thank you for reminding me of the magic."

As if my words were all the encouragement it needed, it dipped its nose beneath the water and slid under me, guiding me onto its smooth back. Unsteady, it floated patiently, motionless as I stabilized myself.

I was unsure of what it wanted from me, but leaned forward to balance my weight, resting my stomach on its back. I could feel its pulse, our hearts synching, beating as one. My body relaxed, suddenly exhausted from keeping myself afloat for so long, which had been the perfect distraction to avoid thinking, feeling, *seeing*.

But now, I wanted to feel everything.

Life had hummed back into every cell of my being.

"Thank you," I whispered again, but no words could express the true expanse of gratitude that overflowed from my heart.

When it started moving toward shore, gliding with more grace than I knew possible, disappointment overcame me. I felt a longing to abide in the abyss of the ocean forever, but as my eyes found Björn, I understood where it was delivering me.

He stood on the beach, with waves sweeping rhythmically up around his feet and back out to sea again. As he watched me, a clear stream of light traveled outward from his chest.

I could see again.

I could *see*.

Seawater splashed across my face as we picked up speed. I sat up as a sense of freedom shot through my chest like a star across the night sky, and squeezed my legs tighter around the whale's back to keep my grip.

We raced toward shore until the bank shallowed. When the whale slowed, I heard a voice. I jumped; the whale and I were the only things floating in the shallow water.

The voice was unlike one I had ever heard. It echoed, words long and drawn out, woven together as if there was no need for breath. The pitch was musical, lyrical, but with a tone so deep it rumbled like the earth. As I listened more closely, I realised it traveled along a thread of soundwaves from mind to mind.

To my mind, from the whale's.

"Understand now Maya. Understand so that you may be free." As words became clearer, I recognized the voice all too well.

Qiaŏhui was using the vessel of the whale to send me a message. She knew I'd block her otherwise.

"You knew my enchantment with whales. You knew seeing one would open my heart enough to hear you."

The whale made a low wailing sound.

"Your people chose their destiny by not honoring their true potential," she told me, aware I had been living with a crippling amount of survivor guilt.

"The Mother created you all with the unlimited power to inform and create your own reality through the manifestation of your intention. The mind is a powerful tool when used with clear intent, but a destructive force when ruled by negatively charged thinking.

When one individual functions in a high enough state of awareness to set positive manifestations in motion that work to benefit all life on Earth, they have the power to not only raise their own consciousness, but the collective human consciousness, for the nature of reality is that no individual has ever been truly separate.

When your minds were hacked by the force of Sky People, the collective human consciousness dropped to a level that it began creating a collective reality of suffering and destruction, in service of their intent to transform earth into an iron planet.

Out of harmony with nature you fell, and so, into your own kind of hell.

You mustn't feel guilty for surviving while the rest of your species died, for their bodies *had* to leave this planet. They no longer had a place in the game of consciousness.

But you, you're different.

You and Björn are expressions of humankind's original potential.

You were created with the *destiny* to escape the System, to withstand your social conditioning and the collective consciousness of the Society. You were born with the capacity to experience extreme pain and the power to transcend it, only through contrast understanding the true value of your inner light.

It has all been mapped. It has all been written. And I have been but a shepherd to guide you toward what was inevitable.

The guilt you carry is resistance to the predetermined flow."

There was a pause. I felt her benevolent presence all around me like a comforting embrace. Within it, a deeper sense of divine trust became available, replacing the fear that had seeped in and wrapped around my heart since the channeling.

"Realize, too, that the grief you've been feeling has been as much the Earth Mother's as your own.

Humans were her children, and pursuing their destruction meant destroying part of herself. She used you, Maya, as the in-between to relieve herself of some of the pain, for in her frailty she might not have been strong enough to endure it. She understood it would be overwhelming for your body to share such a load, but also knew you had the resilience to survive.

Because at the core of your being, you are she as well. The One weaves through it all."

My mind went quiet and I waited for Qiaŏhui to continue, but the channel connecting our minds disappeared. The only sound that remained was the surging of water and waves lapping lightly against the whale.

The whale sounded another echo, signaling that our time together was over. I slid from its back, sinking into the waiting arms of the ocean. I paddled to its nose and pressed my forehead against its cheek once more, then floated backward to give it space as it turned back out to sea. My legs tread the water just enough to stay afloat as I watched it disappear into the ocean's depths.

I swam toward shore and crawled onto to the beach, stopping at Björn's feet. He held a fishing line that lay limp on the ground. I lifted my head as if asking, *"Did that really just happen? Really?"* The expression he wore was all the reassurance I needed. He dropped the fishing line in the sand, extending his hand toward me.

My legs wavered as they straightened to stand. We weren't quite touching, and there were no words to be spoken. I was simply glad to be back.

Back to life.

To love.

To the love right in front of me.

To the love of the One.

He ran his hand along my wet cheek and kissed my cold, wet lips. Then wrapped his hot, sun-kissed arms around my shoulders, chin resting on my head as he gazed out at the ocean.

My resistance to let him in vanished, and gratitude for all he'd done and been for me replaced it in full force.

I tilted my head to kiss him, this time passionately. Every moment that I had ignored him over the past weeks were made up for in the potency of this moment.

CHAPTER TWENTY-EIGHT

WE DIDN'T END UP leaving that morning.

We spent the next week intertwined in the sweetest affair of love.

I'd been afraid that first night; of doing something wrong, of not knowing what to do at all, but my natural instincts stepped in, and when my body moved in rhythm with his it was a dance.

We danced like this on the stone floor of the cave.

And the grass, under tropical trees.

And on the beach, under the sweltering summer sun.

And in the water, under the gaze of the water world.

We became inseparable, melting into one.

That week, my dreams stopped, and the visions and memories that haunted me faded as they lost power. I was safe in the loving arms of Björn. It was as if his love formed a protective sphere around me through which only frequencies aligned with love could enter. Now that I'd let it in, and opened my heart and body entirely, I was swimming in it.

Swimming in an ocean of all-encompassing love.

I was free.

Free of worry.

Free of fear.

Free of pain.

And as I dived deeper into the ocean of love, it became clear that the love I experienced with Björn served as an invitation into the vaster, eternal love at the very center of my being, the essence of *all* being. Nothing else existed but love as I fell deeper and deeper into its infinite well.

How was it possible to experience such an extreme change in emotions so quickly? If I were still in the City, Meredith would have medicated me for bipolar disorder and a plethora of other "mental illnesses." Institutionalized me for sure. I smirked at the thought, amused. *But here, I was allowed to feel and change and express my emotions. I realized after allowing myself to walk blindly into the darkness of grief and sorrow, and feel them in their entirety, they were given the chance to heal.*

I had a suspicion that it was just a reprieve, and another layer of pain would soon surface. But the sweetness of the break was enough to realize that maybe I didn't care.

Maybe both extremes were inevitably fleeting.

Maybe *preference* was the real problem.

"Let go of all craving and aversion, and you shall be free."

"My parents would've called it the 'law of polarity,'" Björn said as we explored the forest just beyond the beach.

The trees were tall, tropical, and thinner than those in the spring village, younger and smoother. Its dense canopy provided shade from the midday sun while containing both moisture and heat to create a damp humidity.

Many trees bore bountiful summer fruits that patiently awaited picking, and Björn's eyes scanned branches for any low enough to harvest. He dug his dagger into the trunk of a coconut tree, climbing upward to gather those that were ripe enough for picking.

"Can you toss me a stick?" he called down, his legs wrapped tightly around the trunk.

He used the long stick to knock down coconuts, and I collected them off the ground into a netted bag.

"They got all scientific about it, but I understood it as the way light can't exist without darkness." He climbed back down, landing with a *thump*.

"Understanding opposites means our experience of each spectrum becomes enriched." He kissed me on the cheek and walked ahead, his voice drifting back.

I watched him from behind, his bare, muscular back and shaggy, white/blonde hair that now fell below his ears. He looked as rugged and wild as the tribe, and I had no doubt I did too.

"Darkness will never last, and neither will light. Just as the day always flows into the night." Looking back toward me, he winked, then glanced around the forest with eyes of awe. His step was buoyant.

"You know what Maya," he said changing the subject, "I'm very grateful to be here with you. If we had stayed in the City, we'd be dead right now. I don't know, I guess feeling guilty is a waste of the gift of extended life we've been given."

I nodded, reflecting. "It's true."

It was midmorning, and we lay on the sand where waves washed ashore and kissed our feet. My head rested upon Björn's chest, soaking in the warmth from the bright morning sun.

Björn stroked his fingers across my bare back, sticky from the mango we shared earlier. An ever-present smile lit my face.

"I think . . ." Björn started lazily.

I lifted my chin, and his eyes were lost in the endless blue sky above.

"You think . . ." I kissed his chest.

"Mmm." He closed his eyes. "That maybe . . ."

"Maybe." I crawled up and kissed his neck. "Maybe we should start our journey home this afternoon?"

"Hey, don't do that," he said, pushing up onto his elbows.

"What?"

"Read my thoughts!" he laughed.

"Because you have sooo much to hide," I teased.

"Hey, I *did*."

"I can't see your thoughts; it was just a guess."

"Hmm." he eyed me, unsure.

"It's okay Even if I could, I respect your privacy."

He was thoughtful, shifting his gaze back up toward the sky. "Sometimes I wish you could see yourself through my eyes."

It was only then that I remembered I had. But only for a fleeting moment after waking up from the in-between. I decided not to share that though. . .

"But yes, let's go back today. They'll be so happy to see you again." He smiled, then rolled over to kiss my lips.

"Soon."

I collected the seaweed I had been drying to bring back with us. After packing our belongings up, we began our travels back to the village, moving without urgency. Our bodies had synced in harmony with the rhythm of the calm ocean.

We walked along the shoreline, wandering in and out of the waves that kept us cool. Once the intensity of the afternoon heat struck, we retreated beneath the shady rainforest.

Our journey home was considerably more alive through my reawakened eyes than our journey there.

Colors were more vivid. The slightest movement of leaves in the breeze sounded more melodic.

Björn whistled with the birds.

The fauna thickened with each step. A carpet of unruly grass now coated the ground, cushioning our feet as we reached the jungle between summer and spring. There was no clear-cut path to follow, but the direction was made clear through patches of trodden earth that led the way home.

Thank you. I whispered internally to the Mother. *Thank you for guiding me home.*

As if in response to the light, twinkling feeling within me, a distant bell-like ringing sounded in my ears. The melodic hymn echoed through the trees. It was a sound I'd heard just once before, but the majesty it carried was imprinted in my memory.

I looked over at Björn, who's eyes darted here and there, before chuckling and directing my attention upward. Three luminous star-like beings floated down towards us, moving with little urgency.

The symphony of sounds became one repeated word.

"Björn."

"Björn. Björn. Björn," they sang in a high-pitched hum.

I looked back at the man to whom the name belonged. His eyes had found the light beings and followed them, his steps delayed and dreamy as they moved toward each other. He was infatuated, eyes sparkling, reflecting their magic.

The Fèya stopped to hover before him. He analyzed the tiny, humanlike bodies that hung from wispy wings.

One glowed brighter than the others and floated closer. Just in the seconds it hovered before us, before speaking a word, it shapeshifted from man to woman in numerous flashes, both equally convincing.

Her feminine expression was graceful. She wore a soft white gown, its skirt made of long violet petals. Upon her silky hair sat a crown of delicate, interwoven sticks that reached royally to the sky. She carried a staff of similarly twisted sticks and vines. In some ways she looked like an extension of a plant, while equally astral for her silver-blue glow.

In masculine form, the same petals wrapped around the Fè's hips and dropped into flowing pants that swayed subtly like a flower in the breeze. His chest was bare, glowing beneath vines that crisscrossed his torso. The masculine expression of a crown was less extravagant than the feminine; shorter and sturdier, branches twisting from his head like woody horns.

"This is Zäphïre, both king and queen of the Fèya Kingdom," the male to Zäphïre's right said.

After flickering again, Zäphïre settled in feminine form and bowed her head, meeting my eyes. Hers were a combination of blue that glowed from her skin and the soft violet petals she wore.

"Maya, we've met through association," she nodded. I felt Björn's curious stare, who was unaware of my visit from the light beings on the mountain.

"Anạrtạ," she welcomed in their formal tongue, and although the size of a dragonfly, her power prevailed beyond her body. She turned her gaze to Björn.

"Björn. You and I have also met." This time I looked to him in surprise. But he was even more so than I.

"Through our visions of your coming," she finished.

"Throughout our history, Fèya traveled to your dimension with different roles to play, but all in the name of maintaining and lifting the resonance of light there. There were Fè of each climate, season, and element. Fè of the oceans, mountains, skies, and forests. And some attached to individual humans.

Your parents were the last humans we contacted before retreating permanently underground," Zäphïre revealed.

"Our final mission was to guide humans to the prophesy. We worked with the Nöahl giants to choose a human still open enough to follow our calls. Nöahl Gabriel· foresaw you as the survivor Björn.

We all expected you to take a lone journey, for a woman was never a part of the visions." She turned to me, bowing her head. "It was a great surprise to see you."

"Björn, we used your parents as the mediators to reach you. You were young when we made our final trip and feared you might have dismissed the story as fantasy if given directly. We carried it to the destroyed town where your parents were led to find it, and they were indeed quick to devote themselves to the mission with more faithful trust than we ever hoped for."

"But you knew they wouldn't be the ones to make the journey?" Björn asked.

She shook her head.

"Gabriel· only saw you."

There was silence for some moments in acknowledgment of their passing, then Lupïta the Fè to her left spoke.

"Some things only the Mother can justify." Her voice was like sweet nectar, gentle, and lyrical. "But know your parent's sacrifice is honored here. Among both Fèya and Samãdhi."

A glassy sheath of tears covered Björn's eyes.

"Thank you." They were the first tears I'd witnessed him shed for his parents. I felt tears of my own in response.

Zäphïre lifted her tiny hand to touch Björn's forehead, and as skin met skin, a bright glow sparked between his brow, hovering for a moment before shooting off like a star. He jumped back.

"May the thanks be to your parents."

After some silence, Zäphïre, Lupïta, and her brother Théodren began ascending, as if called on silent cue in the direction they entered, and in just one blink, disappeared out of sight.

Björn and I didn't move for some time, not even to find each other, heads tilted skyward, mystified.

Just as I accepted the Fèya's erratic nature, a single silver light floated back into view. Then another, and another, appearing sporadically all around the lush sphere until the whole space was lit with drifting stars.

I realized, as I examined the trees we stood among, that they didn't just *appear*, they *emerged* from nooks and crevasses they'd been watching from the entire time.

We'd entered the center of their Kingdom, located so high above that we hadn't seen the tiny dwellings where bark doors enclosed homes in hallows, and little vine-woven swings and bridges hung from branch to branch. It was all built and camouflaged cleverly into nature's bare dispensary.

"Come." Lupïta hovered before us again with Théodren by her side, arms open wide.

I looked up through the treetops, so dense it was unclear how high they truly ascended and was intimidated to attempt such a climb. As if reading my thoughts, or just my expression, the Fèya laughed in symphony beside me.

"It's okay, we'll help you," Théodren spoke in deep bells that echoed through the branches, and in abidance, every body of light now visible swarmed toward us.

Their touch was like the tickle of a feather that began along my arm, then spread over my body, every inch of skin tingling under the contact of pure magic.

Björn glowed blueish-silver beside me, bathed in light-bodies; his feet lifted into the air. As I watched him hover, I hardly noticed my own feet leave the ground, but when I glanced down, I, too, was floating.

"Weehee!" I laughed, to which a symphony of bells chimed, never missing an opportunity to be merry. Björn's distinctive laughter was among the chorus, offering a throaty human sound.

We rose higher as if the laughter fueled their magic. I began to feel light-headed, but the field of vision captured my awe. We were floating among giants, immersed in their hair of branches as if granted access into their ancient minds of wisdom.

The camouflaged Kingdom was a wild but perfect mess. The Fè lowered us down to rest side by side on a sturdy branch that dipped to create an ideal human-sized seat. Once safely placed down, their lights scattered once more. Some perched beside us, sounding sweet high-pitched sighs and unrecognizable words of relaxed chatter. Others glided about the air, swooping and soaring, while some just hovered, watching, being.

Partners twirled along the branches to the tune of their humming, leaving trails of glowing dust behind, and one Fè, after flying in a loop, returned to sit upon my shoulder. She was young, her bright innocence seeping out from wide, curious eyes. I got the feeling she'd never met a human before.

I watched her watching me. She broke into a smile so sweet it was like a flower bud bursting open. She inched closer, touching my cheek, and stared plainly into my eyes.

Reaching up, she wrapped her tiny fingers around the ridge of my ear and used it to swing up to the top of my head, settling there.

The king rose before us. His petallike pants swayed with his movement as he lowered himself between Björn and me.

"That's Echõ," he said. "She's one of our youngest. She's drawn to you because you're born of the same frequency of Light Matter."

My head tingled under her pure and vibrant presence.

"I've experienced a lot of darkness recently," I said, doubting his assumption.

"That might be so, but your experiences don't change your essence. I sense it as she does.

Human experience can be confusing, an ever-changing dance between light and dark. The role Fèya have always played with humankind is to help guide you back to light, to truth whenever the darkness intervenes. And even when darkness arises, we help you understand the preceding beauty and love ever-present beneath."

He paused, studying me.

"It was the fear of shadows that almost broke you, not the shadows themselves."

I shuffled, repositioning myself on the branch.

"It's important you develop a relationship with what you fear so you do not crumble when adversity arises again. The path laid out for you is forecast with more challenges than most have to encounter in their lifetime, and you cannot run from it." His warning was felt like a sharp blade, slicing apart my dream of living out the rest of my life there in peace.

"You must be able to hold love and fear beside each other and allow them to co-exist. For if you don't, you will suffer."

I shifted again on the branch, looking down at the distance between us and the ground, suddenly feeling trapped.

"We should get going now," I blurted.

"Of course," he smiled placidly.

My attention drifted to Björn, who had an influx of light-beings darting around him.

"The Fèya have a special love for Björn. Your Light Matter is similar to ours; the essence of air runs deeply through you. His strength is like the earth. Solid and unbreakable." King Zäphïre's comment sounded like it came from another kind of foresight that I couldn't decipher. He experienced the workings of the metaphysical world as clearly as we experienced the physical.

More light-beings drew toward Björn like magnets upon Zäphïre's silent cue and lifted him into the air. I too, began to feel their light touch locking onto my body.

I rose from the branch, following Björn in his descent toward the ground. Zäphïre met us there in the feminine form again. I felt less threatened by her than the freakishly clairvoyant king, even though they were two faces of the same being.

"Are there more of you?" Björn asked before departing.

Zäphïre shook her head.

"There used to be many of our kind, both here and on earth. But we're the last now. I'm hopeful there will come a day when we'll flourish again."

A chime broadcasted across the Fèya tribe as they dispersed through the trees in their final wave of farewell. I searched the faces for Echõ, who had disappeared after I'd taken flight. I wondered where she'd vanished to.

"We'll see you again," Théodren said.

"Sooner than you might think," Lupïta added.

A mischievous giggle rippled through the twins as they drifted backward.

CHAPTER TWENTY-NINE

WE WALKED FOR SOME time. I sensed that Björn was bothered by something. I could feel it brewing.

"Are you thinking about your parents?" He hadn't spoken of them since we arrived. If he had grieved, he kept it to himself.

He was quiet, searching. "I guess it's all confusing now I know they would have still died anyway . . . and that it was never in their cards to make it here . . . but yes."

I nodded.

Then I had an idea.

"I want to try something. I don't know if it'll work," I warned.

He laughed at the sudden enthusiasm. "I trust you."

"Okay." I ran ahead, leading him to a flat, open patch of grass.

We sat facing each other, holding hands, eyes locked. He was curious and open. A ripple of light energy ran through my body.

"Speak to me about your parents," I prompted. But instead of tuning all my attention to his words, I tuned into the responses moving through his body.

Love and pain surfaced from within his heart.

"Ah. There it is." I closed my eyes and followed his emotions as my body became an open channel, feeling everything that arose within him.

I concentrated on his feelings. Images appeared. Memories. Björn's memories of his parents.

I inhaled, for the emotions of love, pain, and everything in-between were immense. I now fully understood his unwillingness to let them go.

With their image and essence my central focus, I dove into the vast space I'd never voluntarily entered before. I *became* the emptiness where those humans went to die, and we all come from to live.

But this time it wasn't frightening. The void. The nothingness. It simply *was*.

I gently placed my fingertips upon his temples, waiting for his mind to quieten. As we began to share his memories, I drew him into the space with me like a vortex.

"They're here," I affirmed as I connected the essence of Björn's late parents from his memories to the essence that still existed even though they had dissolved back into the One.

The mist of nothingness began to move and dance, merging to create the image of a man and woman standing side by side. They were transparent, formed of pure white Light Matter that moved in streams along the illusionary outline of their figures.

Then the voices of their past reassembled with their bodies and began speaking to Björn.

"Son, we can only reappear for a short time before drifting like waves back into the sea," a gentle masculine voice began.

"But rest your mind in knowing that all that occurred was for the higher good. We had to die to force you to leave when you did. You had to disguise yourself as a regular guard to find Maya on the street that day. You had to take the journey below before nature wiped out humanity.

It was all unfolding in consciousness a step before we could register it. It was all unfolding as planned."

His mother's voice followed, echoing through the emptiness.

"And now we're a part of the very air you breathe and the ocean you swim. We're closer than we could have ever been in body.

I know you carry anger at the Control for designing our deaths. Let it go, for there was nothing but love involved in our death. You may not understand it now, but beneath the ugliness of the Control's actions, the One was preparing a warm welcome for us to come home to.

Understand we are free now. We are home," her warm voice trailed off.

They stood in silence for some time, their love enveloping Björn. Tears welled in his eyes, as they did mine, our hearts united.

"You can surrender now to the divine intelligence and allow all to unfold as it will." His mother's voice drifted off, losing the energy to form words.

"You still have work to do in the physical world son, but one day we will be reunited again in the One. Until then that our love is with you always," said his father before vanishing into the ether.

Silence remained between us as we drifted in the realm behind consciousness, the realm of source. And in the stillness, I searched for the essence of Adam.

If he'd died, I should be able to find him here too. I tuned in more acutely, spreading my awareness further into the vastness. I could feel him *somewhere*, but it wasn't there.

He wasn't empty. His heart still beat.

Björn's consciousness returned to his body, but he didn't disturb me as I searched to locate the realm where Adam's heart beat.

All of humanity died. I saw it.

But Adam's heartbeat was lost in the silence. I waited, unable to reconnect. My awareness was being drawn back to my body.

I released the need of finding him, finding joy knowing that, somehow, somewhere, he was *alive*.

My eyes opened, taking time to readjust. Everything was different yet the same. The two dimensions momentarily merged in my vision.

Color and the illusion of density dissolved. The foundation of all form was exposed. Radiant but minute particles of pure white Light Matter gathered in masses to form trees, plants, birds. Björn was nothing more than a mass of particles close enough together to generate the shape of a body. Nothing was solid, nor was it motionless. The Light Matter moved and vibrated in streams of energy that interconnected *everything*. Even the ether in-between appeared more like a mist of dancing particles.

Björn reached for me. A river of Light Matter ran from the blinding bright light of his heart, along his arm, and into his palm. I reached out, and the moment our fingers touched, a spike of energy shot through my body, so intense it shocked me fully back into the realm of density. I caught my breath. The solidity and color of everything around me returned.

We stared at each other. Frozen. Eyes wide, expressions raw.

Time passed, gusts of wind blew, birds sang, and leaves rustled. All my senses were heightened, processing everything both within and around me at high speeds.

Even the most mundane details of the environment were fascinating while at the same time nothing mattered, nothing seemed *real* anymore. Nothing carried the weight it had before.

Björn's eyes were like the most intricate, advanced computers, processing information like I was. The subtlest of movement across his face was compelling, more mechanical than I'd ever noticed before.

He moved to stand, reaching down to pull me up beside him. Without thought or dialogue governing our movements, we walked once more in the direction of home.

At one point Björn stopped, suddenly overwhelmed by confusion. He lowered to his knees, trying to make sense of his experience, of hearing his parent's words, seeing them again as if still alive, of visiting the in-between.

All that held him together shattered.

He pressed his hand against his chest as if he were experiencing a panic attack. I knelt by his side, resting a hand on his back as he desperately sucked air into his lungs.

"I don't know if it will ever make sense," I said softly. "It's too bit to fit inside our minds. It doesn't work, I've tried."

I shook my head, remembering Nõahl Gabriel's warning about the dangers of delving beyond what we have the capacity to comprehend.

"I'm sorry. I thought understanding would bring you solace but I . . . It was dangerous to go there with you." My curious nature had proved harmful yet again.

"No, it's okay. I finally feel at peace with their passing. It's just strange, where we come from. I feel so much bigger than

I always thought I was, but at the same time insignificant."
But words couldn't express the feeling.

I nodded, understanding the juxtaposition completely.

Björn was quiet for the rest of our journey.

He walked as if witnessing the life of every organism for the first time.

CHAPTER THIRTY

BJÖRN REACHED OUT TO squeeze my hand as we arrived at the village entrance, making sure I understood that his silence hadn't been personal. I squeezed back, understanding. He kissed my forehead, igniting a spark where his lips made contact, and pulled me into a tight embrace.

"I love you," He said.

"I love you," I responded, then kissed him. It was like two flares colliding. He jolted back.

"Did you feel that?"

"Yes," I laughed.

"What about this? Can you feel this?" He squeezed me against his chest and tickled my ribs.

I laughed louder before wriggling away and running through the entrance. We ran down the dirt path to our cottage to drop off our travel packs, waving at everyone we passed along the way but not stopping until we reached home.

When the door swung open, we were greeted with the scent of herbal tea. Candles flickered.

Nala sensed our return and prepared the room for us?

I slowly stepped inside, the wooden floor creaking beneath my feet. A woman with frizzy black hair emerged—a human. One I didn't recognize. She broke into a welcoming smile.

"Björn." They knew each other.

"Farrah." He walked toward her and they embraced.

"What— How—" He was in shock. He didn't know what to ask first.

Through the window, movement in the backyard caught my eye. I dropped my travel pack, heart beating faster than I could breathe. I knew before he came through the door who it was.

"Adam!" I ran to him, slamming into his hard chest. He lifted me effortlessly from the ground, arms almost crushing my ribs.

Within seconds, his shirt was spotted with my tears. I couldn't speak.

"I heard what happened," he said quietly, holding himself together a lot better than I. "I'm glad to see you're okay."

"I can't believe you're here," was all I could manage. I squeezed him tighter.

"Ouch." He leaned back, looking down at the pendant that jabbed his chest. "You still have the seashell." I looked up, his eyes brimming with tears, but none fell. He didn't know what it was to cry, but in the short time he'd been in Santōṣha, it seemed his heart was already cracking open.

"I thought it was the only thing I had left of the earth realm. The only reminder left of you," I said.

Suddenly, it hit me. "Wait, how are you here?" I laughed ecstatically.

Adam looked at Björn with soft, appreciative eyes.

"Björn left the prophesy with me. I woke up with it in my arms. I was so angry I almost ripped it apart. But I couldn't ignore that it was something profound when a picture of the valley started drawing itself on the page, identical to the one you'd painted," he started.

"I *did* spend days stubbornly imagining that you'd stalked her and crafted the whole thing in order to manipulate her, but at some point, it became too obvious, too freakishly polished to be all some master plan of yours," he said to Björn. "No offence."

"I had to convince Maya the same thing," Björn shrugged.

Adam was thoughtful. "It's pretty obvious now that all the spinning thoughts and resistance I felt came from the shadows of Sky consciousness, keeping me from following you to freedom."

He was smart, quick to understand the subtleties of their trap.

"Pretty damn convincing," Farrah said, her voice husky and demeanour tough as I turned to face her.

"I'm still surprised I agreed to come, let alone survived the vortex. It sounded too impossible." Her otherwise emotionless eyes twinkled as she looked at Adam.

"But the map revealed pictures to me too, and after Adam showed me your room, the paintings, a part of me knew something bigger than anything we could comprehend was at play."

My heart beamed with happiness as I soaked in every subtlety of the face I knew so well, and that of Farrah's, understanding much about her just through her mannerisms.

"Farrah worked with me," Adam explained. "I always sensed she was not as tough as she seemed to be. To be honest, when the prophesy started revealing information about having to be 'light' enough to pass through the veil, I was almost sure we wouldn't survive." Adam laughed to himself. "But things were getting bad in the City. It was looking like we might all be dead in a matter of time anyway, and I realized that the way I'd been living, I already kinda was. A slow, drawn-out death . . ."

"What do you mean 'we?' Are there more?" Björn asked.

We moved outside. Björn sat beside me on the warm grass and Adam and Farrah on the porch step as they shared their story.

"When I started believing Santōṣha might actually exist, I wanted to bring as many people that might survive the jump as I could, but we all had chips," Adam said.

"We knew the Creators were the only ones who could get the chips out safely. And for them to do that, the Council would have to approve. The Creators would never oppose the Council."

"So we told Koen about Santōṣha," Farrah continued. "We twisted the pitch so he would think that we could mine Santōṣha's land for everything we needed to keep the City going. If things continued to get worse in the City, we could migrate here. We left out the part about needing to be 'light' to make the jump, knowing that anyone who agreed with our idea wouldn't survive anyway."

"I know it was a risk telling him," Adam admitted, "but it was the best angle we could think of, and it worked."

"Koen sent a small group of officers with us as well as the people Adam convinced into coming. The journey was tightly controlled. The agreement was to return to the City to share what we found," Farrah said.

"They'd have no way of knowing if you all died. It would've been as mysterious as all the explorers in the past who disappeared in the Bermuda Triangle." Björn gathered.

"If they didn't hear from us after a certain amount of time, they were going to send a second troupe. I doubted any other officers would make it. Now it doesn't even matter..." Adam drifted off.

"Only three of us survived the jump. We were stuck in autumn for a while, then winter. We found villages but they were all abandoned, so we kept following the river until it led us here. I remembered that the village you painted was near a river."

Björn and I looked around for the third survivor.

"I think he's with Bŏdhi somewhere, probably annoying the hell out of him," Farrah laughed. "It's like he's on speed or something. He wants to meet everyone and see everything all at once."

"It's Cole," Adam laughed.

Of course! He was always more *alive* than Adam's other friends. Kinder. He kept our secret. He'd seen my paintings from a young age.

"Let's go find him!" My heart burst with more love than I even knew existed. Everything was unfolding impeccably.

There was a celebration that evening. A welcoming for our return home.

Björn was quieter than usual, observing with fresh eyes, a new perspective on the underlying workings of the world. He caught up with Farrah as they'd worked together in the Council, and with the rest of the tribe, while maintaining a depth of internal stillness that was obvious to me.

Cole was as lively and buoyant as Farrah described. I hadn't seen him since Adam left school. He was given farm work and lived outside the City. He barely stopped squeezing me, ecstatic just to be there. To be alive.

"I always thought there was something special about you," he said as we drank warm mugs of Kakáu beside the bonfire.

"I always liked you better than Adam's other friend's too," I grinned.

He shook his head, remembering.

"That time we snuck you into a party." He slapped his knee, splashing hot brown liquid on his pants. "Oops."

"I'd never seen anyone so quiet and afraid. You had no idea how to socialize."

"I just remember thinking that if that's what other teenagers were like, I was grateful I didn't have to go to school," I laughed. "I felt like an alien."

"But then I got you dancing, and all your worries disappeared! Your laugh was so loud and free. You attracted way more attention than you should have, but you didn't even notice."

"Adam did," I said.

"Yeah, he took you home way too early! Ah, that was fun."

The intensity of the flames were hot on my face as I smiled into it, remembering the way Cole had taken care of me that night. Adam never danced in public, he was too 'cool', too popular to make a fool of himself, but Cole was *so* cool that he didn't care.

After that night, he'd started coming over more, hanging out. I winced as I remembered the time we were alone in my room. He tried to kiss me. I was terrified. I shut him out. Adam was furious and stopped inviting him over.

During the celebration I didn't stray too far from Adam. I wanted to catch up on everything we'd missed. The tension he carried was already dropping away. Every belief he'd held tight was being shattered since the moment he fell through the veil.

He'd already formed a friendship with Wolfé, both warriors at heart. Katanä expressed more relief and joy to see me home than I expected she would. The amount of care shown by everyone was overwhelming. Almost. But I embodied the space to carry it now. The love, the care. For I cared for every one of them too.

I no longer felt separate. A deep sense of connection thread us all together, and where I felt shy and nervous in the past, I now felt free to express myself. I was whole, both internally and externally. And from this space, love flooded from, through, and into everything and everyone around me.

The moon was bright and full, glimmering luminously upon us and showering the night with a silvery glow distinctive of the planet's peak time in its cycle. And I was glowing with it.

CHAPTER THIRTY-ONE

NALA AND I WALKED in silence, the only sounds coming from the chirpy songs of the birds and from the leaves whispering in the light breeze. Her presence was calm, still, and I could feel it carrying me, supporting me. My steps were light and mind quiet.

She led me down a narrow, weaving path I hadn't yet explored that widened at an access point to the river. The water trickled along calmly. Sweet and soothing was the sound of it kissing the bordering stones as it moved gracefully through nature's passage.

We sat on a smooth stone at the water's edge.

"I'm so happy you found healing Maya," Nala said sweetly, a rare girlish simplicity shining in her eyes. I smiled up at her, then turned my gaze back upon the stream.

"I think it would be more accurate to say it found me," I laughed lightly in memory of the whale, of Qiaŏhui's eternal guidance, and the way darkness transformed so quickly into light.

I sensed that Nala could see the pictures on replay too, but I could never be sure with her.

"The ocean is like a pool of the Mother's greatest medicine."

We sat in silence for a while before Nala spoke.

"Just before you returned, we received a message."

I listened intently, curious if the message was the same one I received from the whale.

"The Mother speaks to us in many ways throughout each day. It could be through certain animals, the winds and weather, sometimes even godly beings with more symbolic messages for us to interpret. It forces us to always listen, receive. It keeps our divine intelligence alive. It's rare for her to speak directly . . ." she trailed off, studying me for a moment, pausing, considering.

"I'll show you."

"What do you mean *show* me?"

"I don't do this much. It takes a lot of energy." She placed her fingertips on my temples just as I had with Björn in the jungle, then closed her eyes.

The moment she made contact, volts of electricity raced to my brain. There was a bright flash and I felt as if I were spinning as my mind traveled at lightning speed into the past.

Then everything was still.

As before, I sat on a thin cushion in the center of a polished, electric blue stone floor enclosed by three golden walls that met in a tip directly above. The three Nöahls sat hand in hand in a ring around me and the flame of a candle flickered in front of me.

I was in one of Nala's memories inside the pyramid.

I heard the faint sound of flowing water. A transparent sheet of water began trickling down the triangular walls. I also understood it was a signal that the power of the element was present.

It tumbled down from the tip of the triangle, showering us and washing us clean before ceasing abruptly.

In its place, the celestial golden Light Matter rained down. Minuscule glistening particles spreading wide before transforming into the same five godly beings that had visited me the night of the earth's end.

Through Nirmala, I came to understand they were the Âscendants, a prehistoric race of light-beings; manifestations of the highest consciousnesses existing across all realms. The pyramid was a portal through which the Nŏahl's could call upon and communicate with the Âscendants, whose wisdom spanned from the very beginning of time.

A presence emerged directly behind me. A hand rested on my shoulder, and through it, a frequency of light vibrated that was godly.

Without looking, I immediately knew who it was. I knew because Nala knew. It was the Nepalese woman Nala knew by the name of Chaiṭãnya. She was an Âscendant.

The Âscendants settled in a ring behind us, assuming statue like positions behind each Nŏahl. Ídã was the name of the little Nordic Âscendant, and Âdja, the dark-skinned warrior. I knew them all intimately now – again, only because of my association with Nala. jagath, the young boy whose glassy eyes shimmered like they carried the whole universe, held my attention, skin striking against the blazing gold of his simple robe. He barely looked human.

Qiaŏhui stood behind an empty space. She was representing me. And as a fixed, unfaltering stillness prevailed through all of them, I realized they weren't the only celestial being being called upon.

A gust of wind blew through the pyramid, but like the water, there was no opening for it to enter through. It swirled around us, lifting Nala's hair, fanning the candle flame. It reached higher, forming a face.

My face.

The wind died down and the atmosphere stilled, the fire ceasing to but a wisp of white smoke. We remained holding hands, tightening our grip if anything, understanding an all-powerful energy was among us. As our eyes closed in unison, the earth began to rumble from deep below the golden platform we rested on.

Behind closed lids, a dominating white light blinded me and a voice began to speak—the omniscient voice of the Mother.

"I am here for your clarity," she said. Her voice was smooth and airy while at the same time thundered with the volume, resonance, and power of the entire earth.

They didn't have to ask their questions aloud, for she already knew what they were.

"It is true that the deaths of humankind passed through Maya as the in-between. As one of the last living humans, she now carries the history of the whole of human existence on earth within her body, to be passed down to future generations."

Her words echoed in sweeping waves, each one ringing for a time until gradually disappearing on the airwaves and rolling into the next. I could hear in it the rustling of leaves, the whistle of the wind, the rushing of water, birds chirping, and stones crumbling.

"The earth above is being restored for human life again, but we cannot risk history repeating itself. Maya holds the memories of humankind's darkest potential; through witnessing their destructive past, and their lightest potential, through understanding now their true nature.

"When she cocreates and births new life, her children will carry these memories as will her children's children, and so may humankind continue choosing to live in union with nature and avert the temptations of darkness.

"As a future mother and carrier of earth's new Children, it had to be her and not Björn-" Suddenly, Nala cut me out of the memory, but not quite fast enough.

"I'm sorry," she said. "It's dangerous for us to know too much of our future."

I froze, stunned into silence, bewildered, and awestruck. It took some time for my vision to readjust to the color of the natural world, for glistening gold imprinted my mind's eye.

The mystery of the pyramid and the Âscendants was now fully exposed, and its majesty was beyond anything I imagined.

Of everything Nala shared of the Mother's words, it was the last sentence that affected me the most.

The very last word.

Björn.

For it was only then that I fully understood.

It was no coincidence we were falling in love.

It was no coincidence we had survived the extinction of humanity as we knew it.

Well, us, Phöenix, Bŏdhi, Chantara and their kids. And now Adam, Farrah, and Cole.

It was our responsibility to give birth to a new wave of humanity, our responsibility to redeem humankind from absolute extinction. The Mother had planned it all so very seamlessly. We were merely living out the story she had already written.

"It's okay. It's just . . ." I bit my lip, but the Mother's plan was too transcendental to resist.

I couldn't fight it even if I wanted to.

And so, my only option was to surrender.

"I've already seen it. Our future." I took a long breath and lifted my chest. "There's something I have to share with everyone."

CHAPTER THIRTY-TWO

I STEPPED ONTO THE polished stone platform. Bright rays of sunshine beamed down through the round opening above, and I felt a sense of heightened respect from all the leaders present. Since returning from the ocean, something shifted. I was one of them now, there to represent humankind.

The underground hallow was quiet but for the echoes of dripping stalactites, all waiting. I took a deep breath as I sat on the last empty cushion that was embroidered with scarlet red swirls.

Björn smiled from across the circle with the loving eyes I'd come to know. Any fear that arose about our written destiny together vanished, and the warmth of his silent encouragement fueled my words.

"There was a part of the vision I didn't tell you," I began.

"When the City was wiped out, the Sky People were close to having full dominance over humans. I could feel their shadows tangled up in each body that passed through me. They were already overrun. Through wiping the earth of both metals and humans, the Mother eliminated their access to the planet, but she also left a bare, clean slate.

"Nature takes time to regenerate, so in the meantime, she's raw and vulnerable. Even though there's no metal to support the Sky People's invasion, there's also nothing to block it."

"What are you saying?" Ṭarō interrupted. An entanglement of dangling creepers animated the damp rocky backdrop behind him. "You think the Sky People can still take over?"

I took another breath.

"I don't just think it. I know it. I saw it," I finally revealed, ashamed to have been so selfish.

"Something happened when the earth was self-destructing, the future shifted course. The Mother's plan was for nature to regenerate, and for humans and animals to inhabit earth again. The power of the earth realm is in life, in nature, and Sky consciousness gains power in form, in iron. Both realms are at a disadvantage now. Both are weak and lack what they need to be strong. I think the playing field has equalized more than the Mother expected."

"Tell us what you saw Maya," Nala said.

I closed my eyes.

"The whole planet was bare, black. I saw what I could only assume as the Sky People's ships dropping from the sky like bullets. Dark metallic ovals, they spread over the land, maybe more like giant iron eggs. The earth stayed cracked and dry. Stagnant. Dead. And their metals spread over everything.

"If they arrive before nature starts regrowing, she doesn't stand a chance." I paused as the memory sent chills through my body. I opened my eyes, expecting to be met by a bunch of shaming comments and faces.

But I wasn't. Instead, bright rays of sun illuminated the already glowing faces of beings simply processing what it would mean if this future manifested.

If the Sky People indeed dominated the earth in full force, it would only be a matter of time before Santōṣha perished too. Our realms were too closely intertwined, governed by the same Mother, the same essence.

Burning deep in the bones of my body, I knew it wasn't a question of if, but when.

"We can't survive up there," said the female Nŏahl, quick to form ideas that would protect the land from invasion. "You're the only ones that can."

The entire room looked at me, then Björn, whose blank face was unreadable. Tension hung in the air.

"I've made my decision," I said. "I'm returning to earth."

A hush filled the room as concern fell over all, but the Shaman remained steadfast with the divine plan and nodded.

"The warmth of your bodies and beating of your hearts have the power to support nature's growth. You both carry high volumes of light now; your presence can help ward off any darkness." She paused, looked up through the opening, then nodded, her striking eyes staring straight into ours.

"This is your opportunity to truly embody the potential of humankind in a way that's never been fully realized by your species."

The light she spoke of rippled to the surface of my being, and I understood its power as I opened myself wider to allow its full expression. It radiated beyond my body, beyond the cavern, beyond the valley. It was the power of the One itself, and it was within me. Within Björn. Within us all.

"We'll do all the work we can from down here in sending forth light," Nŏahl Çrėę spoke, old eyes kind beneath dark bushy brows. "But ultimately, your power will enrich with numbers. If the other humans here join you . . ."

The unforgettably divine image of ĵagath flickered over Çrėę's form, and I was enchanted as he stared, unflinchingly into my eyes. The slightest smile brushed his etheric features, reminding me of the almighty forces at work beyond our comprehension, and a profound sense of knowing flooded through me.

The Âscendants were with us. The veil between our worlds had thinned, and I was seeing, in moments, two realities, two dimensions, merged into one.

"We mustn't examine this lightly," The headwoman's voice echoed off the cavern's walls.

"The Earth is bare. How will you survive when we don't even know if there'll be water up there, let alone food? As you said, nature takes time to grow, there's no way around that, and even if there are resources, it will be dangerous. Nature can be extremely harsh, especially if you have no shelter to escape rough weather."

Even with all the benevolent entities in the multiverse backing us, food and water *were* kinda important...

"It's been millennia since your species were forced to survive off the land alone, and over time I wouldn't be surprised if your body memory has lost its knowledge on how to do that."

Chief Hân followed her line of truths that were hard to defend. "We've never been in contact with the Sky People. We know they have immense power to manipulate the mind, but we don't know what else they might be capable of. If they do descend and you're stuck there... We've seen how desperate they are to make earth their home.

"Ultimately, it's your decision, but I agree with Athêna; it mustn't be made at all lightly. You'll have to wait until we can at least be sure there's clean water there."

"I can watch from here. I'll know," Nõahl Gabriel said, through whom Ậdja, the dark-skinned warrior was present, morphing in and out of sight, the glowing arrow on his forehead catching my eye.

He was a seer too, an interdimensional traveler of the elle, and far more practiced than me. He didn't have to wait for visions to visit him; he knew how to go to *them*.

The cavern was quiet once more.

Waiting. Contemplating.

A distant ringing drifted in through the high opening, one that sounded like bell chimes. One I recognized well. Every head tilted upward to watch a silvery spark of light float downward and settle in the center of our circle.

In a flash, a tiny body appeared. She bowed her head shyly.

"The stronger of the Fèya will return with you. We can help the plants grow."

"Echõ." I was surprised that of all the Fèya, it was her.

"I followed you home," she said, charming the room.

"You've been here since we returned, and we didn't even notice?" Björn was equally surprised as amused.

"I've never traveled to the Samãdhi village before. I've been exploring." I caught a shimmer over Nala's expression, off which I gathered their worlds had collided at some point.

Echõ looked to me with wide, open eyes. She had known that I was going to call this meeting. That I would find the courage to step up to a future the Fèya tribe already knew would unite with theirs.

"I want to help you," she said, but there was a tone in her voice that offered more than just help, it declared that if I accepted, she was offering to bind herself to me, as the Fèya had done with humans in the past.

A radiant blue-silver light emanated from her body, moving in a river toward mine, and as I opened myself to her in immediate acceptance, I watched a stream of blue-silver light extend from my own heart, floating outward to meet it. The light interlocked like a chain in a bright, blinding flash.

I blinked as the radiance of her presence washed through me and bowed my head in reverence. She rose to hover, then fluttered to land in my cupped hands, the warmth of pure magic soaking the skin she brushed.

The all-knowing Shaman spoke again. "You'll have the support of all we have the power to offer from Santōṣha, and with the abilities of the light-beings beside you, you won't be alone, nor will you be in lack."

I looked back to Athêna and Hân, appreciative of their voiced concerns.

"I have to go back," I said. "I don't know how it'll work. It breaks my heart to leave. But I have to. I can't explain it."

Nirmala nodded her approval, as did Chaiṭãnya, also understanding the call. Illogical, but critical. Unavoidable.

Björn stood. He'd been absorbing the conversation quietly and moved to be by my side, taking my hand in his. He looked out over the circle.

"If you go, I go," he finally spoke, the corner of his lips lifting.

"Be sure to understand this decision doesn't have to be final," Athêna assured us.

"If you decide you don't feel comfortable to step back into unknown territory so soon after all the chaos, we'd prefer you to stay here in safety, with us. And there is no shame in changing your mind," she said with the compassion of a mother.

But when Björn and I turned, we both understood there was no decision to be contemplated. The path was clear.

Frightening, but unquestionable.

Echō twinkled from my hands, her magic tickling my palms as a glowing stream of silver-blue mist diffused into the airwaves from a radiant field around her body, declaring she, too, knew it to be her mission, beyond choice or control.

I reached for the seashell that lay on my chest.

We would return to the ground.

Our homeland.

Afterword

If you connected to this novel in any significant way, your ratings and reviews are valuable to us, and help other readers like yourself find it! Visit the online store you purchased it from to leave your review.

To stay updated with Sita's upcoming releases, you can sign up to her newsletter at
www.sitabennettauthor.com.au

With Love & Gratitude,

Mystic Adventure Press

More Books by

Sita Bennett

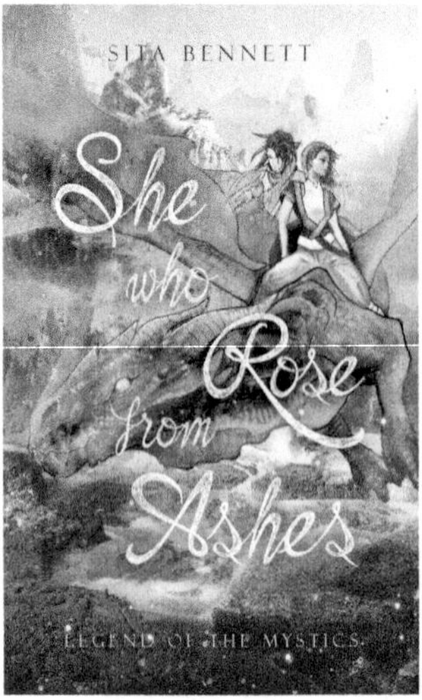
SITA BENNETT
She who Rose from Ashes
LEGEND OF THE MYSTICS

ACKNOWLEDGMENTS

I'm going to keep this brief for a number of reasons. One being, who even reads acknowledgments?

Another being that I've always been quite a loner, so the number of people who have had a significant impact on the creation of this book are few.

But the beauty about these few people, is that because they are very very special to me, their impacts have been immense, so in actual fact, I could write pages on just how grateful I feel for each of their contribution over my journey to publication.

I started writing Maya of the In-between when I was nineteen. The idea was sparked by a conversation with one of dad's friends Jim Banks, about the conspiracy theory of Agartha – a sophisticated civilisation located at the centre of the earth's core. At the time, I was living in a city, missing nature and contemplating climate change, and started dreaming about a fantasy future where humans could retreat underground to this magical inner earth if life above ground was destroyed by global warming. Combined with a bunch of other contemplations about the world, Maya of the In-between was born.

My editors; Christine Florie, Alison Arnold, and Laura Keenan.

My cover designers Thea Magerand and Dion MB.

Because, let's face it, Mum and Dad, you are most likely among the few reading this part, here I take a moment to especially thank the way you've supported and encouraged creativity from such a young age. When I told you I wanted to dedicate my life to artistry, you made me wholeheartedly believe it was possible and held me in all the tears, failures, successes and overwhelming joys this path has bought so far with immense love and understanding. You are true inspirations of people fearlessly following your own unique creative passions and never giving up.

Shyama Paris and Shanti Bennett, you're gentle and loving belief in what I write has given me the courage to remain vulnerable, write from the heart and not sell out to meet mainstream markets.

Frank Bennett, your quiet presence, love and belief is felt and appreciated even without you having to say a word.

Jamie and Shala, you were among my few first readers and made me feel like the book was actually worth publishing in a moment I was going to leave it behind.

Judy Bennett, my grandmother, a special thank you for being my very first reader, giving me honest feedback and supporting the entire process from the very beginning!

A special mention to Rohan Heaton, my mentor who has, much like the Shaman to Maya, helped me find, realise and embody more of the true power within me, and find spaces of deep self-acceptance, love and freedom within.

Lastly, I acknowledge you, the reader, for picking up this book and joining Maya's journey to Santosha. But mostly for being you. Whatever that might be. I'm excited to continue this story with you.

Love Sita

About Author

Sita is a West-Australian Author, Actress, and Filmmaker from the small coastal town of Margaret River.

She writes speculative novels inspired by eastern mysticism and ancient wisdom from multiple cultures, that follow smart, sensitive, resilient & determined young women on quests for truth and freedom in chaotic worlds.

She also co-creates independent films with her brother, Frank Bennett, that explore the mysteries of consciousness. Together, they co-founded Lightdance Productions.

All of Sita's work follow stories of self-discovery, transformation & love as characters find their unique personal power within.

www.sitabennettauthor.com.au

Printed in Great Britain
by Amazon